Praise for
Ludwig's Fugue

A murder mystery with a unique twist. Courtney Miller's complexity of the classic homicide involving the legendary gifts of a Cherokee Shaman provides a different angle to criminal procedures. Set in a small mountain town, a triple homicide rocks the small community and the likeable deputies embark on a mission to solve the riddle. An enjoyable story to follow through each surprising turn of events.

—**Sheriff Shannon Byerly,** Custer County Sheriff

COURTNEY MILLER

Ludwig's Fugue

Books may be purchased in quantity and/or special sales by contacting the author and publisher at:

www.populvuhpublishing.com

Popul Vuh
Publishing

Cover Design: Nick Zelinger, NZ Graphics
Interior Design: Ronnie Moore, WESType Publishing Service
Editing: John Maling, Editing by John, and Georgann Hall
Book Consultant: Judith Briles, The Book Shepherd
Published by: Popul Vuh Publishing
          PO Box 91
          Westcliffe, CO 81252

ISBN: 978-0-9887711-4-7(Hardback)
ISBN: 978-0-9887711-5-4(e-Pub)

Library of Congress Control Number: 2016960972

1. Native American—Fiction   2. Cherokee—Fiction   3. White Feather (Fictitious Character)—Fiction   4. Murder—Investigation—Fiction   5. Wet Mountain Valley—Fiction

First Edition   Printed in USA

Acknowledgments

I am so thankful for those who graciously took time from their busy schedules to answer my many questions and to become a treasured friend.

In the Wet Mountain Valley, Custer County Sheriff Shannon Byerly and his staff, deputies, and detention officers invited me in and gave me a royal reception. Thank you for showing me behind the scenes and enlightening me on procedures.

I want to extend a special thank you to Jim Little, Wayne Ewing and the rest of the staff at the Wet Mountain Tribune for inviting me in and sharing the details of their business.

To Art Nordyke, many thanks for giving me insights into the life of the County Coroner.

On the publishing side, I have been blessed with the best team led by The Book Shepherd, Dr. Judith Briles, editing was done by John Maling and Georgann Hall, cover design was done by Nick Zelinger, and layouts by Ronnie Moore.

And, of course, my wife, Lin, has provided invaluable support, help, and advice.

This book is dedicated to Sheriff Shannon Byerly and the Custer County Sheriff's Office. We are all indebted to our law enforcement officers and in the Wet Mountain Valley, we have the best.

Other Books by Award-winning Author Courtney Miller

The First Raven Mocker
Book 1 of The Cherokee Chronicles
> Has received a Beverly Hills Book Award, International Book Award, and NIEA Excellence Award for Historical Fiction

The Raven Mocker's Legacy
Book 2 of The Cherokee Chronicles
> Has received a Book Excellence Award for "Literary Excellence in Faction" [Fiction based on Fact]

Gihli, The Chief Named Dog
Book 3 of The Cherokee Chronicles (coming soon)
> Finalist in the 2015 Extravaganza Draft to Dream Book Competition

It's About Time
A White Feather Mystery (coming soon)
> Winner of the 2016 Extravaganza Draft to Dream Book Competition

Part I

Wednesday

Chapter One

Shots Disturb the Peace

LIKE A SILENT MESSENGER bringing a subtle, but ominous portent of an event destined to disturb and disrupt the peaceful mountain village, the first breeze of the evening came whispering across the sleepy town.

Residents of Rockcliffe would tell you that they live in the most beautiful place in the world, and they would mean it. The little town was nestled in the Wet Mountain Valley surrounded by massive mountain peaks in south-central Colorado. To the north, Collegiate Peaks shone in the distance with its eight peaks rising above fourteen-thousand feet, or, as Coloradans say, "its eight fourteeners." To the east, the green forested Wet Mountains. To the west and south, the Sangre de Cristo mountain range which hosts ten fourteeners of its own.

Although in a valley, the town's elevation is 7,888 feet above sea level. Despite its incredible scenery and cool high mountain climate, few have ever heard of it. The beauty of the little town of Rockcliffe is so little known because it is not on the way to any of the more well-known destinations. If you find Rockcliffe, it is because you are looking for it. It is a small, remote mountain community normally protected from the crime and hustle of big cities.

The sparse twitter of lazy birds blended with the ever-present but muffled televisions entertaining the elderly, retired, homebound, and those awaiting family returning at the end of the working day. A backup generator started up and whirred loudly to recharge off-grid batteries muffling the crack of gunshots.

Some noticed the three pops interrupting the serene quiet of the neighborhood, but most did not. A fourth shot snapped loudly and caught the attention of a few more. A final fifth shot prompted one or two more to stop what they were doing and divert themselves to their window to peek outside. All but one saw nothing unusual, shrugged, and returned to their T.V.s or sorting clothes or baking or reading. Unconcerned, they filed away the curious sounds in their subconscious memories, because virtually everyone in the valley owned a gun and gunshots were often heard, especially during hunting season. Besides, nothing of note ever happened in their peaceful mountain village.

But Bert was different. He was a keen observer and his hearing was almost as sharp as it was six decades ago when he had become familiar with the sound of gunshots in the war. He dialed 9-1-1.

Chapter Two

Crumpled on the Field

COACH BERLIN JONES CRINGED as he watched his defensive safety flatten the half back in a violent, head-to-head tackle. Concerned by the ferocity of the collision, he blew his whistle and waved the team to the sideline for a huddle and to give the two players a moment to shake off the hit. An assistant coach drew his attention from the field to show him a crudely drawn diagram on his clipboard.

David Ludwig lay crumpled on the field. His head was pounding and his vision fuzzy. He raised his tingling fingers to touch something cool on the side of his face. It was wet. He pulled back his hand and saw crimson blood dripping from his fingers.

Pulling his shredded jersey up to wipe the blood from his face and hair, he looked around and realized that nothing looked familiar! He could not remember the crushing hit he had put on the half back a few moments ago, a hit so violent, it cracked his helmet. Nor did he know that a crippling injury to his cranium had just been sustained—an injury that damaged the connections around the hippocampus, that portion of his brain responsible for managing memories. He did not know where he was. He did not know who he was.

As the dizziness subsided, David stood and removed the mangled shoulder pads that were now partly over his head and partly strapped to his right shoulder. He dropped the pads and the red jersey tangled in the pads onto the ground next to the damaged helmet. On the sidelines, he saw uniformed players crowded around two men busy discussing something on a clipboard. He staggered off the field toward the bleachers where a sparse crowd of—to him—strangers had gathered and were visiting among themselves with indifference to the actions on the field—or him.

A pretty, young red-head ran up to him with two giggling girlfriends in tow. She gave him a flirty, familiar smile. She looked much younger than him, maybe a couple of grades, he thought. Could she be his girlfriend? She seemed confident as she hooked a delicate arm around his bare, muscular one and dragged him over to a bleacher seat.

"Oh, David, you are a mess! You look like you need a big ol' hug! She ducked her head under his arm, wrapped her arms around his waist and snuggled very close, with her head buried into his shoulder.

David? Was that his name? He noticed the surprise and excitement registering on her friends' faces. They giggled giddily while nervously looking about. He sensed this brash girl was doing something they found audacious. He now doubted she was his girlfriend. He now questioned her intentions.

She took a tissue from her hand bag and started dabbing the blood from his head. David felt very uncomfortable at first but then her nurturing attention made him feel more secure in this world of mystery he now found himself. A world where he did not know anyone—not even himself! He was relieved to be recognized, to be accepted.

"We're having another party out at the lake. You should come."

"Party?"

Puzzled, she glared at him, "Your brother went to the last one. Surely, he told you about it."

He was starting to feel uncomfortable again, "My brother?"

She smoothed his hair and dabbed the blood off the side of his face with a tissue, "You can even bring your prudish girlfriend. Just let me know and I'll put you on the list."

The pretty, bold girl pulled back and gave David a mocking, sad look, "You should try to smile more!"

Insecurity rushed back into David as she stood and continued pertly, "See you later, David."

The girl smirked and walked off triumphantly, followed by her giggling coterie. Even though he suspected they were mocking him, he strangely regretted their departure. At the moment, it was as if the only people in the world he might be connected to were leaving him. David turned to look at the three boys sitting behind him. They looked back at him indignantly as though his behavior was strange or improper. "She made me feel very uncomfortable!" David said with slow, slurred speech.

The two boys on either side snorted short laughs but the boy in the middle just stared at David and replied, "Yeah, I'll bet!"

David walked away from the bleachers not knowing where he was going. He felt completely isolated and alone in an alien world. Suddenly, a pretty, petite blond ran up to him and grabbed his arm. "David!" She exclaimed, "You're through already? Great!"

She turned up her nose quizzically and gave David a condescending look, "What happened to you?"

David shrugged. He felt incompetent, inadequate. It was clear she knew him and that he should know her. But he did not. He remained silent hoping she would say something or give him some clue that would spur his memories to come streaming back.

The girl shook her head in disgust, "Aren't you going to shower and change?"

David looked down at his dirty, ragged pants, sweaty half shirt and cleated shoes. He looked all around. *Shower? Where could he go to shower? Where would he change? Where were his regular clothes? Where was he, anyway?*

David looked down at the impatient girl that had put him on the spot, "I don't know where my clothes are!"

The girl dug her fists into her hips, "You didn't bring a change of clothes?"

David shrugged.

"Mercy, David! Come on, let's go. Mother won't be home for another thirty minutes. You can shower at my house and borrow something from Jerry!"

She dragged him to a white, two-door, convertible Mustang where a chunky boy reluctantly climbed out of the passenger seat, pushed the seat forward and climbed into the back.

The young boy pouted in the back seat while the girl happily ran around the car and jumped into the driver's seat. David, realizing that he was supposed to sit in the passenger seat, shrugged his apologies to the sulking boy in the back seat and dropped into the vacated passenger seat. She cranked the car, slammed it into drive and floored the accelerator.

They drove a short distance to a bungalow-style house in a neighborhood full of similar, small bungalow-style houses crammed together tightly. The tires squealed as she swerved into the narrow driveway and slammed on the brakes.

"Jerry, David needs to borrow one of your sweatshirts and a pair of sweatpants!" the bossy blond commanded. "Follow me, David, I'll show you where the bathroom is!"

David threw open the door, rolled out of the car and pulled the seat forward for Jerry. The young boy in the backseat frowned a reply, "Yes, Tammy!" He dragged himself out of the car and begrudgingly followed the rushing twosome onto the porch.

"Jerry", *"Tammy"*. David spoke their names to himself and vowed to remember them. But, of course, he would not.

"Take off those cleats before you come in!" Tammy demanded. David kicked them off by the front door. Rushing and in a huff, the girl grabbed the shoes and ran back to toss them into the Mustang before leading David inside.

She dragged him through two small, split rooms with the formal dining room on one side and the formal living room on the other. A short hallway connected to the den past a narrow, galley-style kitchen. She stepped down into the sunken den and then stepped up to the left to lead him down a narrow hallway where she pushed him into the bathroom. She threw open a cabinet door and grabbed a towel and wash cloth and shoved them into his chest, "Now hurry! Mamma will be home soon and I don't want to have to explain you showering in our house."

She yelled over her shoulder as she left, "And clean up your mess when you're through! Leave the bathroom just like you found it."

David set the towel and wash cloth by the sink and started undressing. *What am I doing?* He thought as he turned on the shower, adjusted the knobs until the water was the right temperature, and stepped in.

As he drew the curtain across, he questioned why he was reluctant to admit to the girl—what was her name?—that he did not know her. Instinctively, he was very uncomfortable to just play along, but he reasoned that he did not want to hurt her feelings. But it was more than that. Maybe he just needed to stall for time until his memory came back.

David heard a knock on the bathroom door and instinctively covered up. The door opened and Tammy's voice echoed, "I am laying your clothes on the counter top! Chop! Chop! Get cracking!"

David ducked under the spray of water. His head stung as the water hit the matted part of his hair. He looked down as blood washed down his body onto the shower floor and down the drain. He touched the tender spot and rubbed the matted hair until the blood washed out. He quickly soaped up and washed off.

He turned off the shower and reached across for the towel. He did not want to get the floor wet, so he placed one foot out, snatched the towel and then stepped back into the tub to dry off.

Chapter Three
Who Are These People?

THERE WAS A DRAWSTRING but the sweatpants were still too big in the waist and the legs too short. *There must be some mistake. These are not my pants.* His memory was slipping again.

He pulled on the sweatshirt and found a comb by the sink to comb his damp hair. Then he looked around. *"Socks, shoes?"*

The clean, but bewildered amnesiac slipped out of the bathroom into the hallway. Tammy came busting around the corner! "Where's your shoes?"

David looked down. She pressed her fingers against her forehead, "Ok, let me think!"

Her eyes lit up, "Wait in there." She pointed toward the door at the end of the hallway. David hesitated, then proceeded down the hallway toward the indicated door. A large informal living room was sunken behind the small galley-style kitchen with a bar cut into the wall. He stepped down and crossed the room to sit on the couch.

Tammy burst into the room and tossed him a pair of sneakers and white socks, then rushed out. When she returned, she seemed pleased that he had slipped on the sneakers. "They were Dad's," she explained.

Jerry entered the room from the hallway, smirked at his sister and commented, "Mom will recognize the sweat suit and shoes, you know."

Tammy frowned, put her knuckles under her chin and squinted at David. "Ok! Jerry, go get the black shoe polish! David, take off the top and turn it wrong side out."

The two boys looked at the crazy, fast-talking girl, dumbfounded. She clapped her hands and shouted, "Move it!"

The bewildered boys "moved it."

Jerry was back in an instant with a round metal can that Tammy snatched, opened and stooped to work on David's shoes. As David's head popped through the neck of the reversed sweat shirt, he opened his eyes to see an attractive, middle-aged woman looking curiously at him from across the room. Tammy was kneeling in front of him painting his shoes and did not see the woman so David tapped her on the shoulder. Tammy looked up. David nodded toward the agitated lady behind her.

"Mamma!" Tammy shrieked, as she jumped to her feet.

"Mamma, this is David Ludwig." Tammy waved her hand toward him. David looked at the girl with surprise. *David Ludwig?*

The pretty woman—Mamma—nodded and introduced herself, "Samantha. Excuse me while I set down these groceries."

She retreated into the kitchen with the girl following her talking fast. David heard the front screen door open and a lady called out as she entered, "Sam ... you home?"

"In here, Penny!" Tammy's mother replied from the kitchen.

Penny entered the kitchen and apologized, "Sam, I hate to be the one to tell you ..."

She stopped short when she looked across the bar into the den. She glared at David and whispered with her teeth clenched like a ventriloquist, "Who's that?"

He heard "Sam" whispering "Tammy's boyfriend" as she grabbed Penny's arm and led her out of his sight into the formal living room. The young girl, Tammy, shook her head in disgust. She shouted into the direction of the formal living room, "Mamma, should I call in our order?"

There was hushed chatter coming from the living room.

The girl persisted, "Maaaammaaaaa!"

The whispers stopped. The mother appeared and approached her daughter. She was visibly shaken. "Tam, we're going to have to do this another time. Something has come up ... I'm sorry."

Tam's face turned to concern, "What is it, Mother?"

A tear rolled down her mother's cheek, "I'll tell you later." Samantha wiped the tear and turned toward the front door, "I didn't see another car, do you need to take your friend home?"

The woman was trembling as she looked back apologetically at David, "I'm sorry ... maybe some other time."

She turned and rejoined her friend in the living room. The young girl turned to him with puzzled, confused eyes. She motioned to him and whispered, "I guess I'd better take you home."

"Can I go?" her brother pleaded.

The girl gave the boy the very clear, negative answer with fiery eyes. As she led David past the kitchen into the formal dining room, he could hear her mother gasp and whisper, "What am I going to do?" Her friend glanced up at them showing her disgust for their intrusion. On a strange, unexpected impulse, he walked into the living room and hugged the weeping mother briefly. As he released her, he muttered, "I'm ... sorry."

The woman's teary eyes were wide and her mouth dropped open as she studied him. His heart dropped into his stomach as he thought to himself, *why did I do that?*

He waited pensively for the woman's reaction. Her eyes softened and the signs of a smile reluctantly crept into the corners of her mouth.

The impatient young girl grabbed him and led him to the front door, "I'm going to take David home, Mamma, and I'll be back in a jiff!"

As they drove away, she began a steady, unending conversation with herself, "That awful Penny is always upsetting Mamma. There's no telling what she said this time. I wish Mamma would just tell her to go away and leave her alone! Of course, she can't. Penny is the sheriff's wife. That would be awkward."

He was glad that she was speaking rhetorically. He felt temporarily safe not having to respond in this strange, new, unknown world.

He wondered where they were going. The young girl chattered on as they drove through changing neighborhoods and winding roads. The houses were getting older; the trees bigger; the air cooler. He liked the feel of this neighborhood. It felt quiet and friendly ... and safe.

David began to consider confiding in the young girl about his predicament. He looked over at her ... *No, not a good idea! She was not interested in him at the moment. He just felt that he should not interrupt her.*

Tammy suddenly swerved and drove the right two wheels off the pavement onto the grass growing past the yard and up to the pavement. There she stopped. He glanced at the young girl who smiled and apologized, "I'm sorry, David. I'll call when I find out what is going on. I know Mother wants to meet you but something has apparently come up."

He sensed that she wanted him to get out of the car, but where were they? He glanced out the right side of the car at the old, craftsman-style house with a large porch in front.

The girl's voice broke into his thoughts, "You don't want to go in, do you? Did you have another fight with your dad?"

He looked back at her, "Dad?"

Chapter Four

White Feather Ponders the Past

Lᴋᴇ ᴀ ɢɪᴀɴᴛ ʀᴀᴠᴇɴ, the old Cherokee wizard was perched on the roof outside the window of the second floor bedroom of the abandoned train terminal. It gave him a spectacular view of the Sangre de Cristo mountain range looming beyond the empty warehouses and old factory buildings left to rust and ruin after the steel and smelting factories had closed so many years before.

He felt a connection to the rotting industrial section of Rockcliffe. Like it, he was a relic, aging and forgotten. He held up his bare arm and studied the wrinkled, bluish flesh sagging on his ancient bones. He brushed his hand across his forearm as if smoothing the skin, then propped his arms on his knees and inhaled the quickly cooling evening air. Soon Grandmother Sun would slip behind the mountains and close the door on daytime.

"The millennial man." That was how the old shaman had described him. Not because of the white man's generational designation, but because she was convinced he had lived for that long! He chuckled to himself, *she's the real deal.*

He too was the real deal; a Cherokee witch who had mastered soul transference. In the old days, before the white man, "before contact" as the white man labeled it, his kind had been called Kalanu Ahkyeliski, "Raven Mocker."

The Raven Mocker's legacy had created many evil witches believed capable of stealing the four souls of a man and thereby acquiring the remainder of his years for themselves. Now they were all gone. He was the last Raven Mocker and, because he was a witch, he had been shunned by the Ani Yun Wiya, the real people, the Cherokee, all his life. Now he lived in obscurity on the fringes of the white man's culture.

He had reverted to his birth name, "Ugidahli Unega", or "White Feather." He hated what the Raven Mockers had become and he wanted no part of it. He did not see himself as an evil man like them.

With the coming of the white man and his arrogance, it had become increasingly easier for a witch to hide. The white man, as a rule, dismissed the supernatural as a sham. The old woman was called a shaman now, as a result. She would have been recognized as a medicine woman and priest in the ancient times. Among many Cherokee there were still believers. But outside the tribe, she was seen as a heretic. And so was he.

Clouds hovered over the mountain range and he watched them changing color gradually in the waning light, reminding him of his dream. "He knows not what he is!" the voice in his dream had said about the smoky figure that was changing continuously, like a ghost-like fog. As the fog thinned, there were the silhouettes of three bodies standing on their heads and a bear passing by, disinterested. The dream was an omen, portending something coming into the wizard's life.

Crack, crack, crack! White Feather opened his eyes and turned his attention in the direction of the center of the village where the disturbing triple discharges echoed off stone and stucco buildings. He recognized the sound of gunshots instantly. Again, a shot, but more muffled this time. A pattern was developing, a story was unfolding, a sinister presage.

Pop! Another shot followed by prolonged silence. Perhaps the story had ended. Or had it just begun?

Chapter Five

David Finds Parents and Flees

Dᴀᴠɪᴅ Lᴜᴅᴡɪɢ ᴛᴏᴏᴋ ᴀ deep breath as he turned to look at the strange house—his house? He slid out of Tammy's car and shut the door. "Don't forget your stuff," she reminded him pointing with her thumb toward the back seat. David gathered up the crumpled clothes and cleated shoes.

The young girl waved casually over her shoulder and stomped on the gas spraying gravel as she spun around in a "U" turn.

Still uncertain, he dragged himself slowly across the uneven, weathered sidewalk through the weedy, unkept yard. He trudged up the steps of the large, covered porch. The aged and buckling slats were well-worn where countless footfalls had smudged off the paint leading to the door.

A hanging swing squeaked as the breeze nudged it. He watched it waggle and then come to rest. The front door was centered behind the steps. The screened door bowed its flimsy wooden frame as David pulled it open. He touched the worn, oval, silver door knob; it was smooth, loose. He grasped it and twisted. Pushing, the door popped open and then stuck on the threshold. He pushed again and the scrape and whoosh sounded weirdly familiar; perhaps his mind had even anticipated the sound, he was not sure.

Inside, the dark living room was quiet, still, gloomy and smelled of sweaty cloth, varnished, rotting wood, and something else—something unfamiliar. Maybe no one was home; maybe he could just slip in unnoticed and observe until he learned more. Maybe seeing something familiar would bring back his memories and tell him where he was and why he was there.

His eyes slowly adjusted to the darkness. As the room materialized, he realized that there was a large body lying on the floor near the couch. Two more slumping bodies on the couch startled him, and he gasped and recoiled. There were three bodies! A man on the floor; a woman and a boy were sitting, slumped on the couch. Were they ... sleeping? Dead?

David dropped the bundle of clothes and knelt next to the large man. He was startled when he noticed that the man's eyes were staring at him. He fell back and noticed a pistol laying in the drying pool of blood surrounding the man. David instinctively picked up the gun, stood and then checked out the woman and boy. His heart was pounding; his mouth was dry and tasted strange. Both bloody bodies on the couch were clearly stone still and lifeless.

He glimpsed movement in the front yard and walked to the window. There was a man in uniform. David jumped to one side and hid just out of sight of the man as he walked up to the window and peeked inside. David stood clutching the bloody pistol. He looked down at the obvious murder weapon; his fingerprints; the blood on him! He glanced at the dead bodies. *Did I do this?*

David bolted out the back door and across the unkempt lawn into the alley. He ducked down below the level of the cedar fences hoping to keep from being seen. He did not know where he was going, but he just kept running through alleys, across streets and through weedy fields. As if gliding through a blurry dream, he ran down dusty roads by abandoned warehouses, on and on until he burst into a large wooded park. He paused momentarily to get his bearings. The thick trees and bushes next to a pond attracted him.

He pushed through thickets into a small clearing next to the pond where a park bench sat facing the water, partially obscured by the thick vegetation. He felt hidden and secure as he dropped onto the bench, breathless. He looked down at the gun he was still holding. Why did he have a gun? Where was he? Why was he there? Why was he afraid? Why did this place seem safe? His incessant fugue clouded his ability to recall even recent events.

He was exhausted and his head felt like it was filled with lead. His ears were ringing loudly and he felt dizzy. He rolled over and lay across the bench. As his weary mind turned loose, his thoughts and his tense body relaxed and the pistol slipped from his fingers as he slipped into a dream.

Chapter Six

Breaking News

THE BUZZING IN HIS pocket woke him from his nap. It had been a busy day at the Wet Mountain Valley Chronicle. Wednesday was always a busy day at the small town newspaper, it was the day they put the pages together and sent a "PDF" file to Salida for printing. Mark Doss blinked and let the sounds of the room sink in. The reporter on the television enthusiastically announced "Late breaking news ..."

The incessant strings of "A Little Night Music" by Mozart reminded Mark that his cell phone was ringing. He rolled to the left in his recliner and fished the phone from his pocket, "Hello."

"Mark, this is Sean."

When Mark did not respond, the sheriff clarified, "Sheriff Bailey."

The drowsy man managed, "Yes?"

"We need your help, Mark. There's been a triple-homicide over at the Ludwig house. Jon, Matilda, and Darren were shot dead. A neighbor reported seeing the older son, David, running out the back door carrying something that might be a pistol."

Mark set up urgently. Bailey continued, "Any chance you could put a notice in tomorrow's paper asking citizens to report any information on the whereabouts of David and warning them he may be armed and dangerous?"

Mark glanced at his watch, it was 6:13 p.m. "We've already sent the paper to Salida, Sean."

This time, Sean did not respond, Mark began to think out-loud, "Depends on whether or not they've started printing ours. I think they run La Veta and Leadville before us. I could call ..." he paused. His mind was shifting into high gear. This was the type of thing journalists lived for; a major story; breaking news!

The sheriff broke into his thoughts, "I've got a picture of David in his football uniform. I could meet you at your office."

Mark's mind was sorting and prioritizing, "I'll call you back."

His daughter, Paige, strolled into the room, "Need anything from the Market?"

He held up one finger as he fiddled with his phone, "Hold on. There's been a triple-homicide."

Paige gasped; her eyes widened. She had inherited her father's love of the business and had worked with her father at the paper since she was a toddler. He put the phone to the side of his face, "Chuck, this is Mark over at Rockcliffe."

He started to speak, but was interrupted. He put the phone on speaker and turned it so that he was speaking directly into the end of the phone, "I said, this is Mark Doss with the Chronicle ..."

Chuck's voice blasted, "That's better, Buddy, watcha need?"

"Yeah, well, have you started on ours yet?"

"The Chronicle? Yeah …"

"Is it on the press?"

"Probably."

"Can you stop it, Chuck? We've got late breaking news!"

"Man! I don't know, Mark. Let me go see."

"Ok, I'll hold."

Paige whispered urgently, "A triple-homicide? In Rockcliffe?"

Mark nodded, "Ludwig family. David was seen fleeing, possibly with a pistol."

Paige sat on the armrest of the large comfortable chair across the room from her father's recliner. She bounced her knees nervously while they waited.

"Mark?"

"Yeah, I'm here."

"You're in luck, Buddy. They are just finishing up Alamosa; yours was next. I told 'em to pull it."

Mark's eyes crossed as he looked at his phone, "Ok! Great! Thanks, Chuck. We'll send a replacement PDF post-haste."

"Try to get it here before seven."

Mark tapped the red dot on his phone and threw forward the lever on his recliner, "Sean said he could meet us at the office with a picture. Want to help?"

Paige jumped up, "Of course!"

He tapped the recall button, "I stopped the run, Sean, we're on our way to the office."

Chapter Seven
The Journal

SAMANTHA MORRISON OPENED THE glass face of the old clock and retrieved the key from the mantle. The metal tag on the back of the door had 1936 engraved on it. Her father had brought it home when she was very little, maybe four, carried it into his study and mounted it over the credenza behind his desk. She had been fascinated with its chiming each quarter-hour and striking a bell for each hour on the hour. It felt like it had always been a part of her life.

She inserted the key and wound the spring just as her father had done every evening at this time after everyone had gone to bed. She removed the key, closed the glass face and placed the key atop the mantle as she stepped down off the hearth. The den was partially lit by the light streaming through the niche cut out of the kitchen wall forming the bar. The house was dark, quiet and peaceful as she crossed the room to check the patio door.

She stepped up from the den to the short hall and passed by the kitchen into the dining room to go check the front door latch. She peeked through the shades at the silvery, glistening grass lit by the almost full moon. Her ex-husband, Sam, was out there somewhere. She wondered if he was in town yet.

The water in the kettle would be about ready to boil so she did not search the night for long. Back in the galley-style kitchen, she switched off the flame below the kettle before it could sing its shrill whistle and wake the kids.

She poured the steaming water over the tea packet resting against the side of the small china teacup. The cup was part of a china set her mother and father had given her for a wedding gift. She had only unpacked the tea cups from the set when she had moved back to Rockcliffe after the divorce and she only used the cups for her private evening tea.

She turned off the burner and set the kettle on the cool back burner of the stove, cupped the tea in her cold hands and held her nose over the steam to inhale the warmth and aroma. It smelled like dry leaves, a dull smell for tea, but it was supposed to be relaxing, not stimulating.

She switched off the kitchen light and strolled back into the short hallway, stepping down into the den for the two steps before stepping back up to her left into the long hallway connecting the bedrooms. The soft light from the old antique lamp beside her bed at the end of the hall provided enough light for her to navigate the hallway.

She paused to check Tammy's closed door to her left. It was dark beneath the door and the room was quiet. "Bong." She synchronized her steps with the old clock's chiming cadence. Three steps past the open door of the bathroom, three steps past Jerry's closed door, five more into her bedroom to the night stand. The clock stopped chiming, the kids were quiet, the house was quiet, it was quiet time for herself now.

She took a careful sip of the hot tea before setting it on the coaster she kept on the night stand. She opened the narrow drawer and retrieved a leather-bound journal, clutching it against her bosom and rolling into bed using her free hand to pull up the layers of covers. She untied the leather strings, opened the journal and laid it across her lap. She had been rehearsing what she was going to write as she had made her final rounds, but she delayed her entry long enough for one more sip of the soothing, warm tea.

> *Dear Journal, I am SOOO angry tonight! How could he return after we have finally settled in and gotten accustomed to his absence? After I have finally gotten used to the idea that we are not a couple anymore; after I have given up, he comes back?*
>
> *Why is he here? Did he come to Rockcliffe to be near us and the job just happened to be available? Or, more likely, the job was available and we just happen to live here. Is he ever going to tell us he's here? Why did I have to find out from Penny? Why couldn't he have had the decency to call me; to warn me; to ask me how I feel about it? No! That would take someone with consideration for another's feelings. That's not Sam Morrison.*
>
> *Tammy reacted as I expected she would— she was furious and yelled her contempt before*

stomping off to lock herself in her room and cry herself to sleep. That's exactly how I felt; exactly what I wanted to do but tried to hold it together for the kids. Of course, I couldn't help reacting to the initial shock when I first heard, which was in front of Tammy's new boyfriend.

What a strange boy. He seemed genuinely concerned about me but at a loss as to what to do. I sensed he has a big heart.

Jerry shrugged off the news like it is "no big deal"—his philosophy of life. He filed away the news and spent the evening absorbed in his video games. I wonder if he will ever reach back and think about it in private? Probably not. His father wouldn't. Maybe that's how men deal with their emotions-they just suppress them—while we gals explode.

That was how Sam responded when I told him I had had enough and wanted a separation. No question. He just clammed up and "took it like a man". I wanted him to drop to his knees and beg my forgiveness. I needed for him to tell me that he was sorry and that I meant more to him than his job or life itself. But he didn't. He just took it and accepted it. He left me no alternative but to shout at him to leave and never come back, but I wanted him to grab me and kiss me and tell me he would never leave. Instead, he just sulked like a scolded puppy and left.

I thought that the divorce papers would snap him out of it. But NOOOO. He signed them and sent them back—the S.O.B. I knew deep down

*that he still loved me, but I needed him to tell me.
I needed him to fight for me. But he left me no
choice. I even moved to Rockcliffe with the hope
that going to that extreme would draw him out.
It didn't.*

*Day after day; night after night; waiting for a
phone call; waiting for him to show up on the
doorstep; knowing that instead he was losing
himself even more in his job; drowning his sorrow
in his work.*

*Now he's here! Tell me, Journal, what should I
do? Should I punch his lights out when he shows
up? ... What if he doesn't show up?*

Part II

Thursday

Chapter Eight
Samuel Morrison

Ex-homicide detective Samuel Morrison stood at the bathroom sink staring into the mirror. He had just lathered his face with shaving cream and was waiting for the energy to lift the razor. It had been a long, tiring drive from Denver and he had not gotten to bed until well after midnight.

Sheriff Sean Bailey had called him from the crime scene around 7 p.m. informing him he had been assigned his first case. "I haven't even gotten there yet. I don't start until Monday," he had protested.

"There's been a change. A triple homicide. We need your expertise. How soon can you get here?"

He had told the Sheriff that he would leave right away.

Sam had been offered a deputy's job in Wet Mountain County because of his acquaintance with Undersheriff Buster Crab of the Wet Mountain County Sheriff's Office. Before moving back to Rockcliffe, Buster had worked in the Denver Police Department, Burglary Division. They had worked together on several cases where homicide and burglary overlapped. They had gained a mutual professional respect for one another and had also become good friends on a personal level.

Buster had been one of only a few supporters in the devastating hearing as a character witness. The hearing had been quick and although the charges were trumped up, the verdict had been widely anticipated. Sam Morrison was found guilty of "insubordination" and terminated from the Denver Police Department.

It had been a bitter pill for Morrison to swallow after dedicating his life to homicide investigation for over twenty years. His dedication had first cost him his marriage and his family. Now his overzealousness and refusal to "play the game" and be a "team player" had cost him his job. The humiliation and disgrace of the hearing and termination before his peers was the lowest point in his life.

Buster had been the first person to call Sam after his forced termination. He cringed to think what he would have done had Buster not called when he did. Buster had mentioned that there was an opening for a deputy in the Wet Mountain County Sheriff's Office and volunteered to put in a good word for him.

Buster Crab was in his sixties and after retiring from the Denver Police Department he had moved back to Rockcliffe, his old hometown. He had found retirement difficult and at the urging of his wife, he had run for Sheriff. He was one of three candidates running for the position. He was up against the Undersheriff from the previous administration and a younger man working for the Pueblo Police Department but living in Wetmore, near the southern border of the county.

It had been a fierce campaign. The Undersheriff had clearly expected to win, but the younger candidate, Sean Bailey, had impressed everyone with his clear ideas and humble appearance. Angered by the result, the undersheriff had resigned and the new sheriff surprised Buster when he offered him the undersheriff position.

Wet Mountain County Sheriff's Office was a small office in a peaceful mountain community and Buster found it enjoyable to be back working again.

Morrison had received the call from Sheriff Sean Bailey the next day. Morrison had accepted the sheriff's offer without hesitating. He did not see it as a huge step down from homicide detective in a metropolis to a lowly deputy in a small, rural town; he saw it as a godsend.

It was not until Morrison had accepted the job, celebrated with a stiff whiskey, and sat down to plan his move to Rockcliffe that the unintended consequences of his decision hit him. His ex-wife and children had moved to Rockcliffe after the divorce. They had moved back to his wife's hometown to get away from him. Now, he was moving to Rockcliffe. How would they take his decision?

Putting aside the possible complication in his new life, Sam checked his watch; it was 6:18 a.m. and he needed to get going. Taking a deep breath, he summoned enough energy to quickly finish shaving. He had agreed to meet Buster at the crime scene at 7 a.m.

Chapter Nine

Waking on a Bench

THE SUN INCHED UP over the tree-tops across the pond and rudely flashed into David Ludwig's face. He threw his arm over his eyes to block the glaring light and tried to hang on to sleep.

His body ached from the wood slats of the bench. The bench? He raised up to find himself sitting on a park bench. He must have spent the night on it. He turned his gaze to the lush green grass and verdant trees and shrubs surrounding him. The bench looked out over a deep blue pond that reflected the orange and blue sky of the rising sun.

"Where am I?" he asked himself as he glanced about looking for clues. Dry blood on his hand caught his eye. More stains on his shirt and on his pants leg. He searched for a wound on his arm, his chest, and then he felt a tingle on his head. It was tender to the touch. He checked his fingers but there was no fresh blood.

He was cold, chilled to the bone from the cold night. He pulled the hood over his head and placed his frozen hands between his legs and squeezed.

Something moved in the thickets to his left. A small dark figure emerged. From his unsteady gait and stooped posture, the youth surmised him to be an old man. The old man did not seem to notice him, at first, then, when he looked up, he paused. For an uncomfortable length of time, the old man studied the youth. The youth squirmed a bit and then waved timidly. Finally, the old man shuffled forward.

"Osiyo!" the old man mumbled.

David did not understand the Cherokee word for "hello", but mumbled, "Good morning."

He studied the odd stranger dressed in a red plaid shirt and blue jeans held up by a brown belt with a large silver buckle sporting an oval, turquoise stone. His long, gray hair was parted so that the top portion was pulled through a short, hollow bone. The sides were pulled back into a pony tail that flowed down his back. His face was wrinkled and weathered. A white feather dangled on one side of his face, the shank tied to the hollow bone. *An Indian.*

The old Native American nodded at the open space on the bench beside the youth. David returned the nod and moved further over allowing the old man to sit beside him. The stranger placed the folded newspaper he was carrying on the bench between them, then offered his bony hand, "They call me White Feather."

David grasped the Indian's slender, fragile hand that felt like a bony, beaded necklace. He opened his mouth, but drew a blank! *Who am I?* he thought. The Indian studied his blood-stained hand and sniffed, then turned his piercing eyes back to the boy's face. The old wizard's eyes wandered to the swollen, bloody wound on his head; the blood on his shirt and pants; then to his shoes.

The young man searched his brain for some fleeting memory, but nothing emerged; not whom he was; not where he was; not how he got there; nothing! He turned apologetically to the old man. The old Indian frowned and studied the youth again, particularly his face. It was as if he were trying to remember his face. Then he picked up his newspaper.

While the old man refolded the paper, David watched the sun's rays now streaming through the trees and illuminating the pond. The air was brisk, the birds were chirping, the trees were still. But for some reason, his stomach was churning, his mind was swirling, and he felt anxious. All memories of his past were lost in his persistent fugue.

After a few moments, the Indian glanced at him, then back to the newspaper, "David Ludwig," he pronounced.

David turned back to stare at him. He tried to smile, but the look of the old man was disturbing. The old man clarified, "You are David Ludwig."

The shocked youth's eyes lit up. "I am?"

White Feather did not respond. David questioned, "You know me?"

The Indian kept his eyes on him as he turned the folded newspaper around so that David could see a front page article. The face of a young man in a numbered jersey was prominently displayed below a headline that read "DAVID LUDWIG MISSING. WANTED FOR QUESTIONING IN TRIPLE HOMICIDE!"

David looked at the Indian again. He cocked his head as if to say, "So?"

"Don't you recognize the picture?" the old Indian asked as he tapped the picture with a bony, crooked forefinger.

David looked at the picture again and shook his head, "No. Should I?"

White Feather chuckled. "That's you."

David's stomach quaked! He studied the picture but it did not resonate. The old Indian handed him the newspaper and nodded toward the pond, "Compare your reflection in the water."

David glanced at the Indian and then turned to the pond. He took the newspaper and lumbered off to the water's edge stiff from a night on the bench. He knelt and peering down, compared his reflection to the picture in the paper. It was him! The face in the dark water matched the picture in the newspaper.

He sat back on his heels and started reading the article ...

Jon and Matilda Ludwig and their fifteen-year-old son, Darren, were found shot dead in their home Wednesday around 6:15 pm. The sheriff's office was tipped off by neighbors reporting a disturbance at the family's home and possible gun shots. The sheriff reported that the bodies were found with fatal gunshot wounds fired from close range. The sheriff is looking for the older son, David Ludwig, for questioning and is asking anyone with information on the whereabouts of David Ludwig to call the sheriff's office. Do not approach the youth as he may be armed and dangerous.

The confused "older son" put down the paper and stared into the pond. *Why can't I remember? Did I kill my family?*

The swishing of White Feather's footsteps in the grass alerted the boy of his approach. David turned to him with fear written on his face. White Feather squinted, looking down at the youth.

White Feather revisited the head wound. It might explain the boy's confusion. He examined the blood on his shirt again. A shooter would have blood splatters on his shirt. The blood on the boy's shirt and pants was not splattered on; it was wiped on. The blood on a shooter's hand would be splatters on the back of the hand. The blood on this boy's hand was on the palm from contact with an already bloody weapon. When he had shaken the boy's hand, there was no sign of gun powder residue nor had he smelled any sign of it. A shooter would have blood splatters on top of his shoe and the soles would be clean. Ludwig's shoes were clean on top with blood on the soles. The blood got on his shoe when he stepped in it.

White Feather reached over and touched the boy's shoulder, "Come with me."

As they passed the bench, White Feather kicked the gun further underneath the bench.

Chapter Ten
Abandoned Train Terminal

WHITE FEATHER LED HIS new friend into an abandoned train terminal residing in the decaying, industrialized part of the old town. The new town had grown away from the terminal after the factories and mining had closed and the trains had stopped coming.

The main room, originally the terminal lobby, was sparsely furnished and poorly lit. The old Indian had set up residence here and still used the old potbelly stove in one corner for heat. It looked as if one day, they just closed the doors and walked away. The ticket counter still lined the back half of the room. Even the signs, "Tickets", "Restrooms", "Café" remained.

White Feather shuffled through the wide entrance under the "Café" sign, "You should eat something."

He motioned to a rickety table surrounded by four dilapidated chairs. David searched the chairs for one strong enough to hold his hefty frame while the old Indian disappeared behind double doors.

Soon, David could smell eggs and bacon frying on a grill. White Feather waddled back out of the kitchen and gathered plates and silverware from behind the bar.

"What are you cooking back there?" David inquired.

White Feather studied David for a moment, "Bacon and eggs, white man's food."

David smiled and nodded approval. He was famished. "What is this place? You live here?"

White Feather placed the plates and silverware on the table as he answered, "Trains stopped here once. No more. Makes a nice home, well built."

David looked around curiously. It did not look like much to him. "The facilities work?" His troubled memory still functioned satisfactorily with regard to certain basic fundamentals.

White Feather was on his way back to the kitchen. He stopped and turned. He seemed puzzled by the question but then nodded and pointed toward the lobby, "Through the entryway, look to your left."

David was surprised to find the bathroom unusually clean and well kept. He entered the first stall and checked the toilet. It had water in it and appeared clean. He flushed it to make sure it worked.

When he left the stall, the stranger in the mirror above the basin surprised him! *Who is that? Where am I?*

He approached the lavatory, noting that his every movement was mimicked by the stranger in the mirror. He reached out to touch the glass, "Me? That's me?"

He turned and headed for the door to explore the strange surroundings. He had already forgotten why he was there or how he got there! The door led to a large, almost empty room with a pot-belly stove in one corner and across the back of the room a long counter with built-in windows atop. Above the counter a sign read "Tickets". *"Tickets for what?"*

"Hello?" he uttered tentatively, "Anyone here?"

He was startled by the appearance of a strange, old man appearing in a wide entryway below a sign reading, "Cafe". "You work here?" David questioned.

The old man shook his head clearly disappointed by the question, "White Feather. Remember?"

"Remember? No, should I remember you?"

The old man studied him with a cold, unreadable stare before speaking, "Your breakfast is ready."

David Ludwig's stomach growled, "OK ... I guess I am hungry."

He followed the strange man into the cafe area where dusty, unused tables and chairs were scattered about the room. One table and chairs had been dusted off and two plates filled with scrambled eggs, bacon, and toast and a glass full of milk lay waiting.

"What is this place?" the stocky boy asked as he eased into the wobbly chair.

"Abandoned train terminal."

"Why are we here?"

The old man, who was obviously Native American, took a deep breath, shook his head in disappointment again and commanded, "Eat your breakfast."

David studied the old man, "Are you my father?"

White Feather giggled, "No. I am just taking care of you for awhile."

David nodded. He did not understand but felt safe with the Indian. Inexplicably, he trusted him. He glanced around the dusky room and then attacked his breakfast.

Chapter Eleven

Meeting at the Crime Scene

Undersheriff Buster Crab was sitting on the porch swing when Sam Morrison arrived at the Ludwig residence. It was 7 a.m. and he was on time. Before turning off the vintage Hemi engine in his Dodge Charger, Sam revved it up. It was a habit established years before at a much younger age. He loved feeling the caged power of a big, powerful engine. He liked to hear the guttural sound of the big engine rev up and then die off when he switched off the ignition.

Buster leisurely rocked the swing back and forth as his old friend and new deputy walked up the porch steps and ducked under the yellow crime scene tape.

"You look like crap," Buster observed.

Morrison ignored his old friend as he plopped onto the moving swing causing it to waggle sideways and force the lounging undersheriff to thrust forward and grab the arm rest. "Real smooth, Morrison!" Buster joked.

Morrison managed a smile. "What've we got?"

The hefty undersheriff looked incredulously at the former metro detective, "Around here we still say good morning and ask 'How ya doin?'"

Morrison rubbed his newly shaved face with his palms and inhaled the crisp, fresh morning mountain air. "Sorry, Buster."

He then offered his hand, "Good to see you, old friend. How ya' been?"

The burly black man bypassed the handshake and surprised Sam by hugging his old friend and grandly patting him on the back. "Good to see you, too."

The befuddled big-city ex-police detective squirmed and pushed away from the too-friendly old friend who howled his delight that he had embarrassed the up-tight detective.

Morrison shifted and collected himself, "I'm ok. I just need some rest."

"Bull pucky! What you need is a nice homicide to get your mind off your troubles."

Buster pulled a manila folder wedged between him and the arm rest of the swing and handed it to the new deputy. Morrison opened the folder and read the typed report. "Shots reported around 5:45 p.m., you got there at 6:10."

Buster added, "Neighbor saw David Ludwig, the older son, run out the back door around 5:55."

Morrison shook his head, "Ten minutes later? That's a long time."

"May have heard Deputy Calhoun snooping around."

Morrison flipped the page to get to the pictures as he asked, "The autopsy?"

"This afternoon."

As Morrison studied the pictures, Crab announced, "There was a break-in last night after our investigation."

Morrison looked up at the old friend, "A break-in? Here?"

"Yep. Tore the place up lookin' for something."

"You know what they were looking for?"

Buster smiled, "Yeah. I think so."

Morrison frowned and waited for Buster to explain, "One of the victims, Jon Ludwig, was a fellow deputy. He fancied himself a photographer. Always insisted on shooting the photos at a crime scene. We found the office camera on a desk in the laundry room sitting next to Jon's computer. When Sheriff Bailey and I checked it, we found some suspicious pictures. We think there may be more on Ludwig's computer. But, what we found on the camera suggests that Ludwig may have been using the camera for blackmail."

Morrison connected the dots, "So, there were incriminating photos of someone in the office?"

Buster nodded his head, "Yeah, maybe. Curious photos of a recent crime scene we worked."

Buster opened up his arms, "We figure he probably transfers his photos to the computer."

Morrison studied Buster and then questioned, "Who's searching the computer?"

Buster shrugged, "CBI took it. If there's anything, they'll find it."

"You think someone from the office broke in last night to get rid of the evidence?"

Buster nodded, "I think it is very likely."

Chapter Twelve
Breakfast with David

WHEN DAVID REACHED UP to scratch his head and flinched, White Feather walked over to try to examine David's head wound. But the boy was reluctant to let a stranger touch him, "How do you feel?" the old Indian asked.

David shrugged and rubbed his head gingerly, "Fine, I guess, just a headache."

White Feather sat down across the table and watched with amusement as his young, brawny guest shoveled down six scrambled eggs, six slices of bacon, four slices of buttered toast in about three bites.

"More?"

David reared back and let out a deep, rumbling belch. He gulped down his glass full of milk and slammed it triumphantly down on the unstable table. White Feather rescued his own glass of juice as the table rocked back and forth. David did not notice, "Naw, I'm good."

The successful cook downed the last of his juice, gathered the dishes and headed for the bar. He placed the dishes in the sink behind the bar and had an idea, "You need to earn your keep; you can wash the dishes."

The boy did not hesitate. He jumped up and rushed over to the sink, "Good breakfast, thanks."

Satisfied that the boy knew how to wash dishes, the Indian turned to walk away. "I better get over to the crime scene and nose around. See what I can find out. You sure you don't remember anything ... anything at all?"

David Ludwig frowned and looked at White Feather with a confused look on his face, "Crime scene?"

"Alright, then. Stay put. If anyone comes nosing around, there's a trap door in the closet behind the old ticket counter leading into the basement. Hide down there."

David followed the old man to the lobby and watched him waddle across the lobby and exit through the front entrance. As he opened the door, he turned and pointed at the closet behind the counter and reminded David, "Trap door in the floor."

"Trap door?" he questioned as he found the closet behind the ticket counter. He glanced around confused as his recent memories faded and left him wondering why he was standing in front of the closet.

Chapter Thirteen

The Crime Scene

MORRISON STEPPED OVER A pile of clothes. "Football uniform?"

Crab explained, "Belonged to the older son, David Ludwig."

Morrison shuffled through the pictures and studied the boy on the couch, Buster clarified, "That's the younger son, Darren. Evidently, David fled the scene. The uniform places David Ludwig at the scene after football practice."

The house was ransacked just as Crab had warned. Morrison walked around the crime scene checking the photos hoping to see some little clue that might have escaped the original investigation. "Who handled the call?"

Buster bumped his thumb up against his chest several times. "Me and Calhoun. Deputy Calhoun arrived first, around 6:00, and I got here around 6:10. Calhoun interviewed the neighbors while I secured the crime scene. Sheriff Bailey got here around 6:20. CBI got here around 8:00."

Surprised, Morrison inquired, "CBI? Why are they involved?"

"Sean called them in on this. A triple homicide is too big for us; we don't have the resources."

Morrison frowned, "So why did he make me drive down in the middle of the night?"

Buster laughed, "It will be a joint investigation. He wants you here to work with their agent."

"Who's that?"

"Miles Blakely."

Morrison smirked, "Smiles? Out of the Springs?" He used the agents nickname that those familiar with him used behind his back.

Crab chuckled, "S. Miles Blakely. That's the one. You worked with him before?"

Morrison nodded, "Yeah. Mr. 'No Nonsense'. Never smiles. Overly dedicated. No personality."

Crab raised an eyebrow, "You two should get along real well!"

Morrison glared at the undersheriff. The comment stung. His colleagues in Denver had described him the same way."

Morrison flipped back to Deputy Calhoun's report. "Five shots?"

Undersheriff Crab nodded, "Yeah, five." He glanced over Morrison's shoulder, "Three short bursts, a pause and then another, a pause and then another. We found five shell casings but could only find three slugs." He glanced around the room pointing out tags scattered around on the floor and sticky notes posted on the walls.

Morrison knelt beside the chalk mark of the father's body and studied the photograph. The outline of a gun was barely apparent in the pool of blood where the blood had dried around it. It was close enough and at the proper angle for the father to have dropped it as he fell.

He heard something fluttering in the kitchen. He looked at Buster and could see that Buster heard it too. In the kitchen, they spotted the window over the sink was raised about three inches. Sitting on the sill outside the screen was a large, black bird. Buster walked toward the kitchen to look closer.

"Raven," Crab remarked from the door of the kitchen. Morrison joined him and glanced around the tousled kitchen, then returned to the living room.

He faced the couch and studied the photographs, "Walk me through it."

Buster cleared his throat and rubbed his chin with his forefinger and thumb. "Well, when I got here the front and back doors were both open. Jessie, Deputy Calhoun, said they were open when he got here, too. I examined the dead man on the floor first. He appears to have been shot through the throat from close range. The shell casings were from a forty-five. The woman was shot from close range in the stomach and the boy was shot in the head. The woman must not've died right away, she appears to have put her arm around the child and tried to nurture him."

Buster waited for Morrison to comment, but his old friend was examining the couch.

Buster continued, "No bullet holes in the couch, so the woman and boy were probably standing when they were shot. The perp' probably left out the back door. One neighbor saw the older son running across the back yard and into the alley. He thought he was carrying a gun

... or something in his hand. But, we haven't found the boy yet."

"Any other relatives in town?"

"None we know of."

"Perp' have a girlfriend?"

"Calhoun's at the school now talking to the football coach. Hopefully he'll learn more about that."

Morrison was examining the walls and ceiling, "Any history of violence?"

"Yeah! We've been called out twice for domestic disturbance calls. Charges were dropped. Neighbors heard him and his father shouting at each other pretty often."

Morrison was staring at the square hole in the wall above the entry into an anteroom. Buster approached him curiously, "Bullet hole. CBI removed the dry wall and took it back to springs with the other evidence."

Morrison pointed at the center of the hole with his pointing finger and pivoted around to trace the line of flight.

They could both see that the line was too steep. Buster offered his explanation, "Must've deflected off the skull somehow. Forty-five's will do that."

Morrison pointed his finger in line with the line of flight and imagined the head of the dead man standing by the couch. Then he placed his finger against his own throat. "Could be a suicide."

Morrison reexamined the photographs. He leafed through them apparently searching for one in particular. When he found it, he scrutinized the picture and then the couch area.

He was ready to share with Buster, "Bruises on the woman's and boy's faces. Scratches on the man's face.

Table pushed back. Lamp knocked over. There was a struggle. The Medical Examiner examining the body this afternoon?"

"Yeah, the coroner in Colorado Springs will set that up."

"Did you find Deputy Ludwig's service pistol?"

Buster check his notepad, "It was in the bedroom still holstered. CBI took in for a ballistics check. Didn't appear to have been fired recently."

Morrison looked at Buster curiously, "Did you know the Ludwigs?"

Buster put away his notepad, "Yeah, I knew Jon, of course. He's been a deputy since before I came on. Not a likeable guy. I suspect he was an alcoholic and probably beat his wife, but they kept to themselves. The other deputies despised him, but he did his job and was sober while he was working."

Morrison stood in front of the couch and studied a picture. "No bullet holes in the couch?"

Buster shook his head, "No, it was searched thoroughly. Bullet didn't pass through Matilda apparently. The boy was sitting." Buster pointed to the blood splatter on the top of the couch.

Morrison pointed his finger at the imaginary head of the boy as if he were sitting on the couch. A section of dry wall was missing in the dining room next to a painting of the Last Supper. He tried different angles, stood back and considered the evidence, shook his head and commented, "Odd angle. I'm anxious to see the autopsy report."

Morrison finished up his notes, Buster headed for the door, "Let's go over to the office. Sean said he expects Smiles to show up around 9:00 and then he wants us to catch up with Calhoun at the school."

Chapter Fourteen

David Explores the Terminal

Dᴀᴠɪᴅ Lᴜᴅᴡɪɢ ᴏᴘᴇɴᴇᴅ ᴛʜᴇ door to the closet behind the ticket counter. He did not know why, but he was expecting to find stairs. Instead, the closet had a normal looking floor. The tip of his foot touched the floor inside the closet and he heard a clicking sound and felt the floor give slightly. When he stepped back, the floor popped up a few inches in front. He dropped to his knees and slid his fingers underneath the narrow gap and lifted. The floor was hinged on the back side and easily opened to reveal steps leading into a basement.

The curious explorer ventured a few steps down the steep staircase into the darkness. David felt the wall to find a light switch with no luck. He backed up and out of the closet and turned to look for matches, flashlight, candle, anything.

An old rusty lantern sitting at the far end of the ticket counter caught his eye. He examined it and determined that it had fuel in the rounded tank that doubled as its stand. David could not remember ever lighting a lantern before, but the knobs and mechanics of the lantern was oddly familiar to him. He fiddled with the knobs on the side. They were rusty and hard to twist, but after working with them, he was able to get the wick to rise and fall. The other knob raised the globe. "Matches! I need matches."

David started looking around and found himself in a dining room full of tables and chairs. He stopped at a sink where dirty dishes were stacked and others sitting to dry, suggesting that someone had started washing the dishes and then quit. He looked around the room filled with dusty old dining tables and chairs. "What is this place?" he whispered to himself.

He ventured through some double-doors, checked the empty kitchen and then returned to the dining room. Next, he went to the big open room, the lobby next to the dining room. Although it had only been a few minutes since he had been in the room, when he saw the long counter down the right side of the lobby, it puzzled him; he was confused.

To his left, a sign over the door read "Restrooms". To the left of the restrooms, a narrow stairway led upstairs. "Hello! Anyone home?"

He climbed the stairs to the second level. The stairs landed in a short hallway leading to the left into a moderate-sized living room, dining room combination. A door connected the living room to a bedroom and bathroom. No one was home.

A sleeping bag lying on the bare mattress of the bed looked to have been used recently, "Hello! Anyone home?"

David walked to the window and looked out, "How did I get here? What is this place?"

Outside the window were rows of unfamiliar abandoned warehouses and factory buildings. A fertile valley stretched out beyond the buildings rising in the distance to become massive mountains. The valley was dotted by an occasional house and barn, and cattle grazed lazily in the large fenced blocks. "Ranchland," he clarified for himself. Explicit memories of the past, even moments earlier, were blank, but skills he had learned in his unknown past were oddly intact.

Bewildered, he returned to the lower level where the curious, mostly empty room with a long counter down one side confounded him again. As he walked to the center of the room, he saw a sign above the counter that read, "Tickets". A large opening connected to a room with table and chairs. Above the opening, a sign read "Cafe".

He explored the cafe and found double doors leading into a kitchen. The kitchen was empty. *Where is everyone?* he wondered.

Coming out of the kitchen and to his left was a bar. Dirty dishes were in the sink. They were the same dishes he had neglected to wash sitting in the same sink he had passed only minutes before, but either his injured hippocampus had neglected to record these events or was unable to retrieve them.

Someone was here recently, he reasoned, "Anyone here?" he yelled.

He noticed the stairs, so he climbed the stairs to find a small kitchen and a living room combination. A door led to a bedroom and bathroom. "Anyone home?" he yelled.

A rumpled sleeping bag was atop the dirty bare mattress suggesting someone had slept there recently. A small hallway led out of the living room where he discovered a stairs leading downstairs. *Maybe there is someone downstairs.*

And so it went for the young man, whose brain could no longer wield his memories, condemning him to search and discover the mysterious rooms of the train depot over and over again.

Finally, the boy tired and went out to sit on the long porch in front of the depot. He watched as an old man appeared and trudged up the street. When the old man drew close, he spotted him, stopped and yelled, "What are you doing outside?"

David shrugged, "I dunno."

White Feather, glanced around, and then rushed up to the boy and said urgently in a low voice, "Get inside! Someone might see you."

David was confused, "Who are you?"

The old Indian shook his head in bewilderment. "It's ok, I'm White Feather. I'm your friend."

The boy seemed doubtful, glancing around as if discovering the depot for the first time, "Where am I?"

White Feather shook his head, "My home. Used to be an old train terminal."

"Why am I here?"

White Feather led the bewildered boy inside and over to the pot-bellied stove. He opened its door and from a pile next to the stove, placed several old, dry, wood shingles in the stove, stirred the embers until they glowed and ignited the kindling.

"Sit!" the fire tender commanded. A long, rectangular, brightly colored blanket lay on the floor in front of the stove.

David dropped to the blanket and sat cross-legged like a small child, fascinated by the growing fire. He looked up at the frail old man, "You cold?"

White Feather chuckled. "The fire is for ... counsel, not warmth."

White Feather sat beside him, pulled the newspaper article out of his shirt pocket and handed it to him. David Ludwig looked at it but nothing registered on his face. White Feather explained, "That's you."

The young fire gazer got serious. After a thoughtful pause, he asked, "That's me?"

White Feather nodded. The boy returned to the article, "I killed those people?"

White Feather studied the boy. He showed only surprise, confusion, and doubt, but no remorse. "Aren't you sad about your parents?"

The boy looked at White Feather, then stared at the fire; "Those are my parents? I don't remember them. I don't know those people in the paper. I don't even recognize me."

If what the boy said was true, it made sense. How could he feel remorse for people he did not remember? That he did not know? But, if he was lying and the amnesia was a cover, he was the most cold-blooded killer White Feather had ever met—next to himself.

Chapter Fifteen

Wet Mountain County Sheriff's Office

Undersheriff Crab proudly led the new deputy into the Wet Mountain County Sheriff's Office. They entered through the side door from the staff parking area into a wide hallway. A large blackboard was attached to the wall to the right. To the left a door opened to a laundry room where orange jumpsuits were stacked neatly in shelves along the opposite wall from several sets of washers and driers. Next to the laundry was a large kitchen with an island counter in the center. Two men in orange jump-suits were busy working and talking noisily.

Buster led Morrison to the right down a short hallway and stopped at the intersection with a long hallway branching off to the left. Buster pointed down that hallway and explained, "Detention is down there."

He pointed to his right, "Bathroom."

They continued straight into a large, open office area with four desks butted up against each other forming a large island in the center of the room. Each desk contained a computer. Buster explained as they walked past them, "These desks are for the deputies to use to do their paper-work," he pointed to his right, "that's the break room."

The next small office contained a desk and filing cabi-nets, "That's the Administrative Assistant's office. She's not in right now."

Buster looked across the deputies' desks and pointed out the other areas of the open office are, "That's UA over there and that's a little conference desk for meetings."

The "UA" was just a desk next to a small bathroom.

He turned and pointed into an office in the northeast corner, "That's Sheriff Bailey's office."

Sheriff Sean Bailey walked out of his office and joined them. The fit, deceptively tall young man smiled brightly and reached out his hand, "Sean Bailey."

Morrison gripped his hand, "Sam Morrison. It's a pleasure to meet you, Sheriff."

"Yeah, you, too. Buster has really bragged on you. Glad to finally get to see you in person."

Bailey smiled at Buster and pointed his thumb, "Go ahead and finish the tour, Chief, then bring Sam back to my office." He turned to Morrison, "See you in a minute, Sam."

Morrison smirked at his old friend, "Chief?"

Buster snickered, "Inside joke at sheriff offices. Kind of a snipe at police chiefs."

Morrison was confused. Buster explained, "Sheriff's wear four stars, police chiefs wear three. Calling the under-sheriff 'chief' is an underhanded slam on their lower rank."

Morrison got it and laughed.

The Chief led Morrison to a short hallway in the northwest corner of the room. As he passed two closed doors, he pointed out, "File and copy room. Evidence Room."

They pushed through the door into an intersecting hallway. They were facing a counter where a young girl put down her paperback novel and smiled, "Mornin', Buster."

"Mornin' Gabby. This is Sam Morrison, the deputy, I told you about. Sam, this is our dispatcher, Deedie, AKA Gabby."

Her face lit up igniting a bright smile, "Oh! Pleased to meet you."

She reached out her hand and Morrison gripped it lightly, "Pleased to meet you, too. What are you reading?"

Deedie blushed, glanced at Buster, and then held up the book for Morrison to see, "Agatha Christopher, Murder Mystery."

Morrison nodded knowingly, "Oh, yes, I like Agatha Christie mysteries."

Deedie's eyes widened, "Oh, not Agatha Christie, Agatha Christopher. She's a local author. But, I like Agatha Christie, too."

She tilted her head and batted her eyelashes, "Welcome aboard."

Morrison nodded and then followed Buster to the left down a long hallway where he first pointed out a small anteroom and then the interrogation room. Next they stepped into an office on the right. An older, distinguished looking woman in uniform stood and glared at the two intruders. Buster introduced Morrison, "Terry, this is our new deputy, Sam Morrison. Sam, this is Terry Kruger our Senior Detention Officer."

They shook hands but the stern officer only nodded, denying him her smile. Buster pointed at a window in the south side of the office, That's men's detention back there. Morrison could see a long, wide open area with two picnic-style tables. Through the narrow window he could make out three cell doors. He assumed there were three more on the opposite side. He remarked, "Six cells?"

Officer Kruger confirmed, "We have six cells in male detention and three in women's detention. Twelve beds for the men, six for women."

Morrison raised his eyebrows, "That seems like a lot of beds for such a small population."

Buster explained, "We contract out to the state. Helps our budget."

Morrison was startled when an inmate charged up to the small window and pressed his face against the glass producing a grotesque appearance through the one-way glass.

Officer Kruger excused herself and rushed into the hallway. As Buster led Morrison out of the office, he could overhear Kruger and the inmate chatting through the large metal door, "Just paint the cinder block wall in front of the shower."

Buster led Morrison down another long hallway running east-west. They stopped at a door on the right with a large glass pane. Inside, two chairs were placed back-to-back and each faced a counter with a thick glass above it. Phone-like receivers hung on the walls. Morrison recognized the tiny visitors area, but Buster confirmed, "Visitor room for detention. To the left is women's detention, men's to the right, of course."

The hallway terminated back at the restrooms. They turned left to return to the main offices where they found two deputies in the open area. Buster introduced them, "This is Deputy Wooten and Deputy Bennet, they take the lead in drug investigations, and this is ..."

Bennet stood, reached out his hand and interrupted the chief's introduction, "Detective Morrison. We've heard a lot about you."

Bennet was average height, trim and fit, with black wavy hair, dark eyes and complexion. Morrison shook his hand and nodded to Wooten who was not inclined to move off the cabinet he was leaning against. The tall, muscular, blond-headed Wooten nodded and continued to work his teeth with a toothpick.

Morrison sensed that what they had heard about him was not good. It had been the Central Vice Control Section of the Denver Police Department that had spurred the investigation to dismiss him. He suspected the fallacious charges had spread far and wide among the cliquish drug agents, even to rural Wet Mountain Valley.

Morrison challenged the confident Deputy Wooten, "Nice shiner!"

Wooten did not blink or attempt to explain his bruised left eye. Deputy Bennet answered for him, "Hazards of the business."

Sheriff Bailey interrupted the macho gamesmanship, "Ok, you've met Drug Enforcement, let's go to my office and get the formalities out of the way."

Wooten and Bennet smiled condescendingly at Morrison. Sheriff Bailey escorted Morrison into his office and closed the door. He stood at the door for a moment staring through the glass vision pane at the open area. "Whaddaya think of Wooten and Bennet?"

Morrison shrugged. The sheriff shook his head and turned to walk around his desk. "Real tough guys, eh? Have a seat."

Morrison sat down in one of the padded guest chairs in front of the sheriff's desk, crossed his legs, clasped his hands in his lap and defended the deputies: "Rough job."

The sheriff nodded, "Takes a special breed to survive in that world. Of course, drug enforcement is just part of their job. We're too small here to specialize. We all have to do everything."

The sheriff pulled out a pistol snapped securely in a holster designed to attach onto a belt and laid it on the desk. He pulled out another desk drawer and found a badge. Morrison stood, took the gun out of the holster and slipped it into the shoulder holster he wore under his jacket. He pulled out his wallet and pinned the badge inside.

Bailey raised his right hand, Morrison copied him, "You solemnly swear and all that crap?"

"I do."

Bailey shook his hand and handed Morrison a multi-paged form. "Get this back to me when you can. You can pick up your security card from Deedie. Did you meet Judy?"

Morrison frowned, "I don't think so."

Bailey pointed to the south, "She's my Administrative Assistant. Her office is next door. Get with her on your uniforms."

Morrison instantly liked Bailey. He seemed like a down-to-earth, unpretentious young man. He knew from talking to Buster that Bailey was in his late forties, but his smooth, round face made him appear much younger.

Bailey started the conversation, "So, where did you grow up?"

Morrison sat back down, "Fowler, Colorado. Dad had a cantaloupe farm. Went to CSU in Pueblo for two years. I met Samantha there and we got married in 1996. Graduated from the Police Academy in Pueblo and landed a job in the Denver Police Department, Homicide Division."

The sheriff smiled and then shifted in his chair, "I didn't know you were married."

"We divorced five years ago. Samantha and the kids moved here, actually, after the divorce."

"That's a coincidence. What are the odds? How many kids?"

"Two. Tammy is 17 and Jerry is 15. Yeah, it'll be nice to be near the kids again."

"No wonder you accepted the job so quickly."

Morrison let it pass and did not correct the sheriff. After getting fired in Denver, he would have jumped at any offer in law enforcement.

The sheriff sat up and looked at his watch, "Well, it's almost ten and Agent Blakeley isn't here yet."

Bailey focused on Morrison, "Did Buster tell you that you'll be working with CBI Agent Miles Blakeley on this case?

Morrison smiled and nodded, "Yeah. Good ole' Smiles."

The sheriff chuckled, "So, you know him?"

Morrison shrugged, "Worked with him on a couple of cases."

The sheriff motioned for Buster to come over. "Heard from Miles?"

Buster shook his head, "Nope."

"Wanna take Sam over to the school and see what Calhoun's up to?"

"Sure. Don't forget I have that thing at noon."

Sheriff Bailey nodded. "No problem. Sam can hang out with Calhoun today."

Chapter Sixteen

White Feather Uses the Crystal

WHITE FEATHER SHIFTED ON the blanket and watched the fire burn down in the stove. He reported to David seated beside him what he had learned at the crime scene from the two deputies, "Three shots, a pause and another shot, a pause and another shot. Five shots in all but only three found their target."

White Feather remembered hearing the shots himself that afternoon while sitting on the roof watching the clouds spilling over the peaks of the Sangres. "One slug was found in the wall near the ceiling. Deputy figured it must have been the shot that killed Mr. Ludwig, although an odd angle for a head wound. Most likely the fifth shot." White Feather paused. It was unnatural for him to talk so much. He was naturally a quiet man, living alone, avoiding people. But, surprisingly, he was enjoying this rare discourse. "The three short shots are curious. Perhaps, Mrs. Ludwig had struggled with her husband causing three shots to be discharged but only one hit her in the stomach. If that were the case, maybe she let go and stepped back, the younger son tried to intervene and the father shoved him onto the couch and shot him, execution style, in the head. His mother fell beside him and put her arm around him to cradle him. Mr. Ludwig may have regretted what happened, turned the gun on himself."

White Feather looked over at the boy staring blankly at the fire. He shook his head. It was an act of futility conversing with the boy. He was leaning toward believing the boy's amnesia excuse, but over his many years, he had seen enough cases to know that memory loss can be caused by many different things and manifest itself in many different ways. In most cases, the person just needed time to recover; time for the wounds to heal.

But, he had also seen cases among the white man, never among his people, where their memory loss was a sham to cover something they wanted to hide. A Cherokee would never consider faking amnesia. It would be lying. In ancient times, a man was killed for lying so that the tendency would not spread to others.

In his experience, the white people who had feigned amnesia were devious and manipulative. He saw no signs of these characteristics in David Ludwig. He decided to test the boy, "We must consult the crystals."

David snapped out of his trance and looked curiously at the Indian. White Feather tried to push himself up to his feet. The young athlete jumped up to assist his new friend but stumbled back holding his dizzy head. After a moment, he shook it off and asked, "What happened? Where am I?"

White Feather did not respond, just shook his head as he disappeared into the "Cafe" and returned with two large beach-type towels. David followed the old wizard like a faithful puppy outside and down an untraveled street to a small stream.

"Strip." The old man commanded.

David was shocked, "What?"

White Feather shuffled toward the stream, "We must do this in the long man. Take off your clothes unless you don't mind getting them soaked."

David looked down, "I don't mind." Then he asked, "Who is the long man?"

White feather chuckled, "The stream. My people call streams and rivers 'Long Man'."

White Feather stepped out of his moccasins and shoved off his jeans and shirt. He stepped into the calm of a knee-deep pond at the base of rocky rapids. When David shuffled up to the bank, White Feather pulled a clear crystal from the circular pouch built into his elaborate necklace. The way the facets branched out from the center, they reminded David of a Star Wars Starfighter ship.

White Feather handed him the crystal, but before letting go he cautioned, "I've had this ... this crystal is thousands of years old. Don't drop it!"

David took a deep breath and gripped the heavy crystal firmly. Then it hit him, "Thousands of years?"

White Feather chuckled and begrudgingly let go. The slippery crystal squirted from David's fingers back into the wizard's hands. The bungling boy gasped, "Nice catch!"

The disgusted old man closed his hand around his precious crystal and turned away from the bungling young fool. Instead of admonishing the young man, he said simply, "You sure you want to wear those sweatpants?"

While David considered the consequences, he studied the nearly naked Indian who was skin and bones and only wore white briefs. Deciding, David took a deep breath, glanced all around and quickly flung off his clothes. Covering his privates, the timid giant made sure once more that they were isolated and then stepped into the pond.

The water was ice-cold and the suddenly freezing giant leaped back out, "Cheeeez!"

White Feather cackled and shook his head, "Wimp."

David looked at the impertinent medicine man and watched him wade up to the rocks at the end of the small rapids. He gingerly stepped back into the icy pond and joined the old man.

Immediately, the Cherokee medicine man began to chant and hold up the crystal to the heavens. David felt very awkward. He did not know whether he should bow his head, beseech the heavens, or say a prayer. He decided to slightly bow his head and remain quiet.

White feather's chant went on for some time. The strange old man occasionally rotated saying his prayer to the seven directions: east, south, west, north, up, down and center.

Then he turned to explain the ritual to the shivering "wimp." "The crystal held under the water reveals the truth. I will hold the crystal under the water and you must look for your image in the many facets. As you search for your image, I will speak to the spirit world. When you find your image, you must tell me whether your image is vertical or horizontal."

David appeared to be confused. The medicine man simplified, "Standing or lying down!"

"Oh! Ok."

White Feather dropped to his knees and carefully cradled the crystal under the foamy white water flowing over the rocks. He closed his eyes and began to chant again in his native language. He moved the crystal around tracing a figure eight and rolled his shoulder to and fro. Ending the chant and holding the crystal steady, he opened his eyes and nodded at David indicating that it was time.

David dropped to his knees in the pool and studied the crystal. He tilted his head first one way and then the other. The icy water splashed off the crystal producing ever changing shadows and images. It was very hard to concentrate on the crystals while flinching and shivering, but he could not see an image of a person in the crystal. He dropped down on all fours and poked his nose to within a few inches of the crystal to focus on the dark images in the crystal facets.

"Vertical!" he shouted proudly.

White Feather studied the boy for a moment and then pulled the crystal away from the rushing waters, replaced it into the pouch in his necklace and grabbed the boy's face with both hands. Looking deeply into his eyes he declared, "Now! Listen! Tell me what you remember."

David's eyes grew large as river stones as he inhaled and strained to remember something, anything, but his mind was blank. Sadly, he admitted, "I don't remember anything."

White Feather studied him for what seemed like forever, then, suddenly, the spindly medicine man released the boy's head, stood and waded out of the stream. "We're done, let's go."

David found the old man drying off with a beach towel. As he stepped out of the stream, White feather handed him one.

"So, you some kind of shaman or witch doctor or something?"

White Feather snorted contemptuously. "Shaman is a white man's word meant to belittle Native American men of medicine."

David slumped under his towel. He was still shivering from the icy waters of the stream. "Oh, sorry. I didn't mean nothing."

White Feather backed off, "If the shamans were white, you would call them a doctor or a priest. In my culture, they are both."

The doctor/priest analogy was correct for shamans. But White Feather neglected to tell the curious lad that he was more. White Feather could more accurately be described as a witch or wizard.

"So, what did the crystal tell you?"

White Feather shrugged, "You are a truthful man."

"You don't sound like you're convinced."

White Feather shrugged. "Get dressed. I need to go out again. I will take you to a safe place."

David nodded agreement, but did not know what he was agreeing to.

Chapter Seventeen
Letter to Self

Wʜɪᴛᴇ Fᴇᴀᴛʜᴇʀ ᴛᴀᴘᴘᴇᴅ ᴛʜᴇ paper with his forefinger, "Write it."

David Ludwig took a deep breath, "You write it."

The impatient Indian shook his head, "Has to be in your handwriting. Tomorrow you won't know me."

David blew out his disgust, "Alright."

As White Feather dictated, the doubtful scribe scribbled the note to himself explaining his relationship with White Feather and his dire situation. When finished, he slapped the pen down on the paper contemptuously. David Ludwig felt disconsolate living in a world within such a narrow history that he could not remember the name of the old man sitting across from him; where he could not remember his own name; where he did not know where he was or why he was there.

White Feather placed his bony hand on the large fist of the lost boy, "We'll get this all straightened out."

The angry boy moved his fist away from the consoling touch of the old Indian. White Feather pushed himself up from the chair, "Ready?"

David shrugged and followed the only person he knew in the world, thus the only person he trusted in the world. White Feather led the boy out of the cafe, turned and slipped in behind the long counter. He turned again, opened the door to a small closet and tapped the closet floor with his foot. It obediently clicked up. David stepped in to save the old man from having to stoop over and lift the trap door. White Feather handed him the flashlight and followed him down the stairs.

The dark, dusky room was filled with miscellanea. White Feather directed the muscular boy to slide an old vanity with a tall mirror mounted in the center over to the center of the room facing an old army cot.

White Feather placed a manila folder on the vanity and boldly wrote "WHO IS DAVID LUDWIG?" on it with a marker. David did not recognize the letter and articles from the newspaper that the old man placed inside. White Feather nodded to the boy and turned to return upstairs.

"Where you goin'?" David cried.

The old man turned, smiled and said reassuringly, "You'll be safe here."

David glanced around at the strange, dirty, cluttered room, "Safe from what?"

The Indian seemed reluctant to answer. *Indians are like that,* He thought to himself, although he did not know where he had derived that bit of information; he was unaware how the brain classified information learned differently than information remembered. The Indian spoke, "Just wait here."

David sensed that the gritty old man had said all he was going to say. He watched the frail man climb the stairs and disappear through the square hole in the ceiling. When the trap door closed, he expected to be left in total darkness, but his eyes had adjusted and there was a small window near the top of one wall that allowed some light through its dingy panes. He switched off the flashlight and placed it on the vanity in the center of the room.

He sat on the rickety cot and wondered if he was in the army. Perhaps his orders were in the manila folder sitting atop the vanity. The folder was addressed to "David Ludwig." Perhaps he should wait for Mr. Ludwig to return.

Chapter Eighteen
Calhoun and the Coach

CHIEF BUSTER CRAB AND Deputy Sam Morrison spotted Deputy Jessie Calhoun in the Wet Mountain Valley High School coach's glass-walled office. Calhoun was facing the coach with his back toward his approaching colleagues. He had his feet propped up on the coach's desk leaning back on two legs of the chair and was telling a tall tale for the amusement of the coach. However, the impatient coach did not appear to be amused.

When the coach spotted the deputies, his face expressed surprise and then relief. He smiled at Calhoun, got his attention, and nodded his head toward his colleagues. Calhoun dropped his head back and craned around to see what the coach was trying to tell him. When he saw Undersheriff Buster Crab, his eyes bulged and while scrambling to remove his feet from the desk, he tipped over his chair, landing with a crash on his back dragging papers and knick-knacks with him. The coach lunged over the desk reflexively trying to catch Calhoun and then burst out laughing when he saw the deputy sprawled on the floor.

As Morrison followed Buster into the coach's office, he heard someone chuckling. He glanced to his left and saw an old man in a blue khaki uniform mopping the floor. Expressionless, Buster stepped over his clumsy colleague and shook hands with the popular coach, "Coach."

"Buster."

"Coach, I would like for you to meet our new deputy, Sam Morrison, fresh out of the Denver P. D."

Morrison reached over Deputy Calhoun, who was trying to roll out of his overturned chair, to shake the coach's hand. "Coach."

"Please have a seat, gentlemen." The coach indicated two chairs set against the floor-to-ceiling glass pane that gave the coach a clear view of the sports training center.

Calhoun stood up holding a stack of papers that were in disarray. He placed the stack on the coach's desk and clumsily tried to straighten the stack to no avail before giving up to step over the overturned chair and extend his hand to the new deputy, "Jessie Calhoun."

Morrison leaned forward and nodded as he shook the flustered deputy's hand.

Calhoun quickly righted his chair, raked up the knick-knacks and scattered them on the coach's desk. Buster Crab frowned at the fumbling officer, "So, what have you learned, Jessie?"

Jessie sat down and pulled out his note book. He flipped the pages over and back several times until he found the page he was looking for, "Ludwig mysteriously left practice early. Sometime around 4:45 p.m. No one has seen him since."

Crab waited, shifted in his seat, "That's it?"

Deputy Calhoun flicked through the sheets of his notebook again and studied several different pages. "Yep! That's it so far."

Morrison addressed the coach, "When was the last time you saw David Ludwig?"

"We were running drills on the field. Ludwig is a defensive safety—a good one. He hits hard and goes full speed all the time. We ran green 51—the fullback up the middle—and Ludwig came up fast and laid out the fullback on the line of scrimmage. What a collision! Ludwig's helmet flew off and it nearly tore off his pads, as well."

The coach smiled broadly as he paused to remember the moment. He shook his head, "What a collision. I called the boys over to huddle up to give Ludwig and the fullback time to pull themselves back together. When I looked up, Ludwig was gone! His helmet and pads were lying on the field but he was gone."

Morrison did not look up from his notepad, "What time was that?"

The coach scratched the side of his cheek, "Like I told Calhoun, probably around ... oh, four forty-five, I guess."

Morrison scribbled notes in his notebook and continued, "How was he that day ... how did he act? Was he any different? Anything bothering him?"

The coach thought about it. Deputy Calhoun squinted at the coach in anticipation. The coach shook his head, "No, not really. He seemed his usual easy-going self."

Morrison nodded, "Do you know if he was having any trouble at home?"

The coach took a deep breath, "Everyone knew he didn't get along with his old man. There were several incidents."

Morrison looked up from his notepad, "Several incidents?"

"Calhoun could probably fill you in on that. I just heard the scuttlebutt."

Calhoun jumped at the opportunity, "Domestic disturbances. Twice called out for domestic disturbances, fighting with his old man."

Buster interjected, "Charges were dropped." He turned to Morrison, "I told you about that."

Morrison was busy writing, "Why was HE called out and not his old man?"

Calhoun looked at Undersheriff Crab and then back at Morrison, "I guess he was the one causin' the fight!"

"Were you there?"

Calhoun sat back smugly, "No, Sir. I believe Deputy Melton answered those calls."

Morrison kept writing, "Coach, how was his temperament after those ... incidents? Was he dejected? Angry?"

The coach looked up toward the ceiling, "Well, as near as I recall, he was just quiet. You know, just stayed to himself kinda."

"Did he ever talk to you about it?"

"No, not really. I called him in after one of the incidents and asked him if he wanted to talk about it but he declined."

Morrison put down his notepad and looked seriously at the coach, "What did you do when you realized that Ludwig had disappeared?"

The coach seemed uneasy and shifted in his chair. His eyes darted about as he replayed it in his mind.

"Well ... I didn't notice immediately. I was going over some ideas with the assistant coach as the boys huddled up. When I looked around and saw that Ludwig was missing, I asked what happened to him? The others were also surprised that he was gone, so I sent Dave, the assistant coach, to the locker room to look for him. He came right back and said that Ludwig wasn't there either."

Morrison raised an eyebrow. The coach continued, "I figured after that hit, he was not feeling well, you know? The helmet was cracked right down the center. I had the manager gather his stuff up off the field."

Morrison made some more notes as the coach continued, "As we continued to practice, I got to thinking about it and decided to knock off early and go check on him. But when I drove up to the house, the sheriff was there so I left. I heard about the murders this morning."

Morrison stared at the coach for a moment, "What time would you say you arrived at the Ludwig house?"

The coach glanced up at the large, round clock in the training center, "Hmm. Must have been around 6:45 or 7:00, I guess."

Morrison made a note in his pad, "How late do practices normally last?"

The coach was surprised by the question, "Seven usually."

Morrison looked at the coach, "So, you only knocked off fifteen minutes early?"

The coach squirmed in his chair, "Well, I INTENDED to knock off early, but things kept coming up. One of the players hit himself in the head with a barbell. So, by the time I got away, it wasn't so early after all."

Morrison finished up his notes and then turned to Buster and nodded. Buster looked at Deputy Calhoun, "You got anything else, Jessie?"

Jessie smugly closed his note pad and placed it in his breast pocket, "That's all I need."

The Chief shook his head, Calhoun tapped his body cam, "It's all right here."

Undersheriff Crab stood and shook hands with the coach, "Thanks, Coach."

Morrison shook hands with the coach, "Do you have a name, Coach? Besides 'Coach'?"

Coach laughed, "Jones, Berlin Jones. But everybody just calls me 'Coach'."

Morrison smiled sympathetically, "I don't have any cards, Coach Jones, but if you think of anything else you can call dispatch and she'll get ahold of me."

The coach smiled, "I will. And welcome to Rockcliffe. It's a nice little town once you get to know it."

Morrison nodded, "I'm sure I'll like it fine."

As they reached the door, Morrison paused and turned for one more question, "Did you know Jon Ludwig?"

The coach seemed nervous, "Not very well. I've met him, I think."

Morrison studied him for a moment noting that the question seemed to suddenly make the coach nervous, then nodded and turned to leave.

Chapter Nineteen
The Principal

THE THREE MEN OF the law strolled down the empty hallway of the school lost in their individual thoughts. Morrison was curious about Calhoun's body cam comment, "Buster, do you record all interviews on your body cams?"

Buster felt his body cam, "Oh, yeah. Even in, or especially in, the interview room. Remind me to get you one assigned when we get back."

Morrison glanced at Deputy Calhoun. He felt sorry for the proud man who had gotten off to such a bungling start with a new deputy. Morrison decided to try to mend the bridge, "Jessie, I'd like your opinion. Do you think the Coach was telling the truth?"

Jessie looked surprised by the question. He puffed up a little and declared, "Oh, yeah! He's tellin' the truth!"

Morrison added, "The WHOLE truth?"

He nodded his head again, "Yep."

Morrison was a little disappointed with the quickness of his answer. "You seem pretty sure."

"Everbody knows Ludwig's the best safety we've ever had."

Morrison stopped and studied his new colleague. He tried to decide whether Calhoun was pulling his leg or was just that dumb. Morrison's scrutiny was making Calhoun uncomfortable.

Calhoun puffed up, "I've seen Ludwig play! He's an animal!"

The unbelieving Morrison looked at Buster. Crab snorted apologetically and shook his head. He pointed to the end of the hall. "The principal's office is down there. I've gotta get going or I'll be late for my appointment. Jessie, take care of Deputy Morrison. Sean wants him to take the lead on this one—wants to see what he can do."

Deputy Calhoun saluted, "No problem, Chief."

Deputy Calhoun led his colleague through the administrative offices of the school to a back office where a distinguished looking older woman sat erect behind her desk, "Hey, Mrs. Pentington."

The woman glanced up, "Hey, Calhoun."

"We need to see the principal."

Mrs. Pentington smirked, "You in trouble again?"

Calhoun's eyes widened like a deer in headlights and his face turned bright red. Mrs. Pentington chuckled as she picked up the phone and pressed a button, "Two deputies to see you. ... Ok."

"Go on in, Deputies."

Pentington looked down and appeared to ignore the deputies as they passed by. Morrison studied her as they entered the principal's office. She seemed to be avoiding eye contact. His scrutiny was interrupted by his new partner's greeting, "Hey, Elton!"

"Elton" was a tall, thin, distinguished looking man with wire-rimmed, round glasses, brown tweed suit jacket, beige shirt and green tie. His hair was gray and thinning, but no signs of balding. When he looked up to see Deputy Calhoun, his kindly smile faded slightly. He stood and reached out his hand, "Good morning, Deputy Calhoun."

Calhoun grabbed his hand and gave it a jarring tug. "This is my new partner from Denver, Deputy Morrison."

Morrison nudged Calhoun aside and shook the principal's hand. "Elton Wheeler, Deputy, nice to meet you. Please be seated."

Morrison began, "We are investigating the Ludwig triple homicide."

"Yes, I assumed you must be. Are you just here for the investigation, Mr. Morrison?"

Calhoun butted in, "He's here for good! Can you believe it? From Denver to little ole Rockcliffe."

The room fell awkwardly quiet for a moment, Morrison picked it up, "Buster Crab and I go back …"

The principal smiled, "Oh, yes, that's right, Buster Crab was in Denver for many years. You must've worked together."

"We were in different divisions, but we worked together on a number of cases that overlapped."

"Buster must think a lot of you to recommend you to work here."

"We got to be good friends. We worked together well. I am grateful for the opportunity to work with him again."

The principal nodded, clasped his hands on the desk and smiled, "So, how can I help you?"

Morrison pulled out his note pad. He was impressed that the principal had the class to not ask more questions. Calhoun grabbed his notepad as well. Morrison sat back and crossed his legs, "Tell me about David Ludwig. What kind of student was he?"

Elton Wheeler pulled his interlaced hands back off his desk to his stomach, took a deep breath, and focused on a point somewhere above Morrison's head. "David was ... is a model student. He gets good, not great, grades. Good enough to play football. I never see him in my office, which is a good thing; it means you're probably behaving yourself." Wheeler paused to chuckle. He was joined by Calhoun but Morrison remained stern. Principal Wheeler continued, "His teachers always speak highly of him. He appears to be respected and liked by his classmates."

As Principal Wheeler finished his praise of David Ludwig, he refocused on Morrison and smiled. Morrison made some notes, "Have you noticed any change in his behavior lately? Any tardiness?"

The principal refocused on the ceiling, "Hmm. No ... No, I can't say as I have. Just a moment ..."

He reached over and pushed a button on his over-sized desk phone, "Mrs. Pentington, could you bring me David Ludwig's attendance records, please."

Morrison interjected, "And the brother, Darren, too."

Wheeler added Darren Ludwig to his request, a staticky voice replied, "Yes, Mr. Wheeler."

"Are you aware of any troubles at home?" Morrison probed.

The elderly, attractive, well dressed Mrs. Pentington charged into the office and handed the principal two legal-sized ledger-like sheets. Morrison noticed a nasty bruise on her cheek under thick makeup.

"Thanks, Dottie." Wheeler responded. As she turned to leave, she noticed Morrison's scrutiny and covered the side of her face with her fingers.

Wheeler studied the cards. "No tardiness issues. Well, except Darren missed his last class yesterday. Hmm. It was Study Hall and it looks like he skipped out on several occasions. As far as problems at home, we knew that David sometimes fought with his father. I understand he was arrested once or twice. Calhoun could probably tell you more about Mr. Ludwig."

Morrison looked up, "Why is that?"

"Ludwig was a deputy; one of their own, so to speak."

He looked expectantly at Deputy Morrison. Morrison kept his head down as he made a note. "Could I speak to their teachers and classmates?"

Wheeler nodded graciously, "Yes, of course. I'll have Mrs. Pentington schedule that for you. Can I have the appointments sent to your office?"

Morrison put away his notepad and stood, "Can I pick it up here ... say tomorrow morning?"

Principal Wheeler stood and straightened his jacket, "I'm sure that would be fine. Would you like for us to call the parents?"

Morrison was confused, "Call the parents?"

Wheeler asked, "Isn't it policy to have a parent present during questioning?"

Calhoun chimed in, "Gotta have a parent present. That's policy all right."

Wheeler smiled, "I'll have Dottie call them."

Morrison nodded, shook the principal's hand and turned to leave, almost tripping over the janitor's mop bucket sitting next to the secretary's desk. Deputy Calhoun jammed his notepad into his breast pocket and jumped up, "Hey, Elton!"

"Hey, Jessie."

Chapter Twenty
Maggie's

Calhoun pulled out of the school parking lot, turned onto Main Street and headed away from downtown. "Hungry, Sam?"

The hair on the back of Sam's neck stood up! "Just call me Morrison."

"Huh? Oh, don't like Sam, eh? Ok, buddy, ya hungry? Company's buying."

Morrison realized that he was famished. "You know a place with really strong coffee?"

Calhoun turned into a small graveled parking lot. An unassuming metal building with only a couple of windows across the front sat in the back of the lot with a large, white sign proclaiming simply "Maggie's".

As they entered the large, dimly lit, square room, Calhoun yelled, "Hey, Maggie!"

The heads of deer, elk, antelope, and buffalo were hanging on walls covered by aged wood. A wide opening connected the main dining room to the bar area. A stuffed bobcat, mountain lion, and rattlesnake were sitting on a stage-like platform above the bar. A short, pudgy lady drying a plate with a stained dish towel yelled back, "Hey, Jessie."

Jessie led Morrison through the bar to an outdoor patio out back, "More privacy back here."

Jessie Calhoun appeared very comfortable in this setting. No one else was dining on the patio but Calhoun made a big deal out of picking the chair with his back to the wall, "Doc Holiday always sat with his back to the wall so nobody could sneak up on him."

"You mean Wild Bill Hickok?"

Calhoun frowned, "Huh?"

Morrison took the chair across from him, "Any gunslingers in Rockcliffe?"

Calhoun laughed loudly, "That's a good one, Sa ... Morrison!"

Morrison picked up the menu stuck in a rack in the center of the table and began searching through the hamburgers.

"Full of Bull."

Morrison looked up quizzically. Calhoun explained, "The last burger on the list. Maggie's 'Full of Bull'. You can't beat it."

Morrison closed the menu and laid it on the table edge. Calhoun leaned across and snatched the menu and placed it neatly back in the rack as their waitress stepped out onto the patio and approached them. "Hey, Darla!"

The waitress was thin and pretty but timid with sad, dark eyes. She nodded and almost whispered, "Hey, Jessie. You havin' your usual?"

"Full of Bull. Can't beat it."

Darla nodded shyly and turned to Morrison, "And you, Sir?"

Morrison started to order when Calhoun cut him off, "Darla, this is Deputy Morrison, from Denver. Can you believe he's come all the way down to little ol' Rockcliffe?"

Darla forced a smile and turned back to Morrison, clearly embarrassed. Morrison was struck by her frail vulnerability. She was attractive in a sultry sort of way that seemed a contradiction. If she came across as provocative, he got the feeling that it was news to her. He suspected that the image she portrayed was nothing like the image she had of herself. He ordered a "Full of Bull" hamburger and strong black coffee.

She wrote something in tiny letters on her pad, nervously glanced at him, turned and strode away with quick, short steps. Deputy Calhoun leaned back in his chair, crossed his legs and clasped his hands behind his head. "Here's how I see it. Old man Ludwig is a neat freak, ya know? But crime scenes are messy, disorganized, everything out of place and it grates on him to have to photograph 'em."

Morrison perked up, "You knew Ludwig?"

"Yeah! Oh, yeah, he's been a deputy since before me. He took photos for us, and dang good at it. Didn't miss a detail and all great photos, ya know what I mean?"

As if appearing from nowhere, Darla set coffee cups and iced water on the table. Morrison dropped an ice-cube in his coffee, stirred furiously, gulped it down and held the cup up to her for a refill. Darla's eyes widened and she gave him a childlike smirk as she refilled his cup. She smirked at him again and shyly strode away. She had a genuine and very attractive smile that drew him in and appealed to his protective nature.

"So, when he goes home he wants eh-ver-reee-thang to be neat and organized. Perfectionist, ya see? But, of course, teenagers ain't neat and organized. So, they fight. You know, just argue at first, then pretty soon they're yelling at each other and the neighbors call 9-1-1. Well, spendin' the night in the slammer ain't no fun, is it? And it's embarrassing at school. Everybody makin' fun of ya. You know? Teenagers is real sensitive to thangs like 'at. So, this time, old man Ludwig pushes him too far and he snaps! Just like a dry twig."

Morrison did not know where to begin, "Why'd he shoot his mother and brother?"

"Huh? Well, uh, he snapped! You know, like a dry twig."

"Where'd he get the gun?"

"Huh? Well, I guess they kept it in the house."

Calhoun was so irritatingly arrogant that Morrison could not resist, "So, in the heat of the argument, David says, 'hold on a minute while I go get the gun' and they wait for him to come back and shoot them?"

"Well, maybe he had the gun with him!"

"So, he beats up his mother and brother first, then shoots them, turns the gun on his father, then scratches his father's face all up?"

"Scratches his face? Who said he scratched his face?"

"There were scratch marks on the face. The lady and boy had bruises on their faces."

Calhoun frowned. Morrison changed the subject, "How was Ludwig received by the office?"

Calhoun frowned again, "Received?"

Morrison crossed his legs and rephrased his question, "How did the other deputies like him?"

Calhoun shifted nervously in his chair, "Well, ok, I guess."

"Was he friendly around the office?"

Morrison could see that Calhoun was not comfortable with the subject. He let him squirm for a few minutes. "Did you like him?"

Calhoun's eyes got big as saucers, "Me? Well ..."

"What about Bennet and Wooten?"

Calhoun glanced all about and then leaned forward, "To tell you the truth, I think they despised him. But they had to work with him, you know?"

Morrison pressed on, "Why do you think they despised him?"

Calhoun squirmed and glanced about nervously, "Well, he was a bully. You know? Like on the playground, except he never grew out of it."

Morrison squinted at Calhoun, "Did he bully you?"

Calhoun licked his lips and rubbed his thighs, "Sometimes. But I just ignored him, you know? That's what you do with bullies, you ignore 'em."

"What if they won't stop?"

Calhoun was perspiring, "What? They? Who?"

"What if the bully won't stop harassing you. What if he embarrasses you in front of your friends?"

Morrison felt that Calhoun was ready to break. He was certain from his reaction that Ludwig had bullied him and embarrassed him. "Maybe he pushed you too far and you'd had enough. Maybe you went over to his house to settle things."

Calhoun bolted up and then sat down and glanced around with bulging eyes, his voice became shrill and whiney, "What? You think I ..."

Morrison did not let up, "Where were you when the call came in?"

Calhoun began to stutter and sweat profusely, "I I I wa-was pa-pa-patrolling."

"You were the first one on the scene?"

Calhoun gulped, "We-well, yeah, I guess ..."

"Maybe you were already there, maybe you shot Ludwig and then ..."

Calhoun was on his feet shaking like a leaf caught in a storm, "Now look, Morrison! You got this all wrong!"

Morrison studied Calhoun's reaction. He raised his hand. It was obvious to him that Calhoun could never come up with the courage to confront a bully. "Ok, Calhoun. Calm down. I believe you."

Calhoun's face grew red as he started pacing around, "Oh, man!"

He turned around and challenged his partner, "You can't do that, Morrison. That ain't right. You know? It just ain't right!"

The waitress backed through the door carrying their orders on a tray. She kept her head down and ignored Calhoun as she quickly placed the baskets on the table, refilled their cups and smiled sheepishly at Morrison. Morrison nodded and she blushed and rushed back inside. Calhoun was breathing heavily and started pacing again. Morrison stood and grabbed his partner's shoulders, "Ok, Jessie, you're right. That was uncalled for."

Calhoun shouted and jabbed his pointing finger down, "You darn right it was uncalled for."

Morrison held up his palms, "You're right. I apologize. But, I don't know you and I have to follow up all leads, ok?"

Calhoun had just taken an angry bite of the juicy burger when his walkie-talkie chattered. He put down the burger, chomped desperately, wiped Maggie's 'special sauce' off his lips and chin, reached down and pulled the bulky device from its pouch, "Calhoun."

The voice of Sheriff Bailey squawked, "Jessie, you got Morrison there?"

The deputy handed the walkie-talkie to Morrison, "Morrison." He mumbled through the chunks of hamburger in his mouth.

"Sam, you alright?"

Morrison swallowed hard, "Yeah, just had a mouth full of bull."

"What?"

"Maggie's 'Full of Bull' hamburger."

He could hear the sheriff chuckle, "Just talked to CBI in Springs. The Medical Examiner is doing the autopsies today. Smiles called in sick this morning, so I talked them into letting us meet with the examiner for a preliminary report. Come over to the office after lunch for an update and we'll go over to see what he comes up with."

Morrison choked briefly on his coffee and then responded, "Sounds good."

As Morrison handed back the walkie-talkie, Deputy Calhoun snatched the walkie talkie without looking at Morrison and slammed it back in its pouch.

Chapter Twenty-One
Waking in a Basement

ABOVE THE SLUMBERING GIANT, a rectangular, metal-framed window was glowing brightly with midday light. David Ludwig opened his eyes momentarily, but the glaring noon day sun forced him to shade his eyes with his hand. Surveying the room, he could make out a large vanity sitting isolated in the center of the room with an old wooden chair askew beside it. A manila folder with bold writing across it angled across the surface of the vanity but the writing was unreadable from his bed.

As his eyes adjusted, a bare staircase materialized across the room attached to the far wall oriented to the left. The large, musty room was cluttered with dusty antiques and crates. Nothing was familiar. He closed his eyes for a moment.

When he reopened his eyes, he reviewed the room again. Still, nothing was familiar. He frowned as he sat up and rotated his legs around to sit on the rickety cot creaking and moaning from his great weight. The young man pushed his bulky frame off the bed and lumbered across the room to the vanity. In bold letters, "Who is David Ludwig?" was scrawled across the folder. He picked it up and sat on the unsteady chair next to the vanity.

"David Ludwig?" He questioned out loud.

The young man glanced around the room confirming he was alone, "Who is David Ludwig?"

He opened the folder cautiously. A section of a newspaper was clipped to a white sheet of paper inscribed with small, neat handwriting. He removed the article from the clip, laid the open folder on the vanity and carefully unfolded the article. The headline read "DAVID LUDWIG MISSING. WANTED FOR QUESTIONING IN TRIPLE HOMICIDE!" The picture of a stocky teenager wearing a football jersey was tagged "David Ludwig". He did not recognize the person.

He reached for the letter. It read, "You are David Ludwig. You lost your memory. Do not panic. White Feather is your friend and will help you."

The letter was signed, "David Ludwig".

He turned the letter over to find a blank page, then flipped it back over. He glanced into the mirror on the vanity. His heart skipped. He picked up the newspaper clipping and studied the picture, then he looked back into the mirror to recognize the face in the mirror to be that in the newspaper clipping. He addressed the person in the mirror, "I am David Ludwig?"

He searched the musty room full of old trunks, furniture, crates and boxes for clues; something familiar. He stood and walked to the window clouded with white and gray film. Outside lay an unfamiliar world of scattered buildings, old railroad tracks, and rusting warehouses.

He walked back over to sit in the chair, picked up the newspaper article and read it. When he finished, he dropped his hand on his knee, "I did that?"

He heard a clicking noise coming from the top of the stairs. Light streamed down the stairway as a small, square portion of the ceiling was lifted. David Ludwig glanced about searching for a weapon or a place to hide.

He ran to the opposite corner from the stairway and pushed his over-sized body into a gap in the tall stack of crates. He listened to the creaking stairs giving way to the steps of a stranger. Creak, creak, creak. The stranger descended the stairs and shuffled closer, ever closer to his hideout. The intruder's shadow fell across the floor in front of him. An old man stepped into view.

The old man smiled, "Osiyo, David."

The frightened young man looked left, then right, "David? Who's David?"

White Feather shook his head, "You are. Come out now. I'm your friend, White Feather."

White Feather turned and walked away. The confused young man warily stepped out, looked around, then dutifully followed him across the room and up the stairs.

The boy inquired, "Where are we going?"

White Feather looked over his shoulder, "Lunch. You're hungry, remember?"

"Oh, yeah, that's right."

Over lunch, White Feather explained to the boy his plight again. Then he shared how he had posed as a janitor at the school in order to listen to the deputy's interview with the coach and principal. The boy listened blankly and he wondered why the old man was telling him all these things.

After lunch, the old man gathered the dishes and carried them to the sink where other dishes were stacked. David stood and offered to wash the dishes, an old habit surfacing from lost memories. The old man seemed to consider his request and then simply replied, "Let's go."

David then followed the mysterious old man back to the basement. "You'll be safe here. Stay put," is all the Indian said before leaving him.

Chapter Twenty-Two

Morrison Quizzes Sheriff About Ludwig

CALHOUN HAD BEEN QUIET since lunch. Morrison enjoyed the peaceful drive back to the office, but felt sorry for the insecure deputy. He was a proud man who wanted to please people. Rockcliffe was a small town where people were family, not like the impersonal relationships in Denver. Morrison felt bad that he had been so hard on him.

Back in the office, Morrison filled a styrofoam cup with coffee and excused himself, "I'm going to go update the sheriff."

Calhoun shrugged, "Sure, no problem."

As Morrison entered the sheriff's office, Sean Bailey was staring at the open area, "What's the matter with Calhoun?"

Morrison glanced back and shook his head, "Well, let's just say Calhoun didn't do it."

Bailey looked at him incredulously, "You interrogated Calhoun?"

Morrison shrugged. The Sheriff laughed loudly, shook his head and handed Morrison a form. Morrison took it, grabbed a pen from the sheriff's desk and sat down.

The sheriff set a body cam on the front of his desk and explained, "That's for your body cam. Explains the rules for when to use it and when it is ok to turn it off."

As he read and filled out the form, Morrison probed, "What did you think of Ludwig?"

Bailey raised his eyebrows, "Didn't really know him. Saw him play in a few games I guess, but …"

Morrison raised his hand, "I mean Jon Ludwig."

Bailey inhaled, "Oh, Jon." The sheriff shook his head, "Not what you'd call a likable guy."

Morrison prompted him, "A bully?"

Bailey squinted at Morrison and then glanced out the glass wall at Calhoun, "Yeah, you could say that. Got a kick out of roiling up Jessie."

"What about the other deputies? They like him?"

Bailey shrugged, "Not much. They put up with him, but there was definitely tension when he was around."

Morrison sipped on his coffee, then looked Bailey in the eyes, "You ever have a run-in with him?"

The sheriff drummed his fingers on the desk, "Yeah, once or twice."

The tall, trim sheriff leaned forward and lowered his voice, "I always suspected he was up to something, but could never figure out what. He was just one of those people you figure is shady and devious."

He sat back and looked out the glass wall into the office, "I always suspected that he had something on

Wooten or Bennet. He got along with Melton. I'm not sure why. They're so different that it just doesn't seem like they would get along."

Morrison set down the form and took a sip of coffee, "What do you think he had on Bennet and Wooten?"

"I don't know. They must be covering up for him on something. The sad thing is that although they're pretty rough, they've cleaned up the drug pushers. Solid convictions on all of their cases."

Morrison challenged, "Too solid?"

Bailey shrugged, "Maybe. I always wondered about that Timmons kid. He had an awfully small amount of crack on him to panic the way they said he did. They said he pulled a gun and they shot him dead. Gun had the serial numbers filed off."

"He have a record?"

"Nothing big. Some stuff when he was younger. His mother said he had gotten his life back together."

Bailey held up his hands, "I believed her, but, you know, Mothers always think that about their sons."

Morrison looked down at the floor, "So, all of the drug problems have gone away?"

Bailey leaned forward, "I didn't say that. We still bust our share of druggies, but they must be gettin' it elsewhere. We haven't arrested a pusher in Rockcliffe since Timmons. Or around that time."

"How'd Wooten get that shiner?"

"Claimed he hit it on a door."

Morrison sniggered. Bailey grinned, "Yeah, I know."

Morrison continued, "Ludwig have any problems with others in the community?"

Bailey leaned back and interlaced his fingers, "There've been rumors of some squabbles, but no one ever filed charges. Always seems to come out clean."

Morrison shrugged, "Maybe not this time."

Sheriff Bailey checked his watch, "We better get going. The Examiner is expecting us."

Chapter Twenty-Three

White Feather Observes the Autopsy

ONE OF THE MORE popular programs the local Wet Mountain Valley Rotary Club provides for the remote community is free rides to anyone "down the hill" to Pueblo, Canon City, or Colorado Springs. Although there is no charge, most passengers donate a small amount based upon their ability to pay.

White Feather sat quietly in the back seat of the van and turned to look out the window when the passenger in the front seat handed the volunteer driver an envelope and proudly explained that her daughter was paying to fly her to Chicago for a visit. The driver confirmed that he was to drop her off at the airport in Colorado Springs where she would catch the shuttle flight to Denver International and then transfer to a flight to Chicago O'Hare airport.

After filling in the information on the form on his clipboard, he looked into the rear-view mirror and confirmed that White Feather was requesting a ride to the Pomar Sports Park in Colorado Springs.

"Can't say I know where that is," the driver remarked as he pulled out his cell phone and typed in the name in his Google Maps App. "Shows I get off at Lake Drive and take S. Circle across I-25?"

White Feather nodded. The driver placed his phone in the cup holder, "Ok if we drop you off first before we head over to the airport?"

White Feather and the other passenger nodded. Pomar Sports Park was not his actual destination. The park was across the river from the El Paso County Coroner's building and the Colorado Springs Police compound. From Pomar Sports Park, he would cross a bridge on a bike and hiking trail that would put him right at the compound.

The tired old Indian was soon slumbering as the van continued the hour-and-one-half drive to Colorado Springs.

Sitting on the steps at the entrance of the rectangular, unpretentious, one-story brick building, White Feather watched the old Jeep Grand Cherokee roll up to park in front of a sign reading "Reserved – Medical Examiner." A large, gray-haired, distinguished-looking man in a wrinkled, well-worn suit rolled out of the Jeep and slammed the door. The man walked to the back of the vehicle, lifted the back door, retrieved a large, heavy, black case and limped over to the door of the building depositing the keys into his pant pocket. White Feather could hear a clicking sound from the Jeep as the doors locked.

White Feather stood, reached for the door and opened it for the man who nodded "thanks" and entered. White Feather followed. The man was recognized by the receptionist and they settled the matter of the weather while he signed in. He handed the sign-in sheet to White Feather and waited for him to scribble his name and time on the sheet.

The man seemed quite familiar with the building and wasted no time finding the stairs to the basement, followed by White Feather. The man looked over his shoulder, "Seen the bodies yet?"

White Feather mumbled, "Not yet"

The CBI medical examiner commented, "Nasty affair."

The bold Indian replied with an indistinct, "Hmmph."

"Did you know the Ludwigs?"

"Just the son, David," White Feather admitted.

"Have you found him yet?"

White Feather paused to select his words carefully, "Still looking."

The medical examiner opened the door at the base of the stairs letting cold air escape from the frigid interior. White Feather shivered and pulled his jacket tight around his neck as he followed the man into the cold room. Three gurneys were positioned side by side in the center of the small room. The medical examiner produced a small oval case, swiped some sort of cream out of it, rubbed it into his nostrils and offered it to White Feather. The obliging Indian accepted a swipe of the cream and copied the examiner's application of the cream to his nostrils. The medical examiner wasted no time getting started. White Feather stepped back into a corner to watch.

The medical examiner removed his suit coat, hung it carelessly on the coat rack, and pulled an apron from the drawer of a metal table. A door opened and an older tall thin man with thinning gray hair slipped in. The medical examiner glanced at him and nodded, "Hi, John, shall we get to work?"

The tall man, the local coroner, also smeared cream in his nose, nodded back at the medical examiner and began assisting him from across the gurney. The medical examiner pulled a hand recorder off the table, loaded a small tape, then clicked it on. In unison, they both donned rubber gloves.

When John spotted White Feather, he frowned and glared at the intruder. White Feather smiled and silently greeted him with a nod. John nodded back as the medical examiner interrupted by demanding a scalpel. The local coroner quickly retrieved the instrument and the two men busied themselves in their grisly work.

Chapter Twenty-Four

The Coroner's Report

DURING THE LONG DRIVE to Colorado Springs, Morrison and Bailey had been quiet for a while, lost in thought. The sheriff restarted the conversation, "So, you and Jessie have gotten crossways?"

"You have a policy against working alone?"

The sheriff laughed. "He's a weird duck alright, but he means well, and really loyal if he likes you. Does surprisingly well in a crisis, too. He'll guard your back."

"My back need guarding?"

The sheriff's smile faded as he considered how to answer. Morrison backed off, "He got on my nerves and because of the timing of his arrival at the crime scene, I asked him some pointed questions about his relationship with Ludwig. I expected him to be a little more professional about it, but didn't expect him to get so rattled. Now I feel really bad. I hope we can patch things up, but it may take some time."

Bailey shook his head, "Yeah, Jessie can get pretty flustered. He'll come around. Learn anything at the school?"

"David left football practice early after a particularly violent tackle. Coach hadn't noticed anything unusual in David's behavior before that. Says he left early to check on David and drove over to his house, but when he saw the sheriff's vehicles, he went on home."

"Principal says David Ludwig was a good student, never tardy, no perceptible concerns recently. We only talked to the principal after Buster left. The principal is getting me a list of teachers and friends for tomorrow."

The sheriff nodded, "Excellent. We'll need to call the parents."

"Wheeler is handling that."

"Got any theories so far?"

"Looks like murder-suicide."

"You don't think David did it?"

"I think he probably walked in after-the-fact; picked up the gun; heard your deputy snooping around and panicked."

"Buster tells me the Ludwigs didn't have a handgun registered. So, we're not sure where the gun came from. What makes you think he picked up the gun afterwards?"

"The imprint of the gun was in the dried blood. If David brought the gun, he wouldn't have laid it down and then picked it back up after the blood had started drying."

"If he's innocent, why would he run?"

"The only violence I'm aware of off the football field was arguments with his dad. Being a deputy, the answering officers were reluctant to arrest one of their own. Kid knew that and figured with his record, he wouldn't get a fair shake."

The sheriff leaned back, rested one elbow on the arm-rest and draped his wrist over the steering wheel, "Hmm. Interesting. Gonna be hard to prove."

"He's innocent until proven guilty."

Sheriff Bailey chuckled, "Okay, okay; what evidence do you have to support your theory?"

"None, yet. Just a hunch."

Sheriff Bailey and Deputy Morrison quick-stepped down the stairs to the morgue. They burst into the examining room to find the El Paso county coroner, John, wiping his just washed wet hands with a towel, watching the CBI Medical Examiner finish up the paperwork.

The sheriff introduced his new deputy. The two men shook his hand, but the medical examiner seemed confused, "So, Sheriff, who was the Indian that was here earlier?"

Sheriff Bailey's brow furrowed curiously, "Indian? Don't know anything about an Indian."

The two examiners looked at each other and laughed. The medical examiner with the CBI explained, "There was an Indian that opened the door for me when I first got here. I assumed he was your new deputy. He acted like he knew what he was doing and like he was supposed to be here. He didn't say much, just stood over there in the corner and watched. Not sure when he left. After we finished, I looked over and he was gone."

Sheriff Bailey looked at the two men skeptically, "You just let anybody come in here to watch an autopsy without questioning them?"

The two men looked at each other, chagrined. Sheriff Bailey took great delight in their humiliation and reared back laughing. The infectious guffaw ignited the others. Despite his uncontrolled chortle, the sheriff managed, "Probably a vagrant looking for a handout."

Eager to change the subject, the CBI medical examiner blandly began his report: "Bruises on the faces of the husband, wife, and boy are consistent with a domestic fight. Husband's face was also scratched, consistent with wife defending herself. Trace amounts of blood and skin were found under her fingernails."

The local coroner added, "Bullet wounds consistent with a .45 caliber pistol."

Morrison confirmed, "An outline of the pistol was in the congealed blood on the floor. Reminded me of a Military issue, M1911A1, .45 caliber pistol."

The medical examiner nodded and continued, "Mr. Ludwig had been drinking and was legally drunk. Time of death for all three was the same and consistent with your report of 5:30 or so."

Then he got to the "good stuff." He handed Sheriff Bailey a diagram of a body showing front and back views. The diagram was labeled "Matilda Ludwig." A thick red line ran pointed to the stomach of the front view. The coroner gave them a minute to digest the implication. The local coroner smiled broadly in anticipation.

Sheriff Bailey looked up, "So, what are we looking at here?"

Morrison answered, "The angle of the arrow."

The examiners nodded agreement.

Bailey looked again. "So, the bullet was fired from below and angled up?"

The examiner smiled and nodded again as he handed the sheriff another diagram, "Bullet was lodged in her liver, she died from a loss of blood. Now this is the boy."

He handed over a similar diagram with a dark red arrow slicing through the skull. Bailey commented, "The red line is slightly angled up?"

But Bailey was puzzled, "What does it mean?"

The coroner chuckled with delight, "You're the detectives. You tell me."

Morrison ventured a guess, "The woman was shot by someone on their knees or from the floor. The boy was shot execution style. Were there powder burns around the boy's wound?"

John jumped in, "Yes, he was shot from point-blank range. Gun was held to his temple."

The examiner produced the diagram of the father. The red arrow indicated the bullet entered the throat and exited near the top of the head. Morrison interpreted, "Upward angle again. More pronounced than the boy."

Bailey pointed his finger under his chin, "Consistent with a suicide."

The medical examiner countered, "But no powder burns. The shot was fired from at least several feet away."

The coroner added his two-cents, "Old man Ludwig socked the shooter, laying him out on the floor. Shooter fired up at Ludwig hitting him in the throat."

Three pairs of doubting eyes trained on the opinionated coroner. Morrison made a note.

Back in the office, Sheriff Bailey called in Buster Crab and Deputies Calhoun and Melton to review the new information from the autopsies. Each one was trying to interpret the examiner's report in his own way.

Deputy Calhoun was confident in his interpretation. Clearly, the report proved to him that David Ludwig was definitely the perp'. "He came home from football practice and got into a fight with his old man. His mother and brother tried to intervene and got roughed up. The old man socked David in the jaw which knocked him on his butt. The kid drew his gun and threatened his old man. The Mom got in the way and took a bullet before he took out the old man. He shot his brother so he wouldn't rat on him."

Morrison was troubled by the report, but it was consistent with the bullet hole up high in the wall. It pretty much ruled out a murder suicide as he had originally speculated. It was even consistent with Calhoun's theory, which was irksome. Still, it did not feel right. He was troubled by the notion that he would shoot his brother in cold blood—that did not make sense. His experience and intuition told him it was inconsistent.

Sheriff Bailey was concerned about the mysterious Indian. "What do you make of the Indian, Morrison?"

Morrison's expression did not change. He did not have an explanation. "It's bizarre."

Deputy Calhoun had a ready explanation, "Homeless vagabond. Thought he was at the soup kitchen."

Calhoun laughed enthusiastically at his own joke. His fellow investigators were silent.

A cell phone rang, "Buster Crab ... Oh, hi, Jeremy ... Oh, ok, good, thanks."

Chief Crab hastily stuffed his cell phone into his pocket and glanced at the sheriff, "That was my friend, Jeremy, over at CBI. He's found something very curious on the computer and he thinks we might want to come over to see it."

Chapter Twenty-Five
White Feather Returns from Autopsy

WHITE FEATHER SHOOK HIS head sadly as he approached the rusting railroad tracks that ran in front of the abandoned train terminal he called home. He could never get used to how callused the white man was when it came to the dead. He softly prayed for the souls of the Ludwigs. Even a Cherokee witch had more respect for the dead than a coroner or medical examiner!

White Feather trudged up the dusty, gravely street that passed by the old train terminal. He paused to look up at his destination. He wondered if David Ludwig was staying put in the basement. Even though the crystal had confirmed that the boy was on the "up-and-up" so-to-speak, he was still very uncomfortable about the whole affair. His amnesia was just too convenient.

He continued up the street and resumed his thoughts. The injury David had suffered on the football field lent support to his claim of amnesia. He had heard that trauma can cause amnesia and the collision the coach had described was certainly a very traumatic event. He remembered the blood on his clothes and palm of his hand. David was definitely at the crime scene.

So, could the amnesia have been brought on by the murder? Was murdering his parents so traumatic that his mind was burying it? It was certainly possible, even probable. But, if it was a ruse, the crystal should have seen through it. He did not need for the boy to tell him what he saw in the crystal. White Feather could see the images for himself.

In addition, the blood stains he had observed at their first encounter were just not consistent with a shooter. He was at the crime scene, but blood stains on his hands, clothes and shoes suggested that he had arrived after the crime, more a spectator than a perpetrator.

The old wizard sat on the aging train terminal porch to decide what to do next. If the boy did not murder his parents, what really happened? White Feather decided he needed to return to the Ludwig home to study the crime scene firsthand.

Chapter Twenty-Six
The Photos

S HERIFF BAILEY SHARED WITH Deputy Calhoun the news of the break-in at the Ludwig house. He gave him a "special" assignment, "Jessie, go canvas the neighborhood around the Ludwig house to see if anyone saw or heard anything suspicious last night."

Calhoun's brow furrowed, his eyes drooped, "Why me?"

"You've interviewed them before; they know you and trust you."

"Oh, for cryin' out loud," the deputy whined as he grabbed his hat and dragged himself out of the office.

With Calhoun out of the way, Bailey, Crab and Morrison headed back to Colorado Springs to see what Jeremy had found on the Ludwig computer and camera.

Jeremy Thornton was a tall, thin, neatly dressed kid with black-rimmed glasses. Morrison guessed him to be about twenty-four. The last of a set of pictures were emerging from the printer as they entered Jeremy's cluttered office.

"Jeremy this is Sam Morrison, our new deputy. He was a homicide detective in Denver."

The polite young man stood to shake the new deputy's hand. Buster nodded toward the sheriff, "You know Sheriff Bailey."

Jeremy nodded, "Yes, sir."

"Hi, Jeremy, good to see you again."

Jeremy offered chairs for his guests. Buster was eager, "So, show us what you found, Jeremy."

Jeremy sat back down and gathered up the printed photos, "These are the ones I found that appear to be crime scene photos. They're pretty old according to the dates. There were a lot of pictures of what are probably friends and family, but there were also a bunch of pictures of ..." He handed Buster a stack of pictures, "her."

Buster whistled as his eyes bulged, "Wow!" he commented as he passed each picture over to Morrison and Bailey. Morrison raised his eyebrows when he saw the nude picture of a pretty, young woman in her late twenties, posing shyly by a bed. The next picture was of her sitting on the bed, then lying on the bed exposing herself seductively. Despite the seductive poses, the young woman appeared to be embarrassed and uncomfortable.

Morrison commented, "She looks familiar."

Buster joked, "Oh? I didn't notice the face, lemme see those again."

Morrison handed the stack of photos back to his chief. Buster shook his head, "Well I'll be darned. She's that shy waitress over at Maggie's. Who'd of ever thought ..."

Morrison remembered her as the waitress that had waited on him and Calhoun. "Calhoun called her Darla, I think."

Crab was shuffling through the photos again, "Yeah, yeah, Darla."

Buster shook his head again and handed the photos to the sheriff, "Looks like Ludwig had a mistress."

Morrison added, "Or, was blackmailing her."

Buster nodded then turned to his grandson, "Let's see what else you found."

Jeremy handed him a stack of about twenty crime scene photos. Buster scanned one and passed it on, then another and another. They were typical photos of a young man from every angle lying in a pool of blood. Buster exclaimed, "Ah! Here it is."

He handed the photo to Morrison and explained, "This is the one I saw on the camera, it's a close up of the gun being placed by the body."

Morrison took the photo, Bailey looked over his shoulder. Someone's gloved hand holding a gun was barely captured in the shot. Buster tilted his head back, "Bingo!"

He handed Morrison and Bailey a wide shot of the man placing the gun. It was Deputy Wooten. In subsequent photos, Bennet was seen placing a small packet of crack cocaine next to the body.

Buster quickly shuffled through the rest of the photos and gave them to Morrison. They were more innocuous crime scene shots. "That's it?" Buster asked his CBI friend.

Jeremy shrugged, "Well, there's a bunch of shots of people on the street or posing beside cars. Stuff like that. Probably just family and friends."

Bailey stood, "Ok. Good job, Jeremy. We really appreciate the tipoff."

Jeremy straightened the photos, "Sure, no problem." He placed them in a manila folder and handed them to

Buster. "I'm not done yet. He might have hidden stuff in system folders. I didn't look there, just the obvious places."

Bailey nodded, "Sure, look everywhere. Call Buster if you find anything else."

Morrison frowned, "What's that vacant slot at the top of the computer?"

Jeremy turned and put his forefinger into the empty slot and rubbed it across the gap, "Disk reader. The door's broken off."

The young man peered inside and then pushed the small button below it, "It's broken."

Sheriff Bailey glanced at Morrison with raised eyebrows. Morrison shrugged.

Chapter Twenty-Seven
Blocked at Crime Scene, Detour to Library

As White Feather walked by the side of the Ludwig house, he caught a glimpse of Deputy Calhoun's vehicle parked in front. He paused and glanced about and then slipped over to a side window for a peek inside. From this vantage point, he could only see through a bedroom into the back portion of the livingroom but assumed the deputy must be inside.

A dog barked at him from across the street startling him. He frowned at the offensive mutt and then headed back down the street. He would have to return another time but feared the crime scene would cease to be fresh enough for critical observation. And, at some point, they would probably clean the house.

As he passed by the house across the alley from the Ludwig place, he felt eyes trained on him. He looked at the house in time to spot a shadow behind the window move out of sight. White Feather crossed the street and casually glanced back at the window. A tall, stooped elderly man glared out at him.

White Feather paused, turned and glared back. They locked in a stare down for a few moments. White Feather figured the man must be the one who called in the shooting. He felt sorry for the old man living next to an unsolved murder, apparently confined to his house; shielded from the investigation; ignorant of what happened or what might be happening. White Feather nodded, turned and lumbered off down the sidewalk.

So that the trip was not totally in vain, he decided to detour by the library. The County Library was in an renovated building in the center of downtown Main Street, Rockcliffe. He was a man of knowledge, a wizard, and all of his life he had probed the depths of mystery and mastered the unknown and unknowable. He treasured the white man's library invention and often used it. As he approached the front counter, a young, attractive woman beamed a bright smile and declared, "White Feather!"

The old Indian blushed, "Osiyo, Ally."

"Can I help you find something?"

White Feather appreciated Ally and considered her one of his favorite people. She understood his homeless situation and his lack of computer skills but never belittled him for it. "Amnesia. I want to research memory loss."

She smiled at him and he realized he had just set himself up for a senior joke, but she let it pass and headed for a computer. "You want to look it up on the internet? Or do you want a book on it?"

White Feather walked over to look at the computer screen, "Just want to know what can cause it and how to cure it or if it just goes away."

Ally nodded and started typing on the keyboard. He admired how natural it was for her. "Oh! Here's an interesting article from the Smithsonian by Joseph Stromberg. She adjusted the words on the screen and began to read:

> On August 25, 1953, a 27-year-old Connecticut native named Henry Molaison underwent brain surgery to treat the seizures he chronically suffered from as a result of epilepsy. When Molaison awoke after the surgery, his epilepsy was largely cured, but removing so much brain tissue—and, in particular, a structure called the hippocampus—led to an entirely new problem for him. From that moment on, he was unable to create memories of any new events, names, people, places or experiences. He also lost most of the memories he'd formed in the years leading up to surgery. In the most fundamental sense possible, H.M. lived entirely in the moment. "It's like waking from a dream. I just don't remember," he explained.

White Feather got excited, "Yes. Tell me about that." Ally seemed to get excited with him and continued to read:

> Although he interacted with the same nurses and doctors day after day, each time he saw them he had no idea he'd ever met them before. He remained a perfectly intelligent, perceptive person, but was unable to hold down a job or live on his own. Without the connective tissue of long-term memory, his life was reduced to a series of incoherent, isolated moments.

He was incapable of storing new information in his explicit memory—the type of memory that allows us to consciously remember experiences and pieces of new information—but could remember pieces of information over a very short time period (up to about 20 seconds), evidence that his short-term memory was somewhat intact. He could also learn and retain new skills, even if he didn't remember the actual act of learning them.

These fine distinctions led scientists to distinguish between procedural memory—the unconscious memory that allows us to perform motor activities, like driving, and explicit memory. Additionally, that H.M. couldn't form new explicit memories but had undamaged childhood memories highlighted the difference between memory encoding and memory retrieval (he could still perform the latter, but not the former). Perhaps most importantly, the fact that he was missing his hippocampus suggested that the structure was crucially involved in the encoding of long-term explicit memories, but wasn't necessary for short-term or procedural memory.

Ally turned to him with sparkling eyes. White Feather was anxious to know, "What happened to him? Did they fix it?"

Ally frowned and silently studied the article, "No. Once the tissue was removed, I guess they couldn't put it back in."

White Feather muttered, "Removed. ... So, where is the hippopotamus they removed?"

Ally giggled, "The hippocampus is in the center of the brain." She turned the screen toward White Feather and pointed, "Here. There are two of them. They look like seahorses."

She shrugged, "Hence the name. Oh, here is a picture of one."

She studied the screen and then clicked on the keyboard. A new screen appeared and she appeared to be scanning the page. "Hmm. It says that the Hippocampus is one of the few areas in the brain where neurons can grow. I don't know if that means it can repair itself, though."

White Feather nodded and looked at his friend, "Ok, thank you."

Ally smiled, "Sure, want me to look for some more articles?"

White Feather smiled back, "No. That's exactly what I needed, wado."

Ally recognized the Cherokee word for 'thank you' since White Feather had used it before, "You're welcome."

Chapter Twenty-Eight
Back in the Office
Search for Apartment

AFTER VISITING THE BREAK room for his addiction of strong, black coffee, Morrison headed for Buster's office. He found the chief on the phone so he stopped and waited. He could hear Buster's side of the conversation, "Ok, Naomi, ok! I'll speak to him. ... Well, maybe tomorrow. ... Ok, ok, I'll come out there now."

He slammed down the phone and motioned for Morrison to come in. Morrison took a seat in the nearest guest chair. Buster tried to smile as he took a deep breath, "So, you got anymore interviews today?"

"No. I'll finish up some paperwork. Thought I would go by and see Samantha and the kids tonight."

Buster stood, "Why don't you take the afternoon off and look for a place. I'm sure Sean would be fine with it."

Morrison nodded, "Want to go with me?"

Buster shook his head, "Nah, I've gotta run out to the retirement home. My Uncle Benny isn't settling in very well. See you in the morning."

Morrison grabbed his cup and stood, "See you in the morning."

Leaving the break room, he stepped out of Buster's office and into the sheriff's next door to request time off to search for a place to live.

As Morrison got to the door to leave, he stopped and turned to the sheriff, "Mind if I take Calhoun? I was pretty hard on him today. Need to patch things up."

Sheriff Bailey looked surprised, "You're not gettin' soft on ol' Jessie, are you?"

Morrison shrugged, "I could do worse for a partner."

The sheriff walked out to Calhoun's desk and conversed with him for a moment. Morrison was happy to see the deputy puff up again.

Chapter Twenty-Nine
St. Jude

Buster Crab punched the accelerator when he spotted the 65 mph sign outside of town heading north on Highway 69. The state road was in good shape, albeit narrow and winding. Having to go to St. Jude's Methodist Retirement Home was an unwelcome distraction.

His mind was already spinning in the midst of the murder investigation; helping his old friend get settled in; and uncovering blackmail photos, not to mention the hundred other little day-to-day tasks required of the undersheriff.

Benny had never been his favorite uncle-in-law, but he was family and someone had to take responsibility for him. He had been a bad husband to his mother's sister. His mother had once commented that the only good thing about their marriage was that there were no children.

His aunt had stuck by her man through thick and thin and taken care of him better than he deserved. When she passed away recently, it was clear that Benny would not be able to take care of himself financially without the income from her various jobs, so Buster had pulled some strings and got him accepted into St. Jude, a retirement home for the indigent.

It was a remarkable place in a grand and storied old building that was built in 1891 to house the Southern Colorado Institute for the Insane. It was one of the four branches of that institute. It was modeled after the Hudson River Institute for the Insane in New York and was considered a grand project at the time. Over time, rumors of rampant abuse and neglect of the residents eventually brought it down. In 1945, it was closed as an institute for the insane and was re-purposed as a county hospital.

In 1975, after a new hospital was built in Canon City, the Methodist Church purchased and remodeled it to become St. Jude Methodist Retirement Home for the Indigent, a home for "lost causes." Benny was definitely a lost cause.

It was not an assisted living facility. Although there was a resident nurse to help with medications and medical emergencies, the residents were, for the most part, relatively healthy and capable of taking care of themselves with minimal help. They were just financially destitute.

Buster watched for the grand old St. Jude building but it was mostly hidden from the road by the lush forest surrounding it. Suddenly, he was right on the intersection. It was an unassuming intersection marked by a modest green sign reading "St. Jude Methodist Retirement Center." The road widened to provide pullouts on either side. Buster slowed and flipped on his left turn signal. It seemed unnecessary since there were no cars in sight in either direction but he felt obligated as a law enforcement officer to set a good example.

As he crossed Highway 69 to continue on the wide asphalt drive up the slope, St. Jude loomed large and proud at the top of the hill. It was a four story, red bricked building with an impressive conical center that rose another story above the rest with two Victorian-style protrusions on either side. It reminded Buster of an English castle.

The parking lot was a small, gravely rectangle cut into the lush front lawn on the left side of the building. He found parking near the entrance and sat for a moment before going in. This would not be a pleasant visit.

The large man's footfalls crunched loudly on the gravel and his boots tended to slip when he pushed off. It was almost like walking on marbles, so he felt like he was walking stiff legged or on stilts. He thought that the entrances were quite unimpressive compared to the grandiose building. Two identical porches framed the two entrances centered in each Victorian protrusion. The one on the right was seldom used.

As he pulled open the over-sized front door, stepped into the anteroom and opened the interior door, he smiled and waved at his cousin Naomi sitting behind a modest wooden desk at the back of the homey reception area decorated with comfortable Victorian chairs and couches. She looked very distinguished in her lavender suit coat and dress. Naomi was only a few years younger, still very thin and seemed in peak health. Naomi had graduated from CSU in the seventies at a time when black students were a rarity. She had been working at St. Jude for almost as long as it had been a Methodist retirement home.

Naomi stood and held out her arms for a hug, "Buster Crab! My favorite cousin."

Buster hugged her warmly. They had shared some wonderful times growing up together. "You never change, Naomi, how do you do it?"

The elegant woman placed her fingertips over her mouth and blushed, "Listen to you!"

She led him to one of the couches and they sat next to each other as they traded health reports on family. Then Buster got to the point, "Benny's not settling in well?"

Naomi rolled her eyes, "Oh, he's settling in alright! Too well. He's driving everyone crazy. I swear I don't know why someone hasn't socked him yet."

Buster shook his head, it sounded like Benny, all right. "Ok, Naomi, I'll speak to him."

Naomi breathed a sigh of relief, "Oh, thank you, Buster. You've got to get him to back off or Miss Edith will throw him out. She may be a patient and compassionate woman, but I think she has had enough of him."

Buster looked at his watch, "What time is dinner?"

Naomi looked at her watch, "They start serving around five, but Benny goes down early so he can secure a table by the window. It's probably the only way he can get anyone to sit with him." She giggled.

"So, he may be in the dining room now?"

Naomi placed her hand on his arm, "I wouldn't doubt it."

Buster stood, "Want to join me?"

Naomi's eyes grew large and she forced a laugh, "Lordy, no."

As Naomi had predicted, Benny was already in the dining room, his huge body sprawling over a chair at a table by the window. He was nursing a large glass of iced tea and frowning at the sun setting over the magnificent Sangre de Cristo mountain range. Buster glanced at the sunset and recognized that the sun had chosen Electric Peak to pass behind. Buster stopped by the table, "What an amazing sunset!"

Benny's head spun around with surprise and studied his nephew, "Buster Crab! What brings you to Geezer Prison? Come to arrest one of these outlaws?"

Buster ignored the jibe, trying not to encourage him, "May I join you?"

Benny rolled his head as if trying to relieve stiffness. His neck crackled, "Go ahead, I can't stop ya'. You bring your handcuffs?"

Buster sat down next to him and glanced out the window at the shadows stretching across the pond reflecting brilliant oranges and blues from the sunset behind. How could anyone not be inspired by the beauty of this place? "You need some handcuffs, Benny?"

The grouchy man laughed loudly, "For these old ladies?"

A cook pushed a cart through double doors into the dining room, Benny held up his glass and shouted, "Could I get a refill, Darlin'?"

The elderly woman with stringy blondish white hair rubbed her hands on a towel and glared at Benny. She blew a strand of hair out of her face as if spitting at him, grabbed a pitcher of tea, stomped over to the table and refilled his glass. She turned and then paused when she saw the undersheriff, "Buster Crab!"

"Hi, Alma, how you been?"

The rough old woman pulled hair from her face and placed her knuckles on her hip, "I been alright. You come to haul this old jack-ass off to jail where he belongs?"

Buster chuckled, "He been given you trouble?"

She expelled air as if she did not know where to begin. Benny snickered, "Sweetheart! You're breakin' my heart. You know you love me."

Alma rolled her eyes and showed him her fist, "It ain't your HEART I'm gonna break."

Benny put out his arms as if inviting a hug, "Gimme a big kiss and let's make up."

Alma popped him with her towel and stormed off. Benny squealed as if she had made his day. When Alma got to the cart she turned and shouted, "I'm sorry, Deputy, you want some tea?"

Buster smiled and nodded, "Thanks," then turned to his obnoxious uncle, "That's what I came to talk to you about, Benny."

Benny squinted at his nephew between snickers, "You got a crush on Alma? Why didn't you say so, she's all yours. I won't get in your way."

Angry now, Buster glared at him in response as Alma handed him a glass of tea and smirked, "See what we have to put up with?"

Benny slapped her on the butt, "You know you love it!"

Buster jumped up as Alma gasped and slapped his face. Buster pointed his finger in his face, "Enough of that, Benny!"

Alma stormed off and disappeared through the double doors into the kitchen. Buster held his finger aimed at

Benny and glared at him as he tried to get his anger under control. Benny squirmed, grabbed his tea and gulped it down, avoiding eye contact with his nephew-in-law. Buster sat back down and took a drink of tea to cool down.

Benny turned his glass up again and drained the rest of his tea. He held it out to his nephew, "Hey, man, could you get me a refill?"

Buster expelled his breath in a huff and shook his head. "You don't get it, do you?"

Benny pulled back the glass and threw out his arms, "Get what? You too lazy to get an old man a glass of tea?"

Buster shook his head angrily, grabbed the empty glass and stomped over to the cart. What could he say? How was he going to get through to the ... to the over-bearing, arrogant slob? As he poured tea into the glass, images of pounding him in the face flashed across his mind. It was something he had pictured many times before when Benny had mistreated his sweet aunt, or embarrassed everyone at family get-togethers.

He took a deep breath. He did not want to have to take him home with him, and there were no other options that he could think of, so this needed to work.

As Buster walked back over, he studied his pitiful uncle fidgeting and glancing around muttering something to himself. Loud and obnoxious behavior was Benny's defensive shield. He was an angry man who had never amounted to much. His one good job, the only one he ever talked about with any pride, was the bellman position he held at the old hotel in Canon City many years ago. Ironically, it had been closed and torn down to make room for the new hospital. The reason the hospital in this building had been closed.

Since then, he had not been able to hold down a job and they had depended upon his wife's house cleaning, nanny and other odd jobs to stay afloat. Buster felt sorry for him in a way, but Benny was going to have to do something for himself now. He shook his head; ironically, all he had to do was just shut up. He was just too stupid to understand that.

When Buster set the tea down in front of the flustered man, Benny half rolled, half nodded his head as if to give a reluctant thank you. Buster sat down and took another swig of his own tea. "Look Benny. I know you are unhappy. I know it's tough since Aunt Ellie died."

Benny first sniffed and then sipped his tea. Buster could see tears welling up in his eyes. "The problem is ... well, it is what it is, Benny. You've got to accept what you've got here and deal with it."

Benny stared into space and Buster could see his temples rippling as he grounded his teeth. Buster took another drink of tea prompting Benny to gulp down some more, as well. "If you don't make it here, Benny, I don't know what you're going to do. It's pretty much your last option, you know?"

Benny slammed down the tea glass, "These morons just don't have any sense of humor."

Buster got tough, "It ain't humor you're dealin' out, Benny."

Benny glared at him, "Oh? What is it, then?"

Buster rotated his glass with his fingers, "Your hatred is showing through, Uncle. You just need to back off. Everyone in here has fallen on hard times. That's why they're in here. You are not special and they don't care about your problems."

"Back off and keep my mouth shut, huh?"

Buster looked at him to measure whether he was getting it yet. "Yeah, actually. That would work."

The proud, angry man stuck out his chin, "Fine! No problem."

Buster finished his tea and studied his uncle for a moment. He hoped he got it. He reached over and patted his wrist, "Ok. Just relax and ..."

"Keep my mouth shut."

Buster stood and waited, but Benny just kept staring bitterly into space. Buster nodded, "Just behave yourself," and walked away.

Chapter Thirty

The Reunion

M<small>ORRISON WAVED AT</small> D<small>EPUTY</small> Calhoun pulling out of the parking lot at the sheriff's office and then collapsed into his car and sucked in a huge breath of air. He was exhausted, but he hoped he had enough left for what he needed to do now. He took another deep breath and pulled out his cell phone. *This is it, Morrison!*

This moment had tormented him all day. No, ever since he had agreed to take the job in Rockcliffe. At first, he was excited about the unexpected fluke of taking a job in the same town where his ex-wife and children had moved. But, then reality set in.

He tried to imagine how Samantha would feel about his moving to Rockcliffe. She would be shocked when she learned that the man she divorced and moved to Rockcliffe to get away from was now moving there! He would tell her, "Think of the kids! It's better for the kids!"

Nah, that wouldn't work. He had never been there for the kids even when they were married. The truth was that the kids were probably as glad to move away as his wife.

Well, maybe not Jerry. The boy had been pretty good about everything, but his daughter had always sided with her mother.

Samantha and Tammy were very close and he was glad since he was never there for her and her mother always was. They had been able to support each other when he had disappointed them so many times. Each disappointment had drawn them closer together until ...

"Make the phone call, Morrison!" Buster appeared beside him and placed his hand on his friend's shoulder. Morrison pinched the bridge of his nose and dropped his head. He pushed his finger and thumb back to secretly blot the tears.

Morrison looked up at his friend and forced a smile. Buster patted him on the back, "You ok?"

"Yeah, thanks."

Buster got it! The shaky voice, the cell phone, the difficult smile. "Wanna go get a beer?"

Morrison shook his head no. "Gotta make the call."

Buster patted his despondent friend on the shoulder, "If you need anything, call me, ok?"

Morrison nodded ok.

Morrison stopped in front of the small, bungalow-style house and stared at the lighted window behind the porch. He was not surprised that the house and yard were well kept. She had always been responsible, organized and a neat freak. He could imagine her mowing the lawn, sweeping the porch, ...

He pulled into the narrow driveway. His daughter's white Mustang was pulled up close to the small detached garage that sat back beyond the house. She had been so proud of that car. For a short time, he had been her hero.

The anxious ex dragged himself out of his car and up onto the porch. Oddly, he hoped there was a door bell. Knocking was such a violent way of announcing your presence. It was too much like a police raid on a house.

Before he could search for the doorbell button, the porch light came on. The heavy, wooden door resisted and his heart leaped as a familiar slender hand slipped around the edge of the door and gripped it to force it open. Morrison pulled open the screened door and stood before his ex-wife for the first time in ... well, a long time. She looked tired, maybe sad, and her eyes were red and puffy. She had been crying and in a heart-breaking way, she looked delicate, vulnerable, sad.

He greeted her, "Sam."

She greeted him, "Sam."

There was an awkward pause before Morrison offered, "You look well."

His ex-wife took a deep breath and stepped back, "Come in. The kids are in the den."

He helped her shove the stubborn door closed and then she led the way past the small, narrow kitchen and down into the sunken den. Tammy was curled up on the couch picking at her nail polish. She did not look up. Jerry jumped up from the large recliner that was once Morrison's favorite chair, "Hi, Dad."

Morrison forced a smile and hugged his overweight son. "You're looking good! Grown a couple more inches."

Jerry shrugged and plopped back down into the over-stuffed chair and resumed watching television.

Samantha coaxed her daughter, "Tammy, can't you say hi to your father?"

Without looking up, the obstinate teenager mumbled, "Hi."

The frustrated mother tried to save the situation, "Anyone thirsty? Sam? I have some fresh lemonade in the frig."

Morrison felt completely unwelcome, like an intruder, "Oh, no thanks, Samantha. Just stopped by to say hello. I'd better get going. I'm pretty tired from the long drive and working all day."

Samantha's sympathetic eyes held her ex-husband's for a moment before she nodded dejectedly, "I'll walk you out."

Morrison faced the kids bravely. "See ya, Jerr."

Jerry jumped up and hugged his father, "Good to see ya, Dad."

"Now that I live here, maybe we can spend some time together."

Jerry shrugged, "Sure. No problem."

Morrison looked at his daughter, "Good to see you, Tammy. Maybe we ..."

The obstinate daughter sprang from the couch and huffed, "Sure! No problem!" as she stomped out of the room.

Morrison's face flushed. His chest felt tight. He turned to leave, "Good night, Jerr."

The supportive son answered, "Good night, Dad. Good to see ya."

"You, too, Son."

Samantha led her dispirited ex-husband back past the kitchen. Morrison rushed ahead to grab the door. "I can fix this old door. Just needs ..."

Samantha interrupted, "The landlord will get it."

He followed her out onto the porch. She stared at the street for a moment. Morrison stood beside her a respectable distance away.

She offered, "She'll come around."

Morrison appreciated her encouragement, but doubted that Tammy ever would.

Samantha looked at him, "I guess you knew that Tammy was dating that Ludwig kid."

Morrison was shocked!

"They'd only been out a couple of times. She brought him over the day of the shooting. Seemed like a nice kid, but I didn't get to visit with him. I couldn't believe he left our house, went home and murdered his family! Tammy was, is devastated!"

Morrison cleared his throat, "I didn't know."

Samantha looked down at the ground, "I guess you'll have to question her about him."

The thought chilled him and made his face hot. "I can get someone else to. Maybe Buster. She still likes Buster, doesn't she?"

Samantha was quiet. She folded her arms and shivered slightly. Morrison could see that she was cold and wanted to hold her and warm her. It seemed strange that he no longer could touch her.

Morrison started to take a step. Samantha interrupted, "No, maybe you should question her."

Morrison frowned. He did not know if deep down he was afraid or if he was nobly trying to spare his daughter, but he disagreed. But Sam knew the children and he knew he should trust her judgment.

"Do you want to ask her first?"

"No, just come by tomorrow evening around six. Take her to dinner and ..."

Morrison knew she had no more to say. "Six o'clock, then."

She turned, rubbed her arms for warmth, "Good night, Sam."

Morrison started to leave, then turned back to her, "What about Jerry?"

Samantha stopped but did not turn, "No, I think it would be better for you two to be alone when you ask her about David."

"No, I mean won't he feel left out?"

Samantha rubbed her arms vigorously, "Oh. Right."

She turned toward him, "Tammy and I are going to Salida Saturday morning. Why don't you and Jerry have a guys' day out."

Morrison nodded, "Thanks."

She turned and walked away. He was relieved that there might be some hope, some minor resolution to the problem of his unwelcome presence. "Good night."

Chapter Thirty-One

Journal for Thursday

I<small>T WAS THAT TIME</small>—late at night—Samantha Morrison called her own; that time when the kids were in bed; that time when she was free from the demands of her job; that time when the phone would not ring; when no one would knock on the door. The old clock in the living room was chiming eleven bells.

She had wound the clock, locked down the house, turned down the bed, and poured a cup of hot "Triple-Leaf Relaxing Tea." She closed the bedroom door and switched off the light leaving the small, antique lamp by her bed, the only light in the house. The soft glow by her bed was welcoming and she could feel her body relaxing as she strolled across the room.

She set her steaming tea on the night stand, pulled open the small drawer and retrieved her leather-bound journal. She had been rehearsing her narrative while shutting down the house, so she was ready to write as soon as she propped up her pillows, slipped into bed and pulled up the covers. She untied the bindings, laid it on her lap, reached over and took a sip of tea, breathed a deep sigh, pulled the pen from its holder and began her entry:

Journal for Thursday, August 10th

Hello again sad journal. What a difference a day makes. Two days ago, I was complaining about bills and the job, Tammy was complaining about school work and her lazy new boyfriend, and Jerry was upset over not reaching the top level of his video game.

Today, our worlds have reached a new level of complication. Jerry was quiet and distant today. He must be torn by his father's return and his best friend's horrible murder. His gentle, uncomplicated world is spinning with emotions he is ill-equipped to cope with.

Tammy is angry that her father has returned and torn by the disappearance of her boyfriend in the wake of his family's gruesome murder. She resents that her father is complicating her life again. She resents the accusations that David might be a deadly killer.

And what about my life! Just when I was feeling normal and comfortable with my lonesome life—HE comes to town!!! I am sorry he lost his job. I know it was everything to him— EVERYTHING. But why has he picked Rockcliffe of all places to go? NOW he needs me? NOW he needs us?

No longer relaxed, with her mental diatribe, she was now angry, trembling, sweating. She was feeling emotions she could not write; she could not express. As tears streamed down her face, she closed the journal, tied the binding and placed it back into the drawer.

As she switched off the lamp and pulled the covers up, a thought visited her mind as if slipping in the back door. Was Dottie at the Ludwig's when the murders occurred? It was curious that she had not heard from her quilting club friends. She relived their Wednesday meeting.

Dottie had received a call from Matilda Ludwig; Jon had beaten her again and she was finally ready to leave him. Dottie called a meeting of the Quilters to plan Matilda's escape.

They decided to have Dottie go with Matilda to get her things and then the members would take turns hiding her.

With all that was going on with her family, the murders themselves, and work, she had forgotten to call Dottie to see what happened. Dottie must have been there when Jon came home since Matilda had apparently not gotten away. Maybe Matilda had changed her mind again. It was so sad. Matilda had almost gotten away.

She made a mental note to call Dottie in the morning.

Part III
Friday

Chapter Thirty-Two
I Know Who I Am

Dᴀᴠɪᴅ Lᴜᴅᴡɪɢ ᴀᴡᴏᴋᴇ ᴡʜᴇɴ the sun glinted through the window above his head. He glanced around the room and was confused. *Where am I?*

He sat up and glanced around the room searching for clues. *How did I get here?*

He noticed a manila folder sitting on top of a dusty old vanity. He stood to read, "WHO IS DAVID LUDWIG?" printed across the folder. He walked over and opened the folder. It had a couple of newspaper clippings and a hand written note. He read it. "You are David Ludwig. You lost your memory. Do not panic. White Feather is your friend and will help you."

"Who is White Feather?" he muttered.

He set the letter on the vanity and considered the sentence, "You lost your memory."

He sat on the rickety little chair next to the vanity. He knew who he was! He remembered going to school. He remembered that he was supposed to meet Tammy's mother after school and they were going to dinner. He remembered getting suited up for practice.

So, how did he wind up in a dusty old room full of junk?

He picked up one of the newspaper articles. His football picture was prominent below the headline, "LUDWIG FAMILY FOUND MURDERED. SON A SUSPECT."

He jumped to his feet, "What?" he yelled.

The creaking sound of a door opening drew his attention to the stairs. Then a stream of light illuminated the top of them. The black cowboy boots of a man stepped down onto the top stair. Slowly and carefully the man descended. He looked like a weathered old cowboy in blue jeans and a red plaid shirt until he noticed the tuft of hair jutting up on top of his head like a hair fountain and a white feather dangling on the side.

"Who are you?" David challenged.

The stooped old man stopped, looked down at him, "I'm White Feather, your friend. Read the stuff?" he asked pointing at the manila folder on the vanity.

David shrugged, "Some of it."

"Come on up, I've fixed some breakfast."

David followed White Feather up the stairs to a long counter fronting a large room. A "Restrooms" sign was above two doors on one wall. To the left, a stairs led up to a second floor. The old man led him around to a dining room adjoining the large room. "What is this place?"

White Feather waved him over to a table set with plates and silverware, "It was a train terminal years ago. I call it home now."

David sat down while White Feather retrieved a couple of plates loaded with scrambled eggs and bacon from behind two double doors. "How long have I been here?"

White Feather sat across from him, "Two days, as of today."

David played with his fork and stirred the eggs, "Why am I here?"

White Feather patiently explained that he had found him in the park and brought him home. He finished by reassuring him, "I don't think you did it, but I can't prove it yet."

David nodded, "Why do they think I did it?"

White Feather stared at him and then focused on his plate. He was subconsciously bouncing the teeth of his fork on the plate. "Oh, sorry. I guess I'm not hungry."

The patient old Indian continued, "You were seen running out the back door of your house not long after the murders."

The old Indian was looking at him strangely. Images of his family flashed into his head. *His sweet mother dead? His timid brother dead? His father?* He felt a tear drop on his cheek.

David looked down thoughtfully for a moment, "So why do you think I'm innocent?"

White Feather glanced at him, "You're too dumb."

David's mouth dropped open. White Feather chuckled. David chuckled good naturedly and reached for his glass of milk. After swallowing, he gave his new friend a very stern look; "Seriously," he insisted.

White Feather finished chewing his food, wiped his hands with a paper towel and sat back in his chair. "For one thing, you are an honest person."

"How do you know that?"

"I am a medicine man. And, I have been to the crime scene and the autopsy. You could've done it based on some of the evidence, but it doesn't add up."

White Feather took a drink of orange juice, "If you had done it, you would have had blood splatters on your wrist, shirt, and shoes. You had blood on your palms and blood smudges on your shirt. There was blood on the soles of your shoes, nothing on top."

David set down his milk and turned the glass between his fingers and thumb, "What does that mean?"

"You were at the crime scene; picked up the gun; stepped in the blood; but didn't shoot anybody."

"You know who did it?"

"I need more time."

David turned to stare out the window, then offered, "Anything I can do?"

White Feather shrugged, "Get your memory back."

David wiped his eyes with the tips of his fingers and shrugged, "Yeah, that would be nice, but it is all a blank after getting suited up in the locker room."

White Feather leaned forward, "You remember a locker room?"

David was surprised by White Feather's question. "I remember up to getting ready for football practice and then it is all a blank."

White Feather nodded his head, "That's more than you remembered yesterday."

David frowned, "Really?"

White feather smirked and nodded. David added, "I don't remember yesterday."

Chapter Thirty-Three

Sheriff Presents Pictures to Bennet and Wooten

The POWERFUL ENGINE OF his Dodge Charger rumbled and rocked Sam Morrison as he sat thinking about his daughter. She was dating the boy suspected of shooting his family and he had an appointment to interview her. What would he say? She despised him.

There was a knock on his windshield. He turned to see Deputy Calhoun grinning at him. He rolled down the window.

"You coming in?" the goofy deputy inquired.

Morrison revved up the Charger engine and turned the key off. The engine grumbled and clattered before stopping. Morrison opened the door and rolled out. He had not gotten any sleep. All night he had rehearsed his speech to his daughter, over and over.

Calhoun seemed filled with an abundance of irritating energy, "We've got interviews this morning."

Morrison dug his hands into his jacket pockets and lumbered forward ignoring his enthusiastic partner. Calhoun inhaled deeply and loudly, "Great morning, eh? That's what I love about this valley, the crisp mountain air. We're at 7,888 feet, you know."

Morrison coughed lightly and lumbered on. Calhoun rushed ahead to open the door for the new deputy. Morrison ducked in and rushed down the hallway to the offices. All he could think of was a strong cup of coffee. Calhoun followed right on his heels, "How 'bout some coffee? You like it strong and black, right?"

Morrison headed straight for the little break room in the corner. Calhoun persisted, "Want me to get it for you? I'll bring it to your desk."

Without acknowledging the friendly overture, Morrison grabbed a styrofoam cup with his left hand as he grasped the coffee pot with the other and started pouring. Calhoun observed, "You need a real cup. Maybe there's one in the cabinet."

As Calhoun opened the door to the cabinet above the sink, Morrison shoved the pot back onto the burner and headed to the desks in the center of the open area. He could hear Calhoun continuing their conversation in the background as he dropped onto an old, unsteady chair. It rolled a few inches and shifted to the right causing him to spill a few drops of the hot coffee on his knee. "Damn."

There were several bulletins strewn across the otherwise clean desk. He was not accustomed to having a clean desk. It was supposed to be cluttered with stacks of case files, bulletins, and miscellaneous crap. Maybe it would be different here.

A note from Deedie caught his attention. Mrs. Pentington, at the school, had called. Their first interview was at nine o'clock.

He tried the coffee. It was bitter, hot, and strong—just the way he liked it. As he turned the tiny cup up for the last gulp, he gathered up the bulletins and dragged them across his desk into the round trash can. He glanced up at Sheriff Bailey's office. His old friend Buster and Sheriff Bailey were standing behind the big glass vision pane staring at him with ominous smiles on their faces.

Morrison set down the empty cup and guiltily dug the bulletins back out of the trash. Bailey waved for him to come to his office. He jumped up and headed for the big office when Calhoun waltzed up, "Found you a real cup."

Morrison grabbed the filled cup out of his hand and continued to the sheriff's office as he gulped down some of the delicious brew. "You're welcome!" Calhoun shouted.

Morrison made a half turn and saluted him with the cup, then ducked through the sheriff's door. Bailey and Crab were seated. Bailey leaned back in his executive chair, "Have a seat."

Morrison gulped down more coffee and set the cup on the small, glass-topped table. Bailey was clearly a neat freak. Nothing was out of place. No clutter anywhere.

Remembering to be friendly, he forced a smile, "Morning, Sheriff."

Bailey smiled grandly, "Gooood Morning, Morrison."

Morrison turned to Buster, "Mornin', Buster." Morrison cringed, "I don't have to hug you, do I?"

Buster laughed loudly, "Not unless you want to, Pardner."

Morrison shoved his clasped fists between his legs and hunkered over in the chair, "Got heating in this place?"

The sheriff glanced around as if bewildered, held out his hands, "You cold?"

Morrison grumbled, not wanting to admit it. The sheriff clasped his hands and got to the point, "Smiles is sick again today. I told his supervisor we have interviews set up at the school. He told us to go ahead and bring Agent Blakeley up to speed when he gets back."

Morrison shrugged. He felt that CBI involvement was a waste of time anyway. He had investigated hundreds of homicides.

The sheriff lifted the case folder, "I've been reading your write-up on our meeting with the Medical Examiner."

Morrison shook his head as Bailey continued, "It just don't add up. Couldn't have been a murder suicide."

Morrison nodded. It seemed obvious to him. Crab continued, "Lends credence to David Ludwig being the shooter."

Morrison shrugged. His old friend cocked his head to one side and studied Morrison. Buster must have sensed that Morrison's mind was not on work this morning, "You see the family last night?"

Morrison nodded and shivered slightly. Buster asked, "How are they?"

Morrison shrugged again, "Fine. Tammy hates my guts."

Buster waited. Morrison remembered something, "I learned that Tammy's been dating the Ludwig kid."

The sheriff raised his eyebrows. Morrison shifted in his chair, "I'm going over to interview her this evening."

Buster studied his friend for a moment, "Want me to do it?"

Morrison sat up, took a deep breath, rubbed his face with his palms, "Yes."

Then he forced a smile, "Sam thinks I should do it."

"You know why?"

Morrison shook his head, "I just know she's usually right about these things."

Buster nodded. The sheriff glanced at his watch. "Bennet and Wooten will be in any minute now. I laid Ludwig's pictures on Bennet's desk in an envelope. I wrote 'Is this what you were looking for?' on it."

Morrison turned and gazed out the door. He spotted the envelope lying on the center of a desk. He heard the sheriff's pistol clatter as he shoved a clip into it, "You loaded?"

Morrison felt of his gun strapped to his side inside his jacket, "Yeah. You expecting trouble?"

The sheriff laid his pistol on top of his desk, "I don't know what to expect with those two. Why don't you two go wait in the break room?"

Morrison nodded, grabbed his new coffee cup and followed Buster casually to the break room. Calhoun joined them, "We got interviews this morning."

Morrison refilled his coffee mug, "Yeah." He glanced at his watch, "I thought we might head over about ten 'til."

Calhoun looked at his watch, "Yeah, that'll give us plenty of time."

Morrison glanced at Bennet's desk and then tried to kill time with idle chatter, "Learn anything on the break-in?"

Calhoun smirked, "Nah. Nobody heard or saw anything. Probably happened in the middle of the night after everyone had gone to bed. I gave my report to the Sheriff this morning."

Morrison took a cautious sip of the hot coffee, "I'd like to talk to the people who called in the murders. Maybe you and me can run over there after our interviews?"

Calhoun shrugged, "Sure, no problem. It's all in my report. I interviewed them that day, you know."

Morrison nodded, "Sure, I'll take a look at your report."

Morrison heard footsteps coming down the hallway. Bennet and Wooten strolled into the break room. Buster backed into the corner as Morrison and Calhoun gave them room also, "Mornin'."

The two cocky deputies nodded, Bennet mumbled, "Mornin'."

Calhoun puffed up, "Busted any druggies lately?" then laughed.

Wooten exited with his coffee, Bennet glared at Calhoun as he filled his cup, then turned and headed for the desks."

Calhoun explained, "They ain't much for talkin' before they've had their coffee."

Buster and Morrison moved closer to the door to watch them discover the envelope. He blocked out Calhoun's weather update from his thoughts as he watched Bennet sit down at the desk where the envelope was sitting. Wooten walked by Bennet's desk to sit down at another desk to drink his coffee. Bennet paused to read the envelope. He whispered something to Wooten, set down his coffee and picked up the envelope. Wooten strolled over and looked over his shoulder as he pulled out the pictures. They studied the photos for a moment and then studied each other.

Calhoun reported from the window, "It's startin' to cloud up now."

Wooten and Bennet continued to study each other as if they were communicating without words. Bennet stood and reached for his holstered gun clipped to his belt. Wooten pulled his revolver out of the shoulder holster. Morrison slid his hand under his jacket and turned off the safety on his pistol.

Calhoun proclaimed, "Yep, something's rolling in."

Bennet unclipped the holster, set down his coffee and headed for the sheriff's office with Wooten in tow. Morrison stepped out of the break room and gripped the handle of his gun. Buster moved up behind him. They headed for the Sheriff's office but did not draw their pistols since Wooten was carrying his revolver by its body not the grip and Bennet's pistol was still in its holster. Sheriff Bailey was watching them from his big chair with his hand on the pistol lying on his desk.

They walked casually into Bailey's office and laid the weapons on his desk and then pulled their badges and laid them beside the guns. Morrison and Buster waited outside the door as Bailey stood, holstered his gun and made the arrest official, "Bennet, Wooten, you are under arrest for placing incriminating evidence at a crime scene. You have the right to remain silent. Anything you say or do, can and will be held against you in a court of law ..."

The Sheriff cuffed them and motioned for them to leave the office. They ignored Morrison and Crab as they walked by. Bailey winked as he passed Morrison and Buster and nodded for them to follow. Calhoun was standing at the door of the break room with his mouth agape. Deputy Melton was standing by the desk looking down at the photos shaking his head.

"What's goin' on?" Calhoun cried. Morrison held up his hand and bade him stay put. Calhoun's face wrinkled up like he might cry. Melton whispered, "Jessie. Come 'ere."

Chapter Thirty-Four
The Interrogation Room

M ORRISON, CALHOUN AND MELTON watched through the one-way glass of the interrogation room as Bailey and Crab sat down across from Bennet. "Tell me about it."

Bennet shifted in his chair, "It's pretty obvious, ain't it?"

Sheriff nodded, "Why'd you do it?"

Bennet clasped his hands and placed them on the table, "We made a mistake. We'd gotten a tip that Timmons was dealing on the street. I guess Ludwig overheard the dispatch and met us as we drove up."

Bennet looked up, "Hell, he probably called it in. Timmons was standing on the corner with his ear buds on. We didn't see the ear buds; at least I didn't. Wooten came in from one side, me and Ludwig from the other. I told Timmons to freeze and hold up his hands, but he reached into his pocket instead. Ludwig shouted 'gun, he's going for his gun!' Wooten plugged him three times. When we searched his pocket, we found his Walkman."

Bennet had a remorseful expression, almost pleading, "I guess he reached in his pocket to turn it off so he could hear us."

Buster shook his head, "So, whose idea was it to plant the gun and crack?"

Bennet slumped down in his chair as if disgusted, "Jon's."

Bennet leaned forward and put his cuffed hands on the table, "He even provided the gun and crack." Bennet fell back in his chair and swept his hand over the pictures, "Looks like while we were plantin' 'em, he was secretly shootin' pictures."

Sheriff Bailey inhaled deeply, "So, then he blackmailed you."

Bennet nodded. Bailey followed up, "So what did he want from you?"

Bennet ducked his head and pushed his fingers through his black curly hair. "He wanted to take over the drug market."

"With your help?"

Bennet nodded. Bailey summed it up, "You got rid of the competition and he took over the customers?"

Bennet took a deep breath, straightened up and leaned back in the chair, "Yep, that was the program."

The sheriff leaned forward and looked into Bennet's eyes, "So where were you between five and six o'clock Wednesday?"

Bennet glanced at Buster uneasily, "Five to six?"

Bennet was nervous as he searched the ceiling for an answer, then he relaxed, "Oh, yeah, me and Wooten were in Pueblo, Drug Seminar."

Morrison and Melton looked at each other knowingly. Melton almost smiled and nodded his head.

"They didn't do it!" Calhoun proclaimed as if astounded by the idea.

Melton turned to leave. Morrison nodded and looked back through the one-way mirror. Bailey was leading Bennet out of the interrogation room. Wooten would be next, but Morrison knew that his interview would not provide anything new.

Then Morrison remembered something that the sheriff had said: *Ludwig got along with Melton. I'm not sure why. They're so different that it just don't seem like they would get along.*

Morrison followed Melton back to the offices and into the break room. As Melton refilled his coffee mug, Morrison struck up a conversation, "I understand that you got along with Ludwig."

Melton shrugged as he stirred sugar into his coffee. Morrison persisted, "You never had any problem with him?"

Melton calmly took a sip of his coffee, then shook his head and headed for his desk as if the matter was settled. Morrison suspected he was more likely trying to avoid the subject. Morrison refilled his mug and followed the senior deputy to the desks. "How'd you manage to stay on his good side?"

Melton leaned back in the chair and propped his feet on the desk, "Jon didn't have a good side."

Morrison sat in the chair beside Melton and stared at Melton until he broke down to explain, "Jon and I go way back. They joined our church way back when Jon was first trying to deal with his alcoholism. I became his sponsor at AA." Morrison raised an eyebrow.

Melton looked at Morrison guiltily, "I've been sober for twenty-two years now."

Morrison tipped his cup to him. Melton took another sip of his coffee before continuing, "Jon's a strong man and for a couple of years he truly tried to turn his life around. But, then one day, he stopped coming to AA and to church. He had fallen off the wagon, of course.

"Pretty soon Matilda and the boys stopped coming to church. I went over to talk to them and they were friendly and hospitable," Melton glanced at Morrison, "even Jon. But, I could smell the alcohol on Jon and I could read the nervousness in Matilda."

Melton set his coffee on his desk, leaned back and interlaced his fingers across his stomach, "I didn't press them. Told 'em I was there for them. But they never returned my calls or tried to contact me. Jon steered clear of me at work. Kept things professional."

Morrison nursed his coffee while he let Melton reflect on the memory. There was one more thing, "Was it awkward for you when you were called out for a domestic disturbance at the Ludwig's?"

Melton threw out his hands, "Actually, not. For some reason, maybe guilt, when I would walk in the door, Jon would calm down and get very reserved and quiet. I could read in Matilda's pleading eyes that she didn't want me to take Jon in. Of course, I had to arrest someone, so I would take in David. Seemed like the best way to keep the boy safe until Jon sobered up."

Morrison tried not to look judgmental as he looked away and drank the last of his coffee. He knew a rationalization when he heard one. Melton continued, "Maybe it was the wrong thing. David wasn't the one causing the problem, but he seemed ok with it. One of the times, it gave us a chance to talk and David and I got to be pretty good friends. He even called me a couple of times when his father ..." Melton did not finish the sentence, just stared into space, remembering.

"He call you after the murders?"

Melton shook his head sadly. "Nah. I don't think the kid did it, though."

Morrison persisted, "What do you think happened?"

Melton stared into space, "More likely Jon did it."

Morrison stood and offered, "Can I get you some more coffee?"

Melton broke out of his trance, "No, ... no, thanks."

Chapter Thirty-Five
The School Interviews

DEPUTY CALHOUN KEPT UP a steady chatter as they drove to the school, but Morrison tuned him out. Painful memories of the days when Tammy was little occupied his mind; days when she looked up to him and he was her hero. He remembered her first Christmas when she toddled up to the tree and slapped the branches and jabbered excitedly to him. Christmas was so wondrous through her little eyes; so innocent; so happy; so trusting.

He turned to look out the window to hide his watery eyes from his annoying partner. They pulled into the parking lot. Thankfully, they had arrived.

Mrs. Pentington had a list ready for them. Morrison surreptitiously checked her cheek. The swelling had gone down but it was still too colorful to completely cover with makeup. He glanced at the list. Clearly, Dottie Pentington was a very efficient secretary. The list was typed with a column for the time of the interview, the interviewee's name, the room number where to find them, and the subject they taught or, in the case of friends, the classes they shared with the Ludwig boys.

"You call the parents?"

Dottie placed her fingers over her cheek, "None of them wanted to be present. They have jobs, you know? So, they agreed to let the school nurse sit in for them."

Morrison checked his body cam as he glanced over the list and handed it to Calhoun. The jabbering partner hushed while he examined the list. Morrison headed to room 104 for the first interview with a Miss Jones, David Ludwig's Algebra teacher.

Calhoun looked up to find his partner striding down the hallway, so he ran to catch up, "Says we meet a Miss Jones in room 104. She teaches Algebra." Morrison knew he was just trying to be helpful, but Calhoun was annoying. He almost regretted that they had managed to patch things up while searching for a place for him to live.

By the time they had interviewed the last teacher, a pattern had developed. David Ludwig was a good student; never caused any problems; made decent grades; was shy and never raised his hand; seemed to be liked by the other students. They had not noticed anything unusual in his behavior the day of the murders.

Darren Ludwig, in contrast, they learned, made his brother appear to be outgoing. He was shy to the point of being withdrawn, private, and moody. On that Wednesday, some teachers noticed that he was nervous, sullen, or distracted. But they had waved it off as one of his mood swings.

The school nurse was present for interviews with the students. Sheriff Bailey had confirmed that it was their policy to have a parent present if the child was a suspect.

But since these interviews were just fact-finding, an exception could be made provided the school nurse was present and the parents were notified.

The first friend to be interviewed was a flaming red-haired, curly-headed, scrawny kid with thick rimmed glasses and freckles dotting his nose and cheeks.

Morrison smiled, "So, Freddie, you are friends with David Ludwig?"

"Yes, sir."

Morrison studied the nervous boy for a moment, "How long have you been friends?"

Freddie shrugged, "Known him since we were little kids. All my life. We used to live next door."

"What's he like?"

Freddie squirmed like he was facing a pop quiz he was not prepared for, "He's ... quiet; friendly; easy-going."

"Does he have any hobbies?"

The curly-headed kid raked his fingers across his forehead to push unruly red curls out of his eyes, "Liked to hunt. We used to go exploring up in the foothills on bikes. He don't like fishin' much, but would go with me when I wanted to. He's a good sport."

Freddie studied the floor as if looking for more, "Likes to read. Oh, and he loves to play cards."

Calhoun straightened up, lowered his notepad and put on his serious face, "What kinda huntin'?"

Freddie's eyes got big and Morrison read in his face that he was worried he had given a wrong answer, "Just birds and rabbits."

Calhoun pressed on, "So, he liked guns?"

Freddie squirmed, "We got pellet guns for Christmas one year."

Morrison decided to rescue the boy, "Ok, Freddie. Did David act any differently the day of the murders? Was he upset or anything?"

Freddie thought about it, "I don't think so. He seemed friendly like always."

Calhoun jumped in, "He talk to you about the fights with his old man?"

Perspiration beaded up on the boy's forehead, "Mr. Ludwig was ... very strict. He was always yelling at me and David. Especially when he was ... you know ... drinking."

Calhoun started a follow up, but Morrison interrupted him, "Mr. Ludwig drink often?"

Freddie shrugged, "Yessir. Most every night, I guess."

Calhoun tried again, but Morrison placed his hand on his knee, then asked, "Did he ever hit you or David when he was drunk?"

The boy scratched his head, "Well, not me. But, he hit Davey sometimes."

Calhoun could not be silenced, "Davey ever hit his old man?"

The boy rubbed his legs, "I don't think so. I never saw him do that."

Calhoun continued, "David own a pistol?"

Freddie's eyes bulged and his face turned as red as his hair, "Pistol? Na-no, sir. I don't think so."

Morrison felt sorry for Freddie. Calhoun had clearly scared the poor boy. Morrison felt that maybe he had had enough, "Ok, Freddie, we don't have any more questions. Thank you for talking with us."

The boy's eyes grew large anticipating escape, "Sure. Can I go now?"

"Sure, thanks."

Morrison made a note to follow up later. The boy had reacted very nervously when Calhoun asked him about a pistol. Perhaps he knew something but he wanted to ask Freddie under more comfortable circumstances without Calhoun crouching over him.

The other friends were not as close as Freddie, but all painted pretty much the same picture. David was a quiet, friendly boy who stayed out of trouble. Some confirmed that they thought his father was harsh and strict and knew about the fights. But most knew little about David's home life.

Then they interviewed the younger friends of David's brother, Darren. The first was a pretty, petite red-head, Jenifer Jones, the coach's daughter. "Tell me about Darren," Morrison began.

Jenifer's eyes sparkled as she smirked mischievously, "Darren was a sweet boy."

Morrison prompted her for more, "Did he ever talk to you about trouble at home?"

She glanced at Calhoun and smiled. Calhoun puffed up and smirked. The flirty girl then grew serious, "Everybody knows his dad was mean. We talked about it. Darren was scared of him. David was the one that stood up to him. Darren was too shy. He couldn't hurt a fly much less stand up to that creep."

Morrison made notes as he asked, "How well did you know Darren's father?"

For the first time, Jenifer's eyes betrayed uneasiness, "Not well."

Morrison noticed the change and made a note, then continued, "Did you talk to Darren Wednesday?"

Jenifer nodded. Morrison prodded her, "Did you notice anything different? Was he troubled?"

She kicked her legs out and back nervously and shrugged. The out-going girl had clammed up. Morrison persisted, "What did you talk about that day?"

She shrugged and inhaled deeply, "His dad had beat up his mom that morning. When he tried to break it up, his dad roughed him up too."

Morrison challenged her, "Was he angry?"

She gave him an indignant look, "Sure."

"Angry enough to do something about it?"

She smirked, "Pshaw. Darren? Are you kidding?"

Morrison finished up his notes and studied her for a moment. As she nervously kicked her feet out and back, she studied the floor in thought. "Anything else you would like to tell us?"

The thoughtful girl jumped as if startled by his question. She looked into his eyes as if searching for some sign or signal. For a moment, he thought she might share something more, but then she shook her head and looked down again. She was a very strong young girl, but there was something deeply troubling her.

Morrison wished he knew how to reach her, but he sensed that her troubles were very personal and not for the ears of strangers. He wrote his name and cell phone number on a blank sheet and tore it out of his notepad. He held it out to the girl, "Ok, Jenifer. If you think of anything else, you can call me."

She glanced at Morrison surprised, "That's it?"

Morrison nodded. She grabbed the note and bolted out of the room. Calhoun tried to smile at her as she left but she avoided his gaze.

Morrison glanced over the list as the next student came in. His son was not on the list. He was glad, he would have a chance to visit with him privately during their Saturday outing.

A young boy stood sheepishly at the door. Morrison smiled at him and motioned for him to sit across the table from them.

None of the remaining friends interviewed noticed anything peculiar about Darren that day. They all described him as a loner, quiet and withdrawn.

The last interview ended conveniently at noon. Calhoun was eager to show his partner a new place in town.

No one notices the janitor or someone pretending to be a janitor. White Feather had learned that if you push a broom or a mop around in the white man's world you are invisible. So, he had been invisible as he listened to the new deputy and his dim-witted partner interview the teachers and friends of David and Darren Ludwig. There were only two interviews that had interested him— Jenifer Jones and Freddie. He suspected that they were both hiding something.

The more he heard the more convinced he was that David Ludwig was innocent. His friends' perception of David Ludwig seemed to match his own image of the boy.

Chapter Thirty-Six

Mexican Joint

Cᴀʟʜᴏᴜɴ ᴘᴀʀᴋᴇᴅ ᴛʜᴇ ᴄᴀʀ on a side street and lead Morrison to a small Mexican restaurant on the corner of Third and Main Street downtown Rockcliffe. "It's a nice day, let's sit out on the patio."

Morrison followed his partner inside and then out to a covered patio area just large enough for four tables. Calhoun leaned his chair back on two legs, "BGT." He proclaimed.

Morrison blinked and struggled to focus on Calhoun, "What?"

"Bacon, guacamole, and tomato sandwich. BGT."

Morrison picked up the menu and glanced through the choices. The waitress rushed up and pulled out her ticket pad, "What can I getcha?"

Calhoun boasted, "I'll have the BGT and tea."

Morrison was not in the mood to search the menu; he put it down, "Sounds good."

The waitress scribbled on the pad and rushed back inside. Calhoun leaned forward, "Did you catch the gun thing?"

Morrison looked at him puzzled; Calhoun leaned back and swelled up, "That Freddie kid admitted Ludwig liked guns."

Morrison took a deep breath and pondered whether to correct him or not, "You think he shot his ol' man with a pellet gun?"

Calhoun frowned, then laughed, "No, but he liked guns. First you get a pellet gun, see, then you decide you like shooting so you move up to a shotgun. Pretty soon, you move up to pistols."

Morrison studied him for a moment, "Is that what you did?"

Calhoun's eyes grew large as he deflated, "Me? Well, no. I mean it wasn't like that for me, you know, I always respected guns."

Morrison nodded, "I forgot to pull your report. Could you tell me about the people you interviewed in the neighborhood that heard the shots?"

Calhoun crossed his legs, carefully leaned back in his chair and clasped his hands behind his head, "Well, most of 'em heard shots but didn't think anything of it. Assumed it was something else. Old Bert was the exception. He's a Vietnam vet, you see, so he knows shots when he hears 'em. He called it in and then saw David Ludwig runnin' out the back door."

"Where's Bert's house in relation to the Ludwig's?"

"Across the alley, directly behind 'em."

Morrison tried to remember what Buster had said, "Wasn't there more than one caller?"

Calhoun raised his eyebrows, "Oh, yeah. Some lady called ... anonymous."

Morrison did not look up, "None of the women you interviewed confessed to making the call?"

Calhoun's eyes betrayed his surprise by the question, "Well ... uh ... no."

Morrison nodded and reached for his notepad, "How many shots did the callers hear?"

Calhoun's face went blank for a moment, then he reached for his note pad and thumbed through the pages, "Anonymous didn't say, obviously, but Bert heard three quick shots, then a pause, then a shot, then a pause, and then another shot."

Morrison frowned, "Five total shots?"

Calhoun counted, "Yep, five."

Morrison made notes. "I need to see the crime scene again."

The waitress burst through the door and placed red baskets in front of them and two glasses of tea. Morrison quickly added, "After we try these BJT's, of course." He was hungry.

"BGT."

"What?"

Calhoun giggled, "BGT. Guacamole starts with a 'g' not 'j'!"

Morrison laughed, "You got me there, partner, you got me there."

As Morrison picked up the sandwich, he noticed an old man standing quietly behind one of the columns next to the corner of the patio staring at them. He wore a blue ball cap and what appeared to be a white feather dangled on the side of his face. He wore a blue uniform ... like the janitor at the school.

They traded stares for a moment and then the old man turned to cross the street. Morrison jumped up and yelled, "Hey, stop!"

Calhoun was startled by his shout and jumped up drawing his pistol and dancing around looking for a villain and shouting, "What? Where? What?"

The patio was enclosed with a four-foot high plaster wall blocking Morrison from pursuing the old man who shuffled past the building across the street and disappeared. Morrison sat back down and then noticed his partner's antics, "Sorry, Calhoun, false alarm."

Chapter Thirty-Seven

Morrison Returns to the Crime Scene

I<small>T WAS THE FIRST</small> time that Calhoun had seen the crime scene since the break in. "Holy Toledo!"

Morrison crossed the room to check the back wall for the two bullets that had not been found. He searched the wall around the entry way into the anteroom where the bullet that probably had killed Jon Ludwig was tagged. He searched the wall behind the couch along the ceiling and along the baseboard. Calhoun was in the bedroom, "Holy Toledo!"

Morrison studied the living room and tried to imagine the scene, a professional habit developed from years on the force as a detective. He mentally projected a line from the hole above the anteroom back into the room. It was probably the shot that went through Jon Ludwig's head and hit the wall above the anteroom. One shot went into Matilda's liver. The bullet that passed through Darren's head was found lodged in the wall in the dining room beside the painting of the Last Supper. So, where were the other two slugs?

Calhoun announced from the second bedroom, "Holy Crap!"

Jon Ludwig probably knocked the shooter down. From the floor, the shooter shot Ludwig. It would be a difficult shot. Maybe it took three shots before one found its target. Morrison pictured the shooter laying on the floor and turning the gun on Ludwig. He speculated on the possibilities. Perhaps one shot went off accidently when the shooter hit the floor? If the gun was in his right hand, the bullet could have hit the wall between the kitchen and the dining room. He searched for it in that wall. Maybe it went into the kitchen. He headed for the kitchen as Calhoun came out of the second bedroom, "Have you seen this?"

"Yeah, come help me look for a bullet hole. It should be in the refrigerator or the wall behind it."

A thorough search yielded nothing. Calhoun stated the obvious, "Must be somewhere else."

Morrison rubbed his chin. The angle was wrong. He returned to the living room and stood in front of the couch. "Search the couch again."

While Calhoun searched, Morrison paced back and forth in front of the couch. He scanned the wall between the living room and the master bedroom, but again came up empty. Out of desperation, he searched the wall opposite the front of the couch. Along that wall was the front door, the entertainment center filled with electronic equipment and the television. A window looked out over the front lawn. There was no sign of a bullet hole.

Calhoun was standing in front of the couch watching him. When Morrison glanced at him, the deputy shrugged and proclaimed, "Nothing."

Morrison nodded, "Search the anteroom for a bullet hole. We are missing two slugs."

Calhoun stepped into the back room to search. There were windows along the back wall and the back door. Below the windows, a washer and dryer, a table, and a shelf holding detergents and other cleaning supplies. On the other side of the door, another table with pencils and pens in a glass; a desk organizer with paper clips, sticky notes, scissors, hole-punch, etc.; a legal sized note pad, and an ash tray filled with butts and ashes. There was a PC monitor and keyboard with cables laying across the vacant spot where the PC had once sat.

Morrison studied the line of the shots again. He walked over to the left side of the couch, turned and pointed with his finger. To shoot Matilda, the shooter would have had to shoot from below his hip. Blood on the floor indicated that Matilda was standing at point blank range near the center of the couch. *A struggle with the shooter? Gun goes off?*

Morrison nodded his head. Matilda could have made her way to the couch with a stomach wound where she bled out. But the boy was shot in the head. Either he was shot while sitting on the couch, or carried there afterward. He turned and searched the floor for more blood stains. Then he remembered blood splatter on the back of the couch where the boy was sitting. *He was definitely sitting on the couch when he was shot.*

The shooter held a gun to his head and shot him while he sat on the couch in his wounded mother's arms? Morrison tried to crook his hand around until the line of the bullet was consistent with the bullet hole by the painting in the dining room.

Suicide? Morrison considered the possibility. *But, how did the gun get way over beside Ludwig?* It did not make sense. But the angle was so awkward. Morrison sighted down the imagined line-of-flight to where the dry wall had been removed in the dining room. It had to be the one from Darren.

When he turned around, Calhoun was studying the scene. Morrison checked, "No bullet holes in the back room?"

Calhoun smerked and rocked back, "Nope."

Morrison waited for the inevitable—Calhoun's take, "So, old man Ludwig shoots his son." Calhoun acts out the shot, "Then the old lady grabs the gun, it goes off and she falls to the floor. But she hangs on to the gun and shoots the old man from the floor."

Morrison grinned, "Interesting hypothesis. But why would he shoot his son when he was just sitting on the couch?"

Calhoun frowned. "How do you know that?"

Morrison pointed out the blood splatter on the top of the couch. Calhoun's eyes widened, "Oh, yeah."

Morrison tested him, "So, what happened to the other two bullets?"

Calhoun glanced around the room, threw up his hands and declared, "He must have missed twice."

Morrison smiled and patted him on the back. "Obviously, but where are the bullet holes?"

Calhoun scanned the living room, "You looked in here, right?"

Morrison glanced up to the ceiling, "Let's look again. This time you search the living room and I'll search the anteroom."

Chapter Thirty-Eight
Outside the Window

WHITE FEATHER WAS LISTENING with interest outside the kitchen window. Once again his attempt to visit the crime scene personally had been thwarted. But, this time he would wait until the deputies left and then slip inside.

He heard the screened door of the house across the alley creaking and sneaked a peek around the corner of the Ludwig house. The nosy neighbor across the alley was standing on his patio deck studying the Ludwig house. No doubt, he had heard the deputies and was curious.

White Feather pulled back and flattened against the wall. This might not be the day he got to visit the crime scene after all.

White Feather stopped by the Dollar Store to buy a paper and a six-pack of root beer. A customer was talking to the teenaged clerk about the murders. He listened discretely as he pretended to browse the paperbacks.

The customer at the check-out said loudly, "I heard his old man was a wife beater."

"What most people who come in figure is he shot her and Darren and then turned the gun on himself," the clerk responded.

"So how come that boy ran?"

"I don't know, but I figure he found 'em dead and figured he'd get the blame." Pausing, the clerk added, "Every time the old man beats him up, the deputies arrest him instead of the old man."

While the customer nodded his head, he rubbed his whiskers, "Ludwig worked for 'em, I think."

The clerk eagerly acknowledged as he stuffed items into a sack, "Yeah. He was a deputy."

A lady standing next in line changed the subject slightly, "I hear we have a new deputy."

The clerk handed a receipt to the whiskered customer, "Yeah, they say he got fired from Denver PD and came down here to start over. His daughter is Tammy Morrison. She was dating David Ludwig."

The lady beamed, "I'll be darned, you don't say? That's a sticky wicket, ain't it?"

The clerk and customers laughed as the whiskered customer left. White Feather picked up a paperback collection of short stories. He smiled thinking how it would have been perfect for David while he had short term memory. He shook his head, *too late now.*

White Feather chuckled to himself as he put back the book and laid the root beer, milk and newspaper on the counter. "Find everything ok?" the clerk asked.

White Feather nodded, and then asked, "You know David Ludwig?"

The clerk handed a receipt to the lady who grabbed her bag, tossed the receipt inside and rushed out the door. The clerk slid the root beer past the scanner and smiled, "He's in my class. He's kind of a loner, though, so don't know him well."

White Feather got to the point, "You don't think he did it?"

The kid stuck out his lower lip, "Naw. From what I hear, it must have been a murder/suicide. I figure Davey came in afterwards."

White Feather nodded, "You know the girlfriend?"

"Oh, sure, Tammy's very popular. She's really friendly and outgoing."

"You surprised she's dating Ludwig?"

The boy's smile faded. He shrugged, "Yeah, a little. But Davey's a good guy, too, just quiet, you know?"

The clerk dropped the newspaper in the sack with the root beer, opened the cash drawer and made change. As he handed White Feather his change, he dropped a bomb on the old Indian, "What d'you think happened?"

White Feather choked out, "Beats me."

"Have a nice day."

White Feather walked the remaining ten blocks to the old train terminal. As he approached, he feared he would find David sitting on the porch again. Or maybe he would be gone altogether. He found the main floor empty and quiet as he waddled through to the kitchen and placed the root beer and milk in the refrigerator. He checked his supply of food and made a mental note to get more eggs and bacon.

He sat down at his usual table and opened the newspaper searching for an article on the murder investigation. There was not one. He was not surprised. The paper in Canon City seldom carried news about Rockcliffe. He decided he should check on David and headed for the basement.

He found David sleeping peacefully on the cot in the basement. He smiled and decided not to disturb him.

Chapter Thirty-Nine
Dinner with Tammy

As Morrison walked up to the neat, well-kept bungalow house, he straightened his tie and rolled his head to loosen up his tight neck muscles. He felt like he was going on a first date. His shoes were shined, he was wearing his best suit, his favorite after shave, and his hair was combed. He paused at the door, reached into his pocket and pulled out his breath mints, laid the thin sheet on his tongue and looked for the doorbell button. But before he could find it, the porch light came on and the door opened.

"Hi, Sam." Samantha Morrison smiled, "Come in."

Morrison stepped in and nervously tugged on the bottom of his suit jacket. Samantha probably felt sorry for him, "You look very nice."

Morrison took a deep breath and blurted out the first thing that came to mind, "I may have found a place. We went looking yesterday afternoon."

Samantha questioned, "We?"

"Oh. Deputy Calhoun went with me to help me find my way around."

Samantha chuckled, "You needed someone to help you find your way around Rockcliffe?"

They laughed as Samantha led him into the den, "Come on in, I'll get Tammy."

Jerry was reclining in the Lazy Boy recliner watching television. Samantha brushed his hair as she passed by, "Your father is here."

Jerry grabbed the lever and popped up, "Hi, Dad."

Morrison hugged his son, "Hi, Jerr."

Morrison took a seat on the couch as Jerry sat back down in the recliner. Morrison shared his news, "I may have found a place."

Jerry seemed supportive, "Oh, really? Where?"

Morrison shifted and pulled down on the lapel of his jacket, "Oh, it's over on Third, a couple of blocks from Main."

Jerry looked into space, "Oh, ok."

Tammy and her mother appeared in the hallway door. Morrison stood. The pretty young woman in a flattering red dress took his breath away. *When did she grow up?* "Hi, Tammy. You look nice."

Tammy frowned, "Thanks."

Samantha gently nudged her daughter into the den. Morrison smiled, "Ready to go?"

Tammy shrugged. Samantha tried to cheer things up, "Where are you going?"

Morrison offered, "I got us reservations out at the Lodge."

Tammy avoided looking at her dad. Samantha intervened, "Oh! That sounds nice, doesn't it, Honey?"

Tammy shrugged. Morrison glanced at Jerry. "See you tomorrow, Jerr?" His son had re-engaged with television.

Morrison smiled, "Ok. Well, shall we get going?"

Tammy shrugged and headed for the front door. Samantha offered an encouraging smile to her ex-husband as he followed his reluctant daughter out.

Morrison fired up his noisy Dodge Charger and tried to start a conversation, "How's your car doing? Still running …"

"Fine." She interrupted.

Morrison nodded, "That's good."

They were both quiet as they slowly drove through town. Pulling onto highway 69, he headed south out of town. Morrison tried again, "How's school?"

Tammy shrugged, "Ok."

"I met some of your teachers and Mr. Wheeler. They all seem nice."

Tammy did not respond, just turned to look out the side window. Who was this young woman? She had traded in her ebullient, effervescent energy for poise and her unstoppable chatter for tortuous silence. Morrison glanced over to see what might have caught her attention. The sun was going down behind the Sangre de Cristo mountain range, "Pretty sunset," he commented.

When Tammy turned her head slightly to look at the mountain, he realized that she had not been admiring the sunset, just avoiding him. "I may have found a place," he offered.

Tammy looked blankly at the valley ranch land. Morrison hoped that this was not what the whole night was going to be like. The Charger headlights came on as he turned right at Rosita Road and headed for the mountains. The pavement ended as they started climbing up the foothills of the Sangres. The dirt road snaked passed many cabins and chalets where woodpeckers hammered on the log siding and veneers. Tammy's penetrating silence continued as they wound their way up through the pines and past a camping area. The Lodge was nestled in the woods beyond the campsite at the base of Venable Peak.

All tables in the Lodge had a great view of Wet Mountain Valley and the Wet Mountains across the valley. Their table was on the upper level and back in a quiet corner. Morrison was pleased that they would have some privacy.

"You know what you want?" Morrison inquired as he set down his menu. Tammy shrugged, "What are you having? Steak, I bet."

Morrison's heart leaped; she spoke more than one syllable! He smiled, "Yeah. You have me figured out."

Tammy smirked and shifted in her chair as she set down her menu. Morrison ventured a guess, "Fettuccine Alfredo?"

Tammy's eyes got big and she could not squelch a giggle as she covered her mouth and shifted around to try to regain her composure. Morrison laughed, "It's always been your favorite."

For a moment, he saw her as the little girl who could barely see over the table. Now she was a pretty young woman. But, the attitude had not changed. She had been intensely independent and rebellious all of her life. She picked up her silverware wrapped in a thick, cloth napkin and unrolled it as she spoke, "So, where's your place?"

Morrison picked up his silverware and unrolled it, "Not far from downtown on Third."

Tammy nodded, "Convenient. Not far from the Sheriff's Office."

Morrison nodded, "Yeah. But, everywhere in town is pretty close."

Tammy chuckled, "Yeah, I guess so. Compared to Denver."

Morrison agreed. "How do you like it here? Must have been a big change."

Tammy shrugged, "I hated it at first. But, it's not so bad. Mom's really happy here."

Morrison arranged his silverware, "I'm glad. She deserves to be happy."

Tammy glanced up to look at him and then looked away. The waitress saved the moment.

Surprisingly, dinner went well and slowly Tammy came around. They traded embarrassing stories of times at restaurants or public places. It was bitter sweet for Morrison as they laughed and goaded each other. He realized that they had a lot of great memories together. But, he was also very sad knowing there should have been many more. He had missed out on a lot of opportunities to be with her because of his dedication to his job. He privately vowed to change.

After dessert, they sat back and agreed that they were both stuffed. They were getting along so well, he decided that he did not want to spoil it. He would talk to her about David Ludwig some other time. But, to his surprise, she brought it up.

"I don't guess you've found David?"

Morrison shook his head, "No. Any idea where he might have gone?"

Tammy shrugged and fiddled with her fork, "I've been thinking about that. I should've noticed that he was acting kinda strange that day."

Morrison leaned forward, "Strange, how?"

Tammy took the cloth napkin and cleaned the fork, "Oh. I don't know. Disoriented. Quiet. Not himself."

"You think something was bothering him?"

"No. I don't think it was that. It wasn't just me. I talked to Bobby at school and he said that David had gotten 'his brains knocked out' at practice and staggered off the field all wacky."

Morrison remembered, "The coach said the hit busted his helmet and left him dazed."

Tammy looked at him with bright eyes, "Dazed! Yeah, that's it."

She set down the fork and picked up the spoon, "Bobby said he acted like he didn't know anyone when he came over to the bleachers."

The waitress brought the check and gathered up the plates and silverware. Tammy sat quietly as her father fished out his credit card and placed it on the small tray with the ticket. The waitress deftly stacked everything on her arm, scooped up the small tray, "I'll be right back."

Morrison ignored the waitress and observed his daughter, "You're worried about him?"

Tammy nodded and smoothed the table cloth, "David couldn't have murdered them. He hated his father, but he couldn't have done it. Not that. Not his brother and mother."

"Did you know Mr. Ludwig?"

Tammy shrugged and shifted in her chair, "I met him once. He was creepy. His mother was really nice though.

She was in Mom's quilting club and Mom really liked her."

Morrison frowned. Samantha had not mentioned that she knew Matilda, "Did David ever talk about ... his father?"

"No. David was quiet and never talked about himself. I think his brother talked to Jenifer sometimes. They were in the same class."

"Who is Jenifer?"

Tammy glanced at her father and then studied her fingernails, "Jenifer Jones, the coach's daughter." She smirked, "Jerry's girlfriend."

Morrison chuckled, "Jerry's girlfriend?"

Tammy giggled, "Don't tell him I told you. He denies it, but he has a bad crush on her."

Morrison sat back, "I'll be darned." Of course, Jerry was old enough, but he just never thought about him having a girlfriend. The young, defiant redhead he had interviewed at the school flashed in his head. She was very pretty. He could understand why Jerry might have a crush on her. He had felt that she was hiding something; that she knew more than she was letting on, or, perhaps, was protecting someone.

Tammy chewed on the edges of her fingernail, "I don't know what he sees in her. She's ..."

Morrison waited; Tammy put down her hand and fidgeted, "She's kind of wild. But she's cute and flirty and all the boys drool over her."

Morrison considered his daughter's description of the girl. It fit. Tammy looked sad and distant. He sensed she was not thinking about her brother or the flirty redhead. "Has David tried to contact you?"

Her eyes welled up; she looked down and shook her head. He could see that she was hurt by his disappearance; that she was hurt that he had abandoned her. He looked out the huge window at the billions of stars glowing in the dark sky. He remembered a time years before when his little girl was fascinated by the night sky and they had shared a moment talking about the constellations. He wondered if she was still interested in the sky.

He looked at her again. She had regained her composure. She was ready to go home.

Chapter Forty
Journal Entry for Friday

As the old clock chimed the eleventh bell, Samantha sipped her tea and opened her journal.

Journal for Friday, August 11

Journal, where do I start! Where do I end? So much has happened today.

Tammy was sad and withdrawn when she came in but insisted that the meeting with her father had gone well. I think she is worried about David and it was hard for her to have to talk about him. I didn't press her when she wanted to turn in.

Jerry still has not shown any sign of change. He acts as if his father moving here is "no big deal". I can't believe he can just stow away his feelings. I'm afraid it will come out in unexpected ways.

I talked to Dottie today, she claims that Jon came home before they could get Matilda packed and that they started fighting. She said Jon had socked her when she tried to separate them and then forced her to leave. It is the first time I have ever seen Dottie break into tears. She blames herself for Matilda's murder. Maggie advised her to keep quiet about her involvement, but I told her she should go to the sheriff with what she knows. I'm afraid she will take Maggie's advice and not mine.

Part IV

Saturday

Chapter Forty-One
Morning with Jerry

Jerry was sitting on the porch steps when Morrison drove up. He pushed himself up slowly like an old man and swaggered over to the car. "Morning Jerr."

Jerry dropped into the front seat of the Charger, "Morning, Dad."

"So, where we going?"

Jerry shrugged, "Mom suggested we go out to Bishop's Castle, maybe the Wolf Preserve."

Morrison backed out of the driveway, "Just tell me how to get there."

Jerry directed his dad to highway 96 and they headed east out of town. Morrison took his time building his speed up to the 65-mile-per-hour speed limit.

Just as he set the cruise, Jerry shouted, "Deer" and pointed to the right side of the road. Morrison slammed on his brakes. "Thanks."

"They're pretty thick along here."

Morrison and his clearly bored son engaged in small talk about the valley, the village, and school as they followed the curvy asphalt road that climbed up over the

Wet Mountains and then descended to an intersection with a ranch named "Hardscrabble" on the right. They turned right and headed up highway 165, a winding road that finally got them to Bishop's Castle. Jerry began to show signs of mild enthusiasm as they parked, "This old man Bishop has been building the castle all by himself since he was a kid. It's made out of big stones and is really amazing. Just don't ask him anything, he gets pretty crazy sometimes."

There was no formal parking, cars just pulled off on the side of the road. Morrison was shocked when he saw the behemoth rising above the forest. It looked like something Disney might have made except more crude. A wall and moat was under construction and beyond the castle rose up like a giant rock house perched on stone legs. A narrow, steep stairway ascended prominently up the corner of the castle leading to wrought iron balconies that wrapped around the second level. The main structure was a three story house with enormous windows and a metal dragon head curling out of the top. Three towers rose ten stories or more with winding stairways inside and bridges connecting them high above the main structure.

"Where do we pay?" Morrison asked his son as they walked up the hill. Morrison silently wondered to himself about how safe the monstrous structure was.

"It's free, but he takes donations." Jerry pointed to a downstairs room with angry signs posted on the walls suggesting the coding department must not have approved his building techniques. The message within the messages was that Mr. Bishop hated government and regulations.

As they climbed the spiral staircases and explored the many rooms, towers and dungeons, Morrison reveled in the excitement and enthusiasm his son was having showing him around. It was as though Jerry was showing him his own private world and Morrison felt accepted and included in his secret club.

After about an hour, Morrison had to admit he was exhausted so they found benches in the shaded patio of the gift shop across from the castle. Dozens of hummingbirds buzzed around them visiting the many feeders hanging around the porch. As they drank their soda pop, Morrison was sure he had never seen his son so happy. He wondered how he could have let himself miss this for so long. He hoped that there would be many more times like this and that maybe, just maybe, they could be a family again.

As they drove back to Rockcliffe, Morrison decided to ask Jerry about the younger Ludwig boy, "Did you know Darren Ludwig?"

Jerry shrugged, "Yeah, he was in my class. Kind of a weird kid, I didn't know him that well."

Morrison did not want to push it, so he just drove for a while before asking, "I hear he was good friends with the coach's daughter? Jenifer, I think her name is."

Jerry squirmed a little and gazed out the side window before answering, "I guess so. She's probably the most popular girl in my class. She's pretty easy to talk to."

"I interviewed her yesterday. She's pretty."

"Yeah, she said you were pretty cool."

Morrison was startled by his revelation. He would have guessed she thought unfavorably of him. Morrison decided to confide in his son, "I sensed she was hiding something; that maybe she knew more than she was letting on."

Jerry turned and studied his dad, "What could she be hiding?"

Morrison shrugged, "I don't know, hoped you might have an idea."

Jerry stared out the windshield, "About Darren, you mean?"

Morrison glanced at his son, "Maybe."

The way Jerry said "Darren" was curious. *Jealousy, maybe?*

Jerry rubbed the side of his face and slumped down in the seat, "He was a weird kid. They *were* always talking and sharing secrets. I don't get it."

Morrison smiled. "Where to next?"

Chapter Forty-Two
Family Meets at Maggies

Samantha had instructed Jerry to invite Morrison to lunch with them at Maggie's at 1:00. They pulled into the gravelly parking lot a little early so they could get a table, and then Morrison excused himself. He looked around for the waitress Darla, but found Maggie in the kitchen, "Hi, I am Deputy Morrison, aren't you Maggie?"

The happy woman's face sagged. She stopped wiping a pot with the white towel, set them down and wiped her hands on her apron. Morrison continued, "I need to ask you a few questions."

Maggie nodded and squinted at him. He smiled to reassure her and took out his notepad, "I understand that you are a member of the same quilting club as Matilda Ludwig?"

Maggie fidgeted and nodded, he continued, "Did she ever talk about abuse at home?"

Maggie shrugged, "We knew about it."

"When was the last time?"

Maggie picked up the towel and wiped the counter top, "Last week, I think."

"Did you talk to her the day of the murder?"

Maggie picked up the pot, finished drying it with the towel and hung it on a hook over the counter, "When was that?"

"Wednesday."

Maggie looked at a ticket laying on the wide pickup window, then stopped to think, "Yeah, I saw her that day."

As Maggie retrieved four hamburger patties from a refrigerator, Morrison persisted, "How did she look?"

Maggie placed the patties on the grill and covered them with an iron, "I don't know."

This was not going to be easy, but Maggie was holding back so he persisted, "Where did you see her?"

She turned and filled a metal basket with fries and dropped it into the fryer, "She was here."

Morrison hazarded a guess, "Quilting club meeting?"

Maggie flipped the burger patties, "Yeah."

"Who was there?"

Maggie shrugged as she pulled cheese slices from the refrigerator, "Everyone."

Morrison was getting impatient, "Maybe we should finish this down at the Sheriff's office where you don't have so many distractions?"

Maggie teared up and turned away. Morrison waited. Maggie slapped the cheese slices on the patties and pulled the fry basket out of the grease pit. As she wiped her hands on her apron, she hollered through the window, "Help in the kitchen!"

She buttered the buns and dropped them on the grill, "Give me a minute. I'll come out."

Morrison nodded and went out to update Jerry, "Jerr, I need to ask Maggie a few questions. I'll be right back."

Jerry nodded, "Sure, no problem."

He found Maggie sitting on a bar stool at the bar smoking a cigarette. Morrison slid onto the stool next to her, "Tell me about the meeting."

Maggie tilted her head back and blew smoke toward the ceiling, "I got a call from Dottie."

As she tapped her cigarette on the ashtray, she glanced at Morrison, "Dottie Pentington from the school?"

Morrison nodded, "We've met."

She inhaled on the cigarette and blew smoke out her nose and mouth, "Matilda had called her. Jon had beat her up again. This time she had had enough and had called Dottie for help. Dottie called all of us and we decided to meet here at 4 p.m. to come up with a plan."

She snuffed out the cigarette in the ashtray and took a drink of some beverage in a short glass, "So, it was me, Dottie, Sam, and Matilda. Matilda's face was bruised and swollen." She pretended to spit at the ashtray, "That sorry ..."

She shook her head, reached into her pocket for her cigarettes, "We decided to take turns hiding her in our houses. Dottie was going to accompany her back to her house to get her things. Apparently, Jon came home."

Morrison made notes and then asked, "So, Dottie was there when they were murdered?"

Maggie lit her cigarette and shook her head, "You'll have to ask her."

"So the quilting club hasn't gotten back together?"

Maggie shrugged and drew deeply on her cigarette.

"Have you talked to Dottie since the incident?"

Maggie blew a steady stream of gray smoke at the counter, "Yeah. She told me that Jon came home and

caught them packing. He was furious and started ...
hitting Matilda. He even hit Dottie when she tried to
stop him."

Maggie drew on her cigarette again and shook her
head in disgust. She said Matilda made her leave."

Morrison stared at her for a moment, then closed his
notepad, "Thanks, Maggie."

Maggie blew out a cloud of gray smoke and nodded.
He stood and remembered one more thing, "Just one
more question, when will Darla come in?"

Maggie stopped and glared at him, "Whaddya want
with her? She's not in the club."

Morrison noted her defensiveness, "It's not about
Matilda. Another matter."

Maggie was not satisfied, "What other matter?"

Morrison liked her spunkiness and admired that she
was so protective of her employee, "It's a private matter."

Maggie turned to face him and put one hand on her
hip while she held up her cigarette with the other, "Private
matter?"

Morrison did not back down, "Will she be in today?"

Maggie blew smoke in his face, "She's off 'til Tuesday.
Can I give her a message?"

"No, it can wait." He jotted his number on a sheet of
paper and handed it to her, "If you think of anything else,
call me." He flipped his notepad shut and stuffed it in
his hip pocket, "Thank you."

She took the paper, looked at it and then stuffed it in
her apron pocket. Morrison rejoined Jerry at the table just
in time to see Samantha and Tammy enter. He stood and
smiled at the girls. They reflexively tossed their hair and

Samantha opened her purse to drop car keys in. Morrison greeted them, "Afternoon, Ladies. Have fun in Salida?"

He was encouraged by a slight smile from Tammy. Samantha looked tired but tried to be pleasant as she reported on their shopping adventure. Then she glanced at her son and then her ex-husband, "What did you guys do?"

Morrison recapped their visit to Bishop's Castle and drive around Rockcliffe and DeWeese Lake. He shocked everyone when he ordered the 'Full of Bull' burger without even opening the menu. Samantha did not let the opportunity slip by, "What an appropriate choice." The impromptu joke livened up the moment.

Morrison enjoyed being with the family again and before too long, pretenses were dropped and the conversation got happy and comfortable, reminding him of old times.

After dinner, as they walked out of the restaurant, he held back Samantha, "You were in Matilda Ludwig's quilting club, I hear."

Samantha pulled her hair back behind one ear and squinted at him, "Yes."

"Did you see her the day of the murder?"

Samantha looked down as she slipped her purse over her shoulder, "Yes."

"How did she look?"

She looked up into his eyes and studied him as if she were considering whether she could confide in him. Finally, she looked down and answered, "Jon had beat her up again."

She looked at him again and he nodded and added, "Did you talk to her?"

Samantha looked out across the parking lot and then looked back, "She called Dottie and Dottie called the rest of us. So we met here in Maggie's little conference room. We decided that Dottie would accompany her back to the house to get her things and then we would each take turns hiding her from Jon."

Morrison pulled out his notepad and flipped it open to a new page, "Was Dottie there when Ludwig and the boy came home?"

"Dottie said that Ludwig came home and there was a fight, so she left. She didn't mention David or Darren."

Morrison made notes and then tried to clarify, "So, Matilda was alive when she left?"

Samantha shrugged, "Yeah, I think so. I haven't seen Dottie since that day. I called her today and briefly talked to her on the phone. We were going to get back together, but haven't yet."

Chapter Forty-Three
Finding Darla

Morrison pitched the room key on the bed of his motel room. The maid had already cleaned his room so the drapes were drawn. He walked over to the window and admired the snow-capped mountains. It was truly a beautiful valley. The Sangre de Cristo mountain range rose up out of the valley like a long, giant row next to a furrow. Jerry had given him the facts, "The Sangre de Cristo range is the longest, straightest mountain range in North America. It has ten fourteeners. It's called "The Blood of Christ" because the tips of the mountains often turn blood red at sunrise."

Morrison had noticed that the valley itself was quite a bit higher than "the mile-high city," Denver. Coming into town, the sign stated that the altitude at Rockcliffe was 7,888 feet compared to 5,280 feet in Denver. It also explained why he was so short of breath lately.

His eyes were drawn to a convenience store across the street from the motel, so he decided to walk over and check it out. There were three pump bays in front and it hosted a Subway Sandwich shop. For a small store, it was well-stocked with a variety of items including some tools, cans of oil, and even balls for trailer hitches. He picked up a small ice chest, a bag of ice, Lay's Potato Chips and a six pack of root beer.

When he got back to the room and iced down the cans of root beer, he switched on the T.V. There was a baseball game and golf but not much else. He switched it off and fell back on the bed. He was restless and did not want to hang out in the room so he grabbed a ball cap and headed out for a walk.

A slight breeze made the air feel crisp and fresh on his face. It was amazingly quiet and there seemed to be no traffic. No one was stirring. He felt like he had the whole town just to himself until an old rusty pickup pulled up to a stop sign from a side street. The bearded driver with a straw hat raised a finger on the steering wheel to greet him. He nodded and crossed in front of him.

He came to a park that consumed a two block area with playground equipment and picnic tables on one end and a baseball field on the other. He found a table in the shade and sat down. As his vision adjusted, he noticed a slender woman sitting on the other side of the park on a bench nestled within a grove of evergreens. Could it be?

The woman was just far enough away that he could not be sure that she was the waitress at Maggie's he wanted to question. He walked toward her to get a better look. As he approached, the woman looked up and stared at him. He managed a smile and nodded. Darla did not respond. She glanced around as if searching for an escape route, and then seemed resigned to the fact that she was trapped.

Morrison strolled up to her and pointed at the spot next to her on the bench. She waved her hand over the spot to grant him the courtesy. "Beautiful day," he muttered as he sat down. She ignored him.

She looked away from him but he could see that she had been crying. He offered her his hand, "I'm Sam Morrison. I think I saw you at Maggie's the other day."

She ignored his hand, "I know who you are. Maggie told me you were looking for me."

Morrison rubbed the sides of his thighs. It was true what they said about small towns—news travels fast. "I want to ask you about Jon Ludwig."

She sniffed and raised a wadded up tissue to her nose. Morrison prompted her, "You knew him?"

She nodded. Morrison persisted, "You knew him very well?"

Tears started to well in her eyes as she opened her purse and started digging for something. Morrison was tired of dragging information out of her, "Tell me about it."

She found a packet of tissues and extracted a fresh one, blew her nose, and stared at the playground, "I loved him."

Surprised by the woman's frank admission, Morrison was touched by her deep emotion. He could tell that the death of Jon Ludwig had broken her heart. Nearly everyone else in town might be celebrating his departure, but Darla had truly loved the much disliked, complicated man. Morrison tried to understand this surprising side of Ludwig, "Did you know that he had ... intimate pictures of you?"

Tears welled up and she dabbed her eyes to save her makeup and scowled, "Jon and his stupid camera. Always taking pictures. It was a compulsion."

"You didn't mind? The pictures of you, I mean?"

Darla shook her head and looked down at her crossed legs as she rocked her foot, "It wouldn't have mattered. Jon did whatever he wanted."

"That didn't bother you? You didn't resent it?"

"Sure. But Jon was ... different. Exciting. Interesting. He was in charge and knew exactly what he wanted and you didn't cross him ..." she lowered her voice, "and you didn't want to."

Darla was painting a picture of a shy, sheltered girl who found Jon Ludwig exciting and domineering. In a crazy, fearful world, she liked to be told what to do; to not have to make decisions. She probably felt safe when she was with him.

"Did you ever wish you could break things off? Get away from him? Live your own life?"

She snickered, "What life? Jon was my life. He gave me a life."

Morrison looked across the baseball field. It looked as though it had not hosted a game in years. It was like Darla before Jon, just waiting for a life; waiting for someone to come along that appreciated what she had to offer; to draw her out; to use her; to need her.

Morrison took a deep sympathetic breath, "I'm sorry for your loss."

Darla dropped her head into her hands and sobbed. Regretting his imposition, Morrison walked away to respect her solitude.

Part V

Monday

Chapter Forty-Four
Questioning Pentington

Morrison related what he had learned over the weekend to his new boss, Sheriff Sean Bailey. Bailey had listened quietly and let his new deputy reveal the new information in his own way. He was touched by Morrison's handling of Darla. Maybe the big city detective was adjusting to the more personal; the more caring ways of rural life. He decided to reward his deputy's apparent transformation. He reached into his desk, pulled out an envelope and tossed it across the desk. "Why don't you give those to Darla next time you see her. I'll have Buster ask Jeremy to erase the files on the computer."

Morrison appeared at first to be surprised, but then reached across and dragged the envelope off the desk, tipped the envelope to his head to salute the sheriff, "Thanks."

Bailey drummed the edge of his desk with his fingers, "So! What's next?"

"I want to talk to Mrs. Pentington. She told her friends she wasn't there at the time of the murder, but I want to hear her story and her explanation for that bruise on her face."

Bailey nodded, "Makes sense."

The sheriff seemed distracted so Morrison waited for more. Bailey drummed his pencil on the desk, looked at Morrison and confessed, "I don't know what's going on with Agent Blakeley."

Morrison tried to read what the sheriff was implying by using Smiles name more formally. Morrison inquired, "He's AWOL again today?"

Bailey nodded but his thoughts seemed to be distant. Finally, he took a deep breath, placed his elbows on his desk and leaned forward, "It's not like Miles to miss work. I've seen him working when he obviously needed to be in bed. And it's not like the agency to let a case go like this. Normally, they would've re-assigned it by now."

Morrison raised his eyebrows, "That IS strange."

Bailey threw up his hands, "Oh, well. At least they're not stopping us from doing our own investigation."

Morrison nodded agreement.

"Ok. You takin' Calhoun?"

Morrison grimaced. Bailey got the message and rubbed his brow, "Let me see ... maybe he could help Melton investigate a break-in out at Cristo Vista."

Morrison gave a relieved smile, "Thanks."

Mrs. Pentington glanced behind her at the principal's office, "Good morning, Deputy Morrison, are you looking for Mr. Wheeler?"

Morrison brushed his hair back with his fingers, "No. Actually, I was wondering if you could spare a few minutes?"

Her eyes widened only slightly and then she straightened and laid her hands in her lap. "Oh! What can I do for you?"

Morrison glanced at the chairs lined up against the wall opposite her desk. He visualized the poor naughty kids who had to sit there waiting to see the principal. He had been in their shoes plenty of times. Mrs. Pentington anticipated his request, "Please, have a seat."

Morrison chose the chair on the end next to the door, "I understand that Matilda Ludwig called you the day of the murder."

Mrs. Pentington did not flinch, "Yes. Jon had beaten her again and she was scared and … frankly, fed up."

"You and Mrs. Ludwig were close friends?"

Pentington shrugged, "We were in a quilting club together. We often share our problems with each other when we're quilting."

"Had she shared her problems with Mr. Ludwig with you before?"

Pentington got to the point, "The beatings? Yes. We all knew about it."

"Why did she call you and not one of the others?"

"I had told her to call me if it happened again."

Morrison scribbled a few notes in his note pad, and then looked up, "What did you do?"

"I told her to meet us at Maggie's and then I called the other girls."

Morrison asked for clarification, "The other girls?"

"Maggie Ross and Samantha," she looked into the deputy's eyes, " ... Morrison."

"What happened at the meeting?"

Pentington took a deep breath and stared at the door, "We decided that we would hide Matilda from that monster. We decided to take turns keeping her. It was decided that I should accompany Matilda back to her house to pack some things."

Dottie Pentington was clearly giving Morrison the impression that she was a very strong, no-nonsense woman. He could see why she had been chosen to accompany Matilda back home. It was not likely that she would lose her cool under pressure. Maggie was a quick-tempered woman that might try to challenge Jon to defend her friend if Jon were to happen home. Knowing Samantha as he did, she was not a strong woman and probably would have resisted being chosen for that assignment. "What happened at the Ludwig home?"

"We parked down the street by the alley so Jon wouldn't see my car if he happened to return. We slipped in through the back door and found the house empty. We were in the bedroom when we heard the front door open. We were very surprised; we hadn't heard a car drive up. It was Jon and when he found us packing, he was furious. Matilda tried to calm him but he pushed her on to the bed and started yelling at me."

Morrison interrupted, "What time was that?"

Pentington looked up toward the ceiling, "Hmm. Must have been a little after five, maybe 5:15."

Morrison made a note, Pentington muttered, "Could have been earlier, I guess."

"What happened next?"

Pentington reached up and touched her cheek, frowned and showed disgust, "Well. I told him what I thought of him and he socked me in the face! He knocked me down!"

She was aghast, "I couldn't believe it! Matilda jumped off the bed and rushed over to help me up. She insisted I leave, arguing that I would just make matters worse if I stayed. Ludwig looked at me in his arrogant manner and said, 'You better listen to her and get your ... you-know-what ... out of here.'"

Pentington took a deep breath, and rubbed her cheek, "I resisted, but she insisted and pushed me out the back door."

She threw her hands up, "So, I left."

Her lower lip started trembling, "That's the last time I saw her."

She reached across her desk and plucked out a tissue to blot her eyes and nose. Morrison finished up his notes, stuffed his notepad in his jacket pocket and stood, "I'm very sorry. If you think of anything else ..."

He turned to leave but as he got to the door he stopped and turned for one last question, "I'm sorry, but I just want to clarify. The Ludwig boys were not there at that point?"

Pentington pulled herself together and wheeled her chair up to her desk to straighten some papers, "No. At that point, they were not there."

Morrison nodded, then thought of something else, "Did you hear the shots."

She rearranged the pencils on her desk, continuing to avoid eye contact, "It must have happened later."

Morrison studied her. It was the first time he had seen a crack in her confidence. She was holding back something.

Chapter Forty-Five
More Pictures

An earsplitting bell rang as Morrison sauntered down the hall of the school heading for the exit. Noisy kids filled the halls and flowed past him busy conversing and exchanging books at their lockers, as though he wasn't even there; it reminded him that he wanted to talk to Jerry's girlfriend, Jenifer, and red-headed Freddie again. He scanned the sea of pimpled faces searching for his son or the coach's daughter or Freddie. Almost as quickly as they had emerged, the classrooms absorbed the hyperactive students and the halls grew quiet and calm as the piercing sound of the bell rang again.

He stood contemplating his options. He could go back and pester Mrs. Pentington again, but he would feel awkward doing so. He could walk the hallways searching for Jenifer or Freddie and then try to catch them at the next break. He could find the coach and ask him to arrange a meeting with his daughter. None of these options appealed to him.

Suddenly, his cell phone rang interrupting and solving his quandary. It was his old friend, "Hey, Buster."

Morrison guessed he was driving since he was shouting into the phone over a loud humming in the background, "Jeremy called. Meet us at the office."

The three men were not looking forward to the hour-and-one-half drive to Colorado Springs. As they pulled on to highway 96, Morrison leaned forward and cleared his throat, "I just saw Pentington."

Buster glanced over his shoulder and then looked back at the road. Bailey shifted around and draped his arm over the back of his seat, "Learn anything?"

Morrison shrugged, "She said she was at the Ludwig house with Matilda helping her pack. Matilda had decided to leave Jon and the quilting members were going to help her hide. Ludwig came home before they got away and was furious. He clocked Pentington and battled with his wife. Matilda made Pentington leave. She claims that they were alive when she left and neither Darren nor David were home yet."

Bailey studied his deputy, "You don't seem convinced."

Morrison crossed his legs, "The timeline is wrong. The club met at four at Maggie's. They discussed the situation and decided to help Matilda hide. Then Dottie and Matilda went over to her house and parked down the street, walked up to the house, spent some time packing; that was between five and five-fifteen according to Pentington; Jon came home and they fought; Matilda convinced Pentington to leave and Jon added his encouragement. Pentington says she reluctantly left, walked to her car, drove off and never heard any shots."

Morrison looked at Buster, "Neighbor reported shots around 5:45."

Buster nodded, "Pretty tight window."

Morrison shook his head, "Possible, but a pretty tight window."

As they drove up over the Wet Mountain pass, the three law officers drifted off into individual thoughts and quiet solitude.

Morrison looked out the window at a couple of horses grazing leisurely just inside the fence along the road. They jerked their heads up when they heard the SUV approaching and watched them pass. He glanced back to see that they had decided the white SUV with the broad, green stripe was of no real interest and returned to their meal.

As they entered the junky office, Jeremy was busy studying the screen of the computer. Buster greeted his friend, "Hello, again, Jeremy."

The tall, lanky young man looked up and smiled, "Hello."

"Find some more pictures?"

Jeremy nodded, "Found some nasty stuff this time. Check this out."

He handed them some pictures of a couple in a car at a motel and through the window of the motel room. Morrison looked at Buster, "Is that ...?"

Buster nodded his head, "Mr. Wheeler and Mrs. Pentington."

Morrison was stunned. Jeremy had more, "Look at these."

It was a picture of the living room of a house with dozens of kids partying. Half were undressed and engaged in an apparent orgy. Jeremy handed them a close-up of the orgy. Morrison pointed to the face of a young girl, "That's Jenifer Jones."

Morrison's stomach sank as he frantically searched the faces for his son, Jerry. Fortunately, he did not find anyone in either picture that could have been his son. Bailey pointed to another kid in the background, "Darren Ludwig."

The boy was sitting on a couch staring at Jenifer with an angry look on his face. Then it hit Buster, "Ludwig took pictures of his own son at a party?"

Bailey nodded his head, "A real piece of work."

Buster pointed to a glass coffee table in the background. There were tracks of a white powder, very likely cocaine. Bailey commented, "I bet we know who the supplier was."

Morrison looked at Buster and raised his eyebrows, "Drugs and blackmail. Ludwig had quite a setup."

Morrison looked at the pictures again. It was clear the Jones girl was stoned out of her mind. She was cute, but now he was having trouble understanding why Jerry was interested in her. He had to assume; he had to hope that Jerry did not know this side of her.

Morrison presented his question, "I'm still wondering what he did with all the money. Surely, it wasn't all paid in favors."

Buster nodded and rubbed his chin, "It don't add up, does it?"

Bailey was looking at the pictures of Wheeler and Pentington and remembered, "We got a call from an anonymous woman reporting shots fired."

Morrison nodded, "Could it have been Pentington?"

Bailey handed him the pictures of the unsuspecting couple, "I would say she also had a pretty good motive."

Buster inhaled noisily, "Anything else, Jeremy?"

"Well, no, sir. But I am going to start working on recovering deleted files. I'll let you know if I find anything else."

Chapter Forty-Six

Bennet/Wooten, Back to the Coach

As they stepped into the parking lot to leave CBI offices, Buster tapped the manilla envelope tucked under his arm and addressed the sheriff, "What'ya think we ought to do about this?"

Bailey shook his head. "There are a lot of parents that are going to be shocked."

Buster grimaced and shook his head, "Yeah. I'm not looking forward to meeting with them."

Bailey amended his previous statement, "We may find that there are a number of parents who won't be surprised."

Buster got it, "Oh, yeah. I bet Ludwig has probably contacted them."

Morrison had an idea, "What do you think Bennet and Wooten would have to say about them?"

The sheriff's eyes brightened, "Good idea."

Bailey, Morrison and Crab waited for Bennet and Wooten to be escorted into the Fremont County Detention's interrogation room. They had been transferred to Fremont County for safety reasons. Deputies would not be safe in the detention facilities where they might be known by the other prisoners.

Bailey scattered the pictures of the partying kids across the table, "Know anything about these?"

Wooten glanced at the pictures and sat back as if disinterested. Bennet leaned forward and picked them up to study, one-by-one. When he finished he glanced at his old partner, "It's Ludwig's fishin' cabin out at Lake DeWeese."

Wooten was staring into space as Bennet explained, "Ludwig let the kids use his lake cabin for parties. We were supposed to patrol to make sure there was no trouble, but we weren't allowed to go in. We suspected what was going on, but didn't know for sure."

Wooten crossed his arms and huffed, "Must've had hidden cameras stuck around the place so he could blackmail some of the kids' parents."

Bennet added, "Probably supplied the kids with drugs to get 'em hooked."

Bailey inquired, "How'd he get the word out?"

Bennet shrugged, "I'm sure he just told a couple of the dope-heads at school and they spread it around."

Bailey followed up, "You know who the dope-heads are?"

The two men glanced at each other; Bennet answered, "Some of them. Jenifer Jones, Willy Madden, Josh Hagen probably."

The Sheriff clarified, "Jenifer Jones? Coach's daughter?"
Bennet nodded.

"Was he blackmailing the coach?"

Bennet shrugged, "Not sure. Probably."

Bailey shook his head. Bennet and Wooten hung their heads down, apparently displeased with this development. Morrison drummed his fingers on the metal table. "Ludwig was a scumbag. There is no telling how many people he was blackmailing; how many kids he had hooked on drugs; how many others. We have a town full of people with great motives for wanting Ludwig dead."

The coach was in his glass office going over something with his assistant. When he saw Bailey, Crab and Morrison, he wrapped it up and invited them in. "Afternoon, gentlemen, have a seat."

As they sat down, Morrison noticed that the coach appeared nervous. He clasped his hands and leaned forward to rest on his elbows. Bailey took the lead, "Don't suppose you've heard from David Ludwig?"

The coach's face relaxed slightly and he sat back, "No. Any leads?"

Bailey nodded his head and patted the envelope lying on his lap. "How well did you know Jon Ludwig?"

The coach shrugged, "Not that well. Like I told your deputy, I think I've met him a couple of times."

Bailey got to the point, "You know anything about parties out at his cabin on Lake DeWeese?"

The coach's eyes betrayed his surprise. "Parties?"

The sheriff pulled out the photos from the envelope and dropped them on his desk in front of him. The coach frowned and glanced back and forth between the sheriff, Crab and Morrison. He leaned forward and picked up the pictures. He gasped and started choking. Buster jumped up and patted him on the back, offering the standard antidote. "Drink some water, Berlin."

He handed him the bottle of water sitting on the edge of his desk. Coach Jones gulped down a swig and pounded his chest with his fist. His face was red and looked swollen but he managed to get his coughing under control.

"What is this, Sheriff?"

Bailey crossed his legs and stared at him. Coach Berlin Jones wiped a tear from his eyes as he rocked back in his chair and swiveled to one side. Bailey prompted him almost in a whisper, "Want to tell us about it?"

The coach took a deep breath, opened out his hands, opened his mouth but words did not follow, just quivering lips. Bailey tried to help him, "Was Ludwig blackmailing you?"

Coach Jones turned to the sheriff with watery eyes, "You know?"

Bailey nodded, "Tell us about it."

"When he showed me the pictures, I was shocked, Sean. I had no idea that Jenny was into that stuff."

He pinched the bridge of his nose and sniffed. "I couldn't let it get out. It would've ruined her life … and mine."

"What did he want from you?"

"No money. He just wanted me to look the other way, you know? He wanted to push his drugs to some of the players."

Morrison pulled out his notepad, "You know which ones?"

The coach took a deep breath and looked up at the ceiling, "Yeah, I know some of them. Willy Madden, Josh Hagen, Skooter Wilson."

Bailey stepped in, "What did you do?"

The coach glared at him for a moment, shrugged and admitted, "I looked the other way."

Morrison tilted his head to one side, "That's all?"

The coach stared at him as if he did not understand, "He was pushing drugs to your daughter and your players and you just looked the other way?"

"Well, I talked to Jenny and ... tried to help her."

"Tried?"

"We had a big fight; several big fights. She didn't want to listen."

Morrison leaned forward, "So, you went over to talk to Ludwig."

The coach's eyes grew large, "What?"

Morrison persisted, "When you saw what he was doing to David, your players, your daughter, you got fed up and you went over to talk to him."

"No!"

Morrison kept the pressure on, "You said you went to check on David, but the sheriff was there. But that's not how it happened, was it? When you got there, you found Ludwig beatin' up his wife and kid and you tried to stop him, but he punched you, knocked you down. You pulled out your pistol and shot him in self defense."

"No!" the coach yelled, "No! I tell you the sheriff was already there when I got there. I drove on by and went home."

The sheriff stepped in, "Berlin, do you own a pistol?"

Berlin stared at the sheriff. Bailey added, "We can check for a registration."

The coach buried his head in his hands, "Yeah. A Glock."

He opened a drawer of his desk and reached inside, Morrison reached for his pistol. The coach retrieved a pistol from the drawer as Morrison stood, pulled his weapon and leveled it on the coach. The coach laid it on his desk, raised his hands and rolled back away from the desk and the gun, "Don't shoot!"

Bailey stood and put his hand across Morrison as he reached to pick up the coach's gun. Morrison holstered his weapon. The coach volunteered, "I brought it in here after Ludwig started blackmailing me. I don't know what I thought I would do with it."

The sheriff confirmed, "It's a 45."

Morrison resumed his questioning, "Can you prove what time you left here that night?"

The coach studied Morrison for a moment then glanced out at the players and coaches in the training room. "Surely someone saw me leave."

Bailey glanced at Morrison and nodded toward the office door. Morrison walked out to the training room. The players and coaches were huddled in a frenzied discussion. They shut up when they saw the deputy. They started to disperse, but Morrison interrupted, "Wait. I have some questions and they apply to all of you."

Everyone gathered around, "I want you to think back to Wednesday, the day of the Ludwig murders. Can any of you tell me when the coach left that day?"

The players and coaches looked around at each other. The assistant coach looked at his watch. "Well, we ended practice early that day. Coach said he wanted to go check on David. I think that was around 5:30."

One of the players raised his hand. "That was the day I gashed my eye. Coach stopped to help bandage it."

Another older man chimed in, "Oh, yeah, that's right. Willie dropped the bar and it hit him above the eye. Coach rushed over and helped me treat the wound and bandage it. Probably took about ten minutes."

"He left at ten 'til six." One of the players blurted out, "I was in the parking lot putting my stuff in my trunk. I saw him pull away and looked at my watch. I was surprised he hadn't left yet since he had said he was leaving early."

Morrison made a note, "You're sure?"

"Yeah, like I say, I looked at my watch as he drove by."

"Ok, thanks." Morrison closed his notepad.

"Does that clear him?" one of the players asked.

They all seemed eager to hear his answer. Morrison reopened his notepad and found a page. He had written that a neighbor had called in gun shots around 5:45. "Yeah, I think it just might."

The players and coaches appeared relieved as he returned to the coach's office.

Chapter Forty-Seven
Wheeler/Pentington Arrest

As they pulled away from the athletic building of the Wet Mountain Valley High School and turned into the main parking lot, they saw Dottie Pentington and Elton Wheeler rushing out of the front door. Sheriff Bailey punched the accelerator and intercepted them. "Just the people we wanted to see."

Dottie clasped her hands, pulled them close to her chest, and glanced around angrily, Wheeler forced a smile. He offered an excuse, "We were just ... running an errand."

Bailey looked away from them, then turned back, "Could we have a few minutes of your time?"

Pentington gasped and protested in a huff, "Right now?"

Bailey calmly looked back into her eyes, "We have something to show you we think you will want to see. Care to follow us to the office?"

Dottie was clearly upset and was nervously glancing around the parking lot as if searching for an alternative.

Elton got the message and he nodded, "We'll follow you over there."

Crab dropped off Bailey and Morrison in front of the lobby of the sheriff's office and then drove to the staff parking lot. Bailey and Morrison stared out the window at Wheeler and Pentington sitting in their car, Bailey commented, "Getting their stories straight."

Morrison chuckled, "You think we caught them about to run?"

Bailey looked at him, "It's possible, I suppose."

Bailey pushed open the door to the offices and turned to the dispatcher, "Gabby, I want you to listen in on the interrogation."

The young girl fresh out of high school, glanced up from her paperback novel, "Listen in?"

"See if Mrs. Pentington sounds like the lady who anonymously called in about hearing shots at the Ludwig house."

Gabby marked her place, set down the book and pulled up the log on her computer screen. Morrison stepped over to the sheriff and whispered, "Here they come."

Elton Wheeler got out of the car and walked around to get the door for Dottie Pentington. Elton respectfully helped her out of the car and held her arm as they slowly dragged themselves to the front door of the Sheriff's Office. Bailey noted, "They look like they're going to a funeral."

As the couple entered the front door of the sheriff's office, Morrison met them in the reception area and ushered them through the security door into the hallway by the dispatch office. Morrison offered to get them coffee. They both accepted and then the sheriff escorted them down the hall to the interrogation room. Crab joined them as Morrison returned with the coffees and dragged in a chair for himself.

Bailey took a deep breath and reached across the plain, metal desk to lay the slanderous pictures in front of the clearly upset couple. Principal Wheeler glanced at the stack of pictures and gasped. Mrs. Pentington squeaked, "Oh!"

Bailey glanced at Morrison. They were thinking the same thing, this is not what they expected; it was not what they thought they were being brought in for.

The couple grasped each other's hands for support and as Dottie wept, Wheeler nodded and explained, "Yes. We've seen them."

Bailey glanced at Crab, and then addressed Wheeler, "Ludwig was blackmailing you?"

Wheeler nodded. Bailey sought clarification, "What did he want from you?"

Mrs. Pentington blew her nose and looked around for a fresh tissue. Crab pulled out a box of tissue from a cabinet in the corner as Morrison placed the trash can beside her. She grimaced and nodded her appreciation. Wheeler shifted in his chair, "Fifty-thousand dollars."

"Phew!" Bailey remarked. Wheeler continued, "We were allowed to pay five installments of $10,000."

Bailey interjected, "In exchange for?"

Wheeler shrugged, "His silence and all copies of the pictures once we paid up."

Morrison cut in, "Were you aware of any of Ludwig's other dealings?"

Wheeler and Pentington looked at Morrison with confusion written on their faces; Wheeler asked, "Other dealings?"

Bailey clarified, "Did you know of anyone else that Ludwig might have been blackmailing?"

The couple looked at each other and then shook their heads. Wheeler answered, "No."

Morrison continued, "Were you aware that Ludwig was dealing drugs at the school?"

Pentington gasped, "At the school?"

Bailey added, "We have evidence that he may have sponsored some drug parties for the students."

Wheeler's face turned red, the veins in his temples swelled and his lower jaw jutted out, "That sorry lowlife."

Pentington shook her head sadly, "What a despicable monster."

Morrison and the sheriff looked at each other. Which one would be the bad cop? Morrison decided to spare the sheriff in front of his friends, "Fifty grand is a lot of money."

The couple nodded their heads, readily agreeing. "Exposure of your affair, in your positions of trust, in a small town, would be ..."

Wheeler looked sadly at the front of the desk, "Devastating."

Dottie added, "It would have destroyed us."

Morrison shifted in his chair, he really did not believe at this point that they had taken the matter to the extreme, but he had to put it to rest, "You had plenty of motive to want Ludwig dead."

They gasped and glared at Morrison with shock on their faces. Dottie put her hand over her mouth. Elton turned to his friend, "Buster, you don't think we killed him!"

Sean Bailey leaned forward and tilted his head to one side, "We have to ask, Elton. You did have a good reason to want him, well, out of the way."

Morrison looked directly at Mrs. Pentington, "And you have already admitted that you were at the house around the time of the murders."

"Oh!" she gasped. Wheeler leaped to her defense, "Dottie was just trying to help her friend escape from that monster."

Morrison persisted, "You told me that you were there when Jon Ludwig returned home."

Pentington blotted her eyes, "Yes." She addressed the sheriff, "I was helping Matilda pack her stuff. I was going to take her home with me."

She blew her nose quietly, then shook her head, "He was furious. He lit into her and started cursing and slapping her around. I tried to intervene, but he punched me in the face and knocked me down."

She rubbed the bruise on her face, "I think I was out for a moment. The next thing I remember is Matilda trying to help me up and begging me to leave. I protested, of course, but Jon jerked me up and yelled in my face. He told me that I'd better do as Matilda suggested. Matilda grabbed my arm and pulled me to the back door and whispered that she would call me later. She insisted that he would calm down eventually."

The remorseful woman snatched several tissues out of the box angrily, "So I left."

The sheriff looked at his deputy. They exchanged knowing glances. Morrison slipped out of the room as Buster offered them more coffee. Morrison ducked into the room behind the one-way mirror and closed the door, "Well?"

Gabby was standing by the window listening carefully. "I'm not sure. I need to replay the disk."

Morrison nodded, led the young woman to the dispatch desk and helped her load the disk. The woman on the tape sounded hysterical, "Shots! I, I heard shots at the Ludwig house."

Morrison exchanged looks with Gabby, Gabby tilted her head to one side, "It's her, isn't it?"

Morrison inhaled, "Bring the player into the interrogation room."

"Yessir."

Morrison returned to the room just as Buster was entering with fresh coffee cups. They found the couple sitting quietly. Morrison whispered to Bailey, "I've asked Gabby to bring in the disk player."

Dottie's eyes showed enormous concern, "Disk player?"

Gabby slipped in and placed the player on the desk. Morrison hit the "play" button. Mr. Wheeler was surprised and confused, Dottie just listened resignedly. Morrison clicked off the machine. The sheriff nodded to Gabby, "Thanks, Gabby."

Gabby turned to leave but Morrison stopped her, "Gabby, how long after the first call did this one come in?"

Gabby fidgeted, "I'd have to check the log. Maybe five or ten minutes. Want me to check?"

Morrison turned to Dottie Pentington, "That sound about right, Dottie?"

Pentington seemed indignant, "I don't know what you mean."

Morrison shook his head and excused Gabby, and then started pacing, "I think the reason it took you so long to call in the shots, Dottie, is because you were in the house when the shots were fired and you called it in after you left."

Wheeler jumped to his feet and challenged Morrison, "That's outrageous, Deputy, she's already told you she left before any shots were fired!"

Dottie grabbed her lover's arm and bade him to sit back down. As he reluctantly sat, he pleaded, "That's right, isn't it Dottie? That IS what happened, isn't it?"

Dottie broke down into uncontrollable sobs. The sheriff took a deep breath and stood, "I'm sorry, Dottie, but I think I had better inform you of your rights."

Chapter Forty-Eight
Hiding in the Depot

THEY HAD JUST FINISHED lunch, David Ludwig was about to do the dishes, and White Feather was about to open the front door, headed for the Valley Grocery Store to get some groceries when he spotted the men stepping up onto the porch.

He slipped over to the cafe entrance and whispered, "We've gotta hide!"

David turned off the water and grabbed a towel to dry his hands, "What is it?" he whispered.

He followed White Feather to the closet behind the old ticket counter where White Feather stomped on the floor and explained, "We have company."

David glanced at the front door and saw the door knob turning. White Feather pushed him down the stairs and pulled the closet door closed as he followed. He pulled the trap door down and switched on his flashlight as they slipped down to the floor of the basement. They could hear the intruders talking and laughing as they entered the depot lobby so they stopped to listen.

"It's in better shape than I expected."

"Yeah, well, I've tried to keep it up. Put fresh paint on the exterior last summer. The shingles are two years old."

"Looks like someone's been campin' out in here."

"Hmm, the stove is still warm."

"That hobo will have a long wait before the next train leaves."

The men laughed loudly. The floor creaked as they moved across the room toward the cafe.

"They just left all the tables and everything?"

"It was a bankruptcy foreclosure. It all happened pretty fast when the steel mill in Pueblo shut down."

"How far do the tracks run?"

"Oh, just out of town, no further."

White Feather nudged David and pointed at the back corner of the basement where crates were stacked high. He whispered, "See if you can build us a hideout. I'll fold up the cot."

Quietly, they went to work while the tour continued upstairs.

"That hobo must have been here a while. Look at all these dishes."

White Feather flinched when he heard the hiss of water running and then the clank of pipes when the water was shut off, "Hobo turned the water on. Better check your bill next month."

The men laughed again.

David managed to build a narrow entry to a cave-like area behind the crates. White Feather folded the cot and then set it back up in the cave. He removed the folder that was marked "Who Is David Ludwig" from the vanity and tossed it on the cot. "Don't need that no more." White Feather noted.

David sat on the cot to wait. White Feather went over to the corner of the room and scooped up a double handful of dirt and then sprinkled it over the vanity and chair where they had rubbed off the dust. David gave him a thumbs up.

Then they heard a frightening suggestion from above, "There's a basement, but the door got boarded up years ago and I've never gone to the trouble of opening it back up."

"That's alright. No tellin' what's down there!"

The men laughed. White Feather and Ludwig remained quiet as they followed the men's creaking footsteps wandering throughout the terminal.

White Feather and David heard the front door lock and ventured back upstairs. White Feather checked out the front window to make sure the men had gone. David Ludwig stood beside him and looked over his shoulder. "Think they'll be back?"

White Feather nodded.

"Why?"

"By now, they've called the sheriff to report a hobo."

David wiped muddy sweat from his brow, "I'm gonna go clean up."

White Feather did not respond. After a few minutes, David returned, "They turned the water off."

White Feather nodded, "I'll turn it back on later."

David was nervous, "Is there some other place we can hide?"

White Feather rubbed his chin, "There's a warehouse, but it's not pleasant. We should eat and then pack our stuff."

"What's that?" David whispered urgently. White Feather looked out to see the sheriff's SUV pulling up and stopping a couple blocks away.

White Feather looked back at David. He got the message. They headed for the basement again.

Chapter Forty-Nine

Searching the Depot

CRAB HAD EXCUSED HIMSELF and gone home to eat lunch. The sheriff and his deputy stared blankly at the menu at Maggie's restaurant. Arresting Dorothy Pentington left a bad taste in Morrison's mouth. She was definitely holding something back, but he just could not picture the refined woman shooting anyone. Bailey had also been very quiet since the arrest. He set down his menu and expelled the air from his lungs then inhaled a fresh supply.

Morrison felt someone behind him and glanced back. Darla stood meekly with her ticket book clutched against her chest. She was staring at him with sad eyes like a wounded cat that had resigned to its fate. Bailey broke her spell, "I'll have the Full of Bull hamburger and iced tea."

Morrison added, "Same for me except strong, black coffee."

As Darla shuffled off, Bailey shook his head, "Somethin' jes' ain't right, Sam."

Morrison nodded. "You don't think she did it?"

The big man shifted in the creaky chair, "No," he shook his head again, "No, I don't. But, she must've been there when the shots were fired."

Morrison nodded, "She clearly knew about the shots. She might not have been in the house, but she knew about the shots."

Bailey swiped his mouth, "Maybe she left, like she said, but waited in her car thinking she might go back in."

"It would be hard for someone like Mrs. Pentington to just leave her friend in danger."

Darla returned, set a large glass of iced tea on the table, set down a cup of dark coffee and laid two sets of silverware wrapped in paper napkins on the table. Morrison patted his jacket pocket and felt the envelope containing the pictures of her. Bailey reached over and grabbed the sugar and poured a generous amount into his glass, picked up a teaspoon and started stirring. Morrison watched the slender, attractive waitress stroll back to the bar. She slid onto one of the bar stools, raked her fingers through her hair, rested her elbows on the bar and then laid her face in her hands.

Morrison could not help feeling sorry for the poor woman. He had an intense urge to go sit by her and try to comfort her. His heart ached watching her and feeling the pain she must be enduring. "Excuse me, Sean, I have something that belongs to Darla."

Morrison pulled out the envelope and Sean nodded. He walked over to the bar and stood beside her as he stealthily slipped the envelope in front of her, "I think these belong to you."

Darla was startled by his presence and jerked her head around to study him. Then she looked down at the envelope and opened it. She only had to peek inside to understand. She looked at him questioningly. He added, "The files will be been deleted. No one needs to know."

Tears welled up in her eyes as he smiled and then returned to his table.

Morrison and Bailey ate quickly and silently and then returned to the office.

As they entered the open area, Calhoun was hanging up the phone at his desk; he looked up and beamed, "Some old hobo's been living in the train depot."

Morrison studied him for a moment, "There's a depot in Rockcliffe?"

As Calhoun checked his empty coffee cup, Bailey explained, "It's been abandoned for fifty years. Train used to come here to haul coal and coke to the steel mill over at Pueblo."

Calhoun added, "Started coming here way back when they were mining silver out of the Wet Mountains."

Calhoun stood and headed for the break room as the sheriff took over, "Then they built all those ovens and smelted coke until the mill fell on hard times."

Bailey waited for Calhoun to return and put the conversation back on track, "So, who reported the hobo?"

Calhoun explained, "Raymond Ray. He said he's been livin' there for a while. The old stove was warm; he had a blanket thrown down by the heater, dirty dishes in the sink in the old cafe."

Morrison looked at Bailey, "Ludwig?"

The sheriff's eyes narrowed and he frowned, "Calhoun, call Ray and have him meet us down the street from the depot with the key. You and Melton drive over and cover the back."

The deputy switched into panic mode, "You think Ludwig's the hobo?"

Sheriff Bailey glanced at Melton to make sure he heard. The older deputy was strapping on his gun belt. Bailey and Morrison headed for the back door.

Calhoun darted back and forth in an exercise of conflicting intentions. Melton came over from his desk and put his hand on Calhoun's shoulder, "Call Ray."

Raymond Ray pulled up beside Sheriff Bailey's SUV. Morrison read the magnetic sign attached to the side of his Land Rover, "Wet Mountain Valley Properties."

The passenger window slid down and a thin man in his fifties with a thin, white beard smiled and asked, "What's up?"

The sheriff lowered his window, "Afternoon, Raymond. You reported someone living in the depot?"

Raymond pushed the gear shift into park and turned off the engine. "I was showing the place to some retired railroaders this afternoon. We found an old blanket by the pot belly stove in the main room. Stove was still warm. There were dirty dishes stacked in the sink in the dining room."

"Could you tell how long he's been hiding in there?"

Raymond shook his head, "Judging from the dishes, at least a week."

Morrison asked, "Seen anyone hanging around?"

The realtor shook his head, "Shoot, I ain't even been over here in months."

Bailey and Morrison got out and met the realtor in front of his big SUV. Raymond held up the key and started toward the old depot. Bailey grabbed his arm, "Better wait here, Raymond."

Raymond Ray raised his eyebrows and nodded as he gave Bailey the key. Buster pulled out his radio, "Calhoun, ya'll in position?"

Static squawked on the unit as Calhoun responded, "Roger, that."

As they approached the depot, Morrison was surprised to find the old building to be in better shape than he had expected. Half of the building was two-story, the other half had two large garage doors dominating the wall. It had fresh shingles on the roof, freshly painted wood slats on the walls. Morrison commented, "Pretty good shape."

Bailey nodded, "Yeah, they're trying to get it registered as a historic building. Ray had plans to make it into a museum, but couldn't get enough investors. A couple of old retired railroaders have moved into the county and revived interest."

They crossed the rusting tracks, slipped up on the long porch and unlocked the door. Bailey pulled his pistol, turned the knob and pushed open the door slowly. Morrison pulled his pistol and followed him in. To the left was the large potbelly stove with the colorful blanket spread out in front of it. The floor was swept, but there was a lot of dust collected on the counter that ran all along the back wall. A sign said simply "Tickets" above the windows built over the counter.

To the right a wide opening joined the old dining room where dusty old tables and chairs were still scattered around the room. They found the dishes Ray had mentioned in the sink. Bailey turned on the tap and a spray of water belched into the sink followed by the hiss of air. "Ray must've turned the water back off."

Morrison nodded. They found the kitchen behind double doors in the dining room that proved to be empty. Then they returned to the dining room and spotted the stairs across the room and searched upstairs. Morrison commented, "Wrinkles in the bed and the sleeping bag suggest someone may have slept here."

Bailey nodded.

Back downstairs, they found a door to the old baggage garage with the two big doors they had seen from the street, but there was only a couple of old antique baggage carts and some crates inside. Morrison shook his head, "Looks like they just walked off one day."

"They probably locked it down when the bank foreclosed." Bailey explained. "Makes a good hideout."

A door below the stairs appeared to have been boarded up for years.

They returned to the main room and while Morrison checked the restrooms, Bailey searched behind the ticket counter only to find an empty closet at one end. Morrison reported the restrooms clear. Bailey added as he holstered his pistol, "We better keep an eye on this place."

Chapter Fifty

Vacating the Depot

WHITE FEATHER WATCHED THE sheriff's SUV and the Land Rover slowly drive by and circle the depot. David Ludwig was nervous, "We gotta find another place."

White Feather acknowledged by rolling up his blanket. David pressed his friend, "The old warehouse you mentioned, maybe?"

White Feather shook his head, "They'll be patrolling this whole area. How 'bout your place?"

David was confused, "Where?"

White Feather explained, "They won't suspect someone moving in to the crime scene."

David's eyes got large, "Oh!"

White Feather placed the rolled blanket on the ticket counter. David remembered, "What about the neighbors?"

White Feather beckoned for the boy to follow him back into the basement, "Come pack. We'll slip over after dark. We'll be quiet and won't turn on any lights ..."

Back at the sheriff's office, Morrison smiled and nodded at his old friend Buster Crab who was sprawled across one of the little metal chairs in the break room drinking tea from a super-sized glass. Morrison anticipated his question, "Missed him. The place was empty."

Buster nodded, "Yeah, Melton told me."

Morrison pulled out a chair for himself and sat down to join him. Buster's cell phone rang, "Buster Crab."

Buster frowned and listened. Morrison could hear the incessant protesting of a woman's voice, but could only catch bits and pieces. Buster finally got his turn, "Ok, Naomi, I'll come out but I doubt if there's much I can do."

He clicked off the phone and stuffed it in his shirt pocket. "Got to go out to St. Jude again."

Morrison nodded, "Your uncle?"

Buster chuckled, "Now he won't come out of his room. Naomi's afraid he's going to starve himself to death." Buster looked at his old friend, "What you doin' tonight?"

Morrison shrugged, "Supposed to meet the landlord at seven, get the key, sign the papers, etcetera."

Buster stood and grabbed his jacket off the back of his chair, "Wish me luck."

Morrison looked up, "See you tomorrow."

Chapter Fifty-One

Back at St. Jude

Naomi was glad to see her cousin again but appeared to be a little embarrassed, as well. "Hello, Buster, sorry to bother you with this again, but I'm just worried about him."

Buster hugged his cousin and consoled her, "Not a problem, Naomi. So, he's locked himself in his room?"

Naomi placed her hand to the side of her face, "He's locked himself in and won't let anyone in and won't come out to eat."

Buster shook his head as he exhaled with exasperation, "Ok, let's go check on him."

When they arrived at Benny's room, they could hear giggles and muffled voices inside. Buster and Naomi frowned and studied each other. Buster tried the door, but it was locked. He knocked and the voices hushed inside.

Buster waited but there was no response so he knocked again, "Benny, this is Buster. Open up. I want to talk to you."

There was still no response. Buster turned to Naomi, "Do you have a master key?"

Naomi's eyes widened, "Oh. No. I'll go get Miss Edith."

Buster touched her arm, "Don't the residents share a bathroom?"

Naomi's eyes brightened as she looked down the hall to the next door. Then she frowned, "That one is vacant. We keep the vacant room's doors locked."

Buster shrugged, "Oh, well, I guess we'll need Edith."

As his cousin rushed off, Buster pounded on the door again, "Open up, Benny, I know you're in there."

Neighbors cracked open their doors to peek into the hallway. One old gentleman ventured out, "Who are you?" he challenged.

Buster smiled and introduced himself, "I'm Undersheriff Buster Crab. Benny is my uncle-in-law. We are worried about him."

Buster reached out his hand; the old man took it and introduced himself, "Al Stein."

Buster added, "Nice to meet you, Mr. Stein. You know my uncle?"

Stein, a short, thin man with a large nose and wild hair surrounding a round kippah, nodded, "Everyone knows Benjamin."

Buster chuckled, "He ever come out of his room?"

Mr. Stein waved off the suggestion, "He's just being stubborn for show. You should ignore him like we do."

Buster wanted to chuckle. This serious, distinguished old gentleman looked too much like the actor, comedian Woody Allen, so Buster found it hard to take him seriously.

The little man studied Buster for a moment as if deciding whether to reveal more, "It has been nice, actually."

Buster nodded, "Yeah, I understand." Buster shrugged, "We're just worried about him not eating."

Stein chuckled, "Not to worry. Katie Mae will take care of him. She sneaks food up."

The old man turned and headed back to his room. Buster glanced at Benny's door, and then caught the old man's eyes as he paused at his door. Buster put up his thumb and winked. Stein nodded and disappeared into his room.

Buster pounded on the door again, "Last chance, Benny! If you don't open up now, I'm leaving and you can starve for all I care."

Buster waited for a few moments and then stomped off noisily. When he got to the end of the hall, he turned down the intersecting corridor, paused and peeked around the corner to spy on his uncle's room. After several minutes, the door squeaked open just enough for an old lady with well-coiffed, shiny black hair to check the hallway. Buster pulled back his head to hide. When he peeked around again, the door was closed.

Buster shook his head as he chuckled and headed down the corridor to the elevator. The elevator door opened as he approached and Naomi and Edith started to step out. Buster stopped them and then joined them in the elevator. As he pushed the button for the ground floor, he placed his finger over his lips, "Shhh."

When the doors closed, Buster opened up, "Benny is fine. He has a lady friend covertly taking care of him; sneaking him food."

Edith laughed, "You're kidding? How funny."

Naomi just shook her head, "That old reprobate!"

As the elevator doors opened, Buster led the ladies down the corridor to the reception area where they could have privacy, "Look, I don't know what you think, but I think we let him keep up his charade."

Then he chuckled, "If for no other reason than for the sake of the other residents. I met a Mr. Stein who is elated to have Benny locked in his room."

Edith Barkley laughed, "I bet he's not the only one."

But the burden of responsibility fell ultimately upon the Head Administrator of St. Jude. She started thinking out loud, "We will have to check on him periodically to make sure he is eating well and staying healthy."

She crooked her forefinger around her chin as she contemplated the dilemma. Naomi offered her opinion, "I say let him starve."

Naomi shook her head and returned to her desk. Edith placed her hand on Buster's arm, "We can't let him starve, but maybe we can figure out a way to let him continue his little game."

Buster patted her hand, "Thanks, Edith. I'm sure the other residents will appreciate it. Call me if there is anything I can do."

Edith smiled, "I will. Thanks, Buster."

As Buster walked over to hug his cousin, his cell phone erupted. It was dispatch.

Chapter Fifty-Two
Albert Stein

ALBERT STEIN LEANED BACK against the door of his small room and sighed. Benjamin would be alright; he was fortunate, Katie Mae liked the old bully for some odd reason and would take care of him. It was not completely true that she was the only person who liked Benjamin as he had told the undersheriff. Truthfully, Albert did not dislike the contemptuous, egotistical, rascal. He believed that Benjamin was actually a lonely, insecure man who acted up to cover his disappointment and feelings of failure and destitution.

Albert felt sorry for the desperate man who felt helpless and who feared that he had lost control of his life. But, Albert had to admit that the dining room had been peaceful since Benjamin's self-imposed isolation in his room.

Albert understood all too well what Benjamin was feeling. He suspected that most of the residents of St. Jude knew the feeling. They were in St. Jude because their lives had not worked out; they were destitute; time had run out on them. St. Jude was a home for those who had no other options. St. Jude was a place for people like him and Benjamin. Most of the residents were grateful to St. Jude for giving them a shelter and food and a decent life, but they resented their situation and were bitter for what life had dealt them.

Chapter Fifty-Three
The New Hideout

DAVID LUGGED THE HEAVY suitcase behind the wiry old Indian wearing a large, hiker's back pack. He looked up at the dark sky filled with billions of bright stars. The Milky Way arched over the sky like a silvery river of glitter. "Man, look at that sky," David whispered.

The Wet Mountain Valley was an astronomer's dream. The surrounding mountains protected the darkness from city light domes in distant big cities. The high altitude and dry climate produced an atmosphere clear as a crystal. Even the light from the tiny town of Rockcliffe was contained by hooded lighting thanks to the local astronomer's "dark skies" project. Their efforts had gotten Wet Mountain Valley designated as was one of ten dark sky sites in the world.

White Feather stopped and looked up. The dark skies of Rockcliffe reminded him of the old skies. The skies he knew as a child. The elders had told him the stories of the spirits that sat by the billions of campfires in the night sky looking down on them. The white man's "constellations" were weird and dull with little substance or meaning.

He looked back at his new friend. Someday he would take him out and tell him the stories portrayed in the night sky. He looked up again and chuckled.

David was curious, "What's so funny?"

White Feather gazed up and swept his hand across the sky, "When I was a boy, this was our HD, 3D, big screen T.V."

David laughed as the old man continued on down the street. He glanced back up to the sky and then followed him.

When they got to the house, White Feather led him around to the front door. A yappy dog barked across the street and White Feather stopped, glared and pointed his fingers at him. The dog whimpered and got quiet. White Feather stepped over the crime scene tape that the wind had blown loose. He suspected it would soon be blowing down the street. Except for the tape, it all seemed so familiar to David.

White Feather turned and twisted the door knob to enter the house. It was locked and the door handle would not turn, but the door with a push, lurched open. White Feather examined the damaged door frame. Someone had broken in. It was still locked, but had not been fixed yet. He flicked on his flashlight and flashed it around the living room. The room was in chaos. No one had bothered to clean up the scene yet. David noticed, "Good grief! What happened?"

White Feather pushed the door closed. "Probably a burglary."

David watched the circle of light scanning the litter on the floor, White Feather remarked, "Must have been looking for something."

White Feather led David past the couch, careful to keep the flashlight away from the gruesome crime scene, and into David's old bedroom. They dropped the suitcase and backpack on the floor. White Feather secretly studied the boy and noticed signs of apprehension. He could see that David had memories of the house and the past, if not the murder.

White Feather headed for the kitchen to search for food while David wandered around lost in his distant memories. He still could not remember anything after getting ready for football practice. As he explored the now familiar dark, quiet house, it felt strange. He wandered into his parents' bedroom expecting to find his father snoring loudly, but the bed was empty and the room in shambles.

He entered the living room, "Where did the murders take place?"

White Feather paused, turned and watched the boy approach the kitchen. "Your father was found lying on the floor in front of the couch. Your mother and brother were sitting on the couch."

David recoiled, lurching to one side as if the couch might attack him. It was too dark to see it as more than a dark shadow. After a moment, he joined White Feather in the kitchen, "What were the burglars looking for?"

White Feather opened the refrigerator, "Hard to say. Something small."

With the door open, the stench of spoiled food radiated out and gave David the urge to throw up. White Feather seemed unaware. David scratched his head, "Something small? Why do you say that?"

"They opened even the small drawers."

David was impressed, "Did they find it?"

White Feather shrugged, "I don't think so."

David looked at White Feather, "How do you know?"

"There is no sign they stopped looking."

White Feather set a jar of peanut butter and a can of sardines on the counter. "Your choice."

David scooped up the jar of peanut butter and opened a drawer to get a spoon, "Want a fork?"

He heard the pop and grate of the lid being pulled off the sardine can. In the shadows, he could see the old man pinching a sardine and stuffing it in his mouth. David found two glasses in the cabinet and filled them with tap water to drink. They moved to the dining room to sit. David stared out the front windows at the shadowy street as he chewed the sticky peanut butter. It tasted good. He was hungry. He wondered what Tammy was doing. Did she believe he was a murderer? Was she afraid of him now?

Almost fearful, he turned to look into the living room where the murder had occurred. White Feather finished off the smelly fish, wiped the oil from his hands on his jeans, stood and carried the empty can to the door leading out of the kitchen and tossed it into the backyard.

While David continued to smack and suck on the sticky peanut butter, White Feather found a quilt folded and laying on a chair beside the television; he took it and spread it over the blood-stained couch.

David joined him to help cover the couch. The old man stared at the kitchen, "Pizza."

David glanced at the kitchen, "Pizza?"

White Feather was still hungry, "You call the pizza place and I'll walk over to get it. I like pepperoni."

Chapter Fifty-Four

Back at the Lonely Motel

MORRISON SWITCHED OFF THE headlights, revved up the big Hemi engine of the vintage Dodge Charger and turned off the ignition key. He waited for the grumbling engine to shut down, grabbed his briefcase from the passenger seat, and then slid out of the car and dragged himself up to the door of his motel room. He fumbled around in his pocket to find the plastic, diamond-shaped tag of the room key. Finding it, he pulled it out of his pocket dragging with it a metal key that dropped and jingled on the concrete. He looked down and smiled as he bent down to pick up the key to his new apartment.

With any luck, tomorrow he would be exchanging the temporary, unsettled feel of the motel for the permanent, settled feeling of an apartment. He shoved the room key into the lock, twisted and pushed open the door. Switching on the light, he set his heavy briefcase on the small round table by the window, removed his shoulder holster, and sat to remove his boots from his tired and swollen feet.

After making a pit stop in the bathroom, he stopped to splash water on his face. As he dried off with a hand towel, he heard a soft knocking on the door. He paused to listen. Maybe it was the door of another room.

He heard it again and determined that it was definitely the door to his room. He tossed the towel on the counter and rushed across the room. After engaging the chain on the door, he peeked through the tiny hole in the center of the door. The outside light illuminated the area in front of the door but no one was standing there.

He slipped over to peek through the window when he heard the knocking again. Carefully, he pulled open the door until the chain was taut. A woman in a black coat covering a blue dress moved into view. Her long, dark hair covered her bowed face. Slowly, she pulled her hair back and looked through the cracked door. He recognized Darla.

She smiled shyly and looked down. Morrison pushed the door to, slid the chain off the bracket and opened the door. Before he could react, Darla glided past him and appeared to explore the room as if searching for clues to his personal life. He glanced outside guiltily and pushed the door closed. She touched the briefcase and then walked over to stand by the bed and removed her coat. She turned to face him. The bosom of the woman that looked so modest beneath her waitress blouse, looked voluptuous beneath the silky, loose, top of the blue, low cut dress.

Darla smiled proudly when she discovered his fascination with her chest. Morrison blushed and frowned, "What are you doing here, Darla?"

Darla smiled seductively as she unbuttoned the three buttons below the deep dipping "V-neck" of the dress. Morrison reached out, "No! Don't ..."

The three buttons loosened the top of the dress enough for her to slip it off her shoulders exposing her perfect breasts. Morrison gasped, "No! Pull that back up ..."

She pushed the dress to the floor and stepped out of her matching, blue heels to stand nude before him. Morrison rushed up to her and grabbed her shoulders and scolded her in his most authoritative voice, "Don't do this, Darla ..."

Ignoring his command she dug her fingers into his shirt, closed her eyes, tilted her head back inviting him to kiss her. When he hesitated, she halfway opened her eyes and started unbuttoning his shirt. He grabbed her wrists and pushed her back, "Stop this!"

She pulled her hands to her chest so that his knuckles pressed against her breasts. He released her and threw up his hands. She took advantage of the opportunity to finish unbuttoning his shirt, pull it open and press against him. Panic, fear, excitement attacked his senses as she wrapped her arms around his neck and hugged him tightly. With his head swimming and his heart racing, his mind struggled to hold on to reason, she pulled his head to her lips and his arms reflexively wrapped around her.

He felt vibrating on his upper thigh as she wriggled and rubbed against him. It was not until the obnoxious chirping revved up that he realized his cell phone was ringing. Darla revved up as well as if competing with the rude phone for his attention. Reality raced back into his consciousness and he pushed her back to dig the phone out of his front jeans pocket.

It was Buster. Morrison swiped the phone, "What's up?"

"Just got a report that someone is in the Ludwig house."

"Right. I'll meet you there."

As he pressed the "End Call" icon, he looked at the sensuous seductress. She resignedly stepped into her dress and pulled it up. He quickly buttoned his shirt and stuffed the shirt tails into his jeans. As she buttoned her dress, he slipped his shoulder holster on and sat to pull on his boots. Darla stepped into her heels, pulled on her coat and strolled dejectedly across to the door. As he slipped on his jacket, she disappeared into the night.

Chapter Fifty-Five
Discovering David Ludwig

Morrison shut off his headlights and engine as he coasted up to the Ludwig house and stopped behind the sheriff's SUV. Buster and Sheriff Bailey were leaning against the side of his vehicle staring at the house. Morrison wiped his mouth with his hand and whispered, "What have we got?"

"Neighbor called dispatch. Said he heard voices in the Ludwig house."

"They still in there?"

Bailey pushed off the SUV, "Let's go see."

They slipped up to the front door and pulled their pistols. They stood on either side of the door and listened. They heard giggling and juvenile voices. Morrison glanced at Bailey, "Kids?"

Bailey reached across and pounded on the door, "Sheriff! Open up."

The voices hushed. They could hear shuffling. Buster nodded, kicked the door open allowing Morrison to rush in holding his gun out at arm's length. "Freeze!"

Bailey reached in to flip on the light switch and then rushed in to stand between Crab and Morrison. A shirtless David Ludwig sat on the couch with his hands raised. Next to him, a young girl was frantically buttoning her blouse. Her skirt and shoes were on the floor. Morrison gasped, "Tammy!"

Timidly the girl responded, "Daddy?"

The sheriff pointed his pistol at David and commanded, "Put your hands behind your head and stand. Now!"

Ludwig clasped his hands behind his head and leaped to his feet. Tammy jumped up, "No! He didn't do it. Leave him alone, he's innocent."

Morrison holstered his pistol as Buster rushed forward to put his cuffs on Ludwig. Tammy jumped in front of her boyfriend, "You can't do this, Daddy, he's innocent."

Morrison gritted his teeth, "Get dressed, Tammy." He pushed his daughter aside as Buster reached up to seize one of Ludwig's hands and twist it around behind his back to cuff him. Tammy attacked her father, pounding on his shoulder, "No! No! No!"

White Feather noticed a white Mustang parked beside the neighbor's house across the alley from the Ludwig place. It had not been there when he left. He heard someone stirring and saw the old veteran standing on his patio holding a rifle and staring at the back of the Ludwig house. There was shouting inside the Ludwig house.

White Feather ducked below the fence and trotted up to the front of the Ludwig house. When he saw the sheriff's office vehicles and a Dodge Charger, he sat down, cross-legged, opened the pizza box, and tore out a slice.

As he enjoyed the delicious, lukewarm pizza, the front door to the Ludwig house opened and David was escorted out by the sheriff and a deputy. The new deputy followed, wrestling with a very angry teenaged girl. White Feather shook his head and muttered, "Hormones." White Feather found the white man's language very interesting, especially etymologies, a word he liked because it sounded a bit Cherokee-ish. He smiled as he broke the word hormone into two words—"harm one." "Appropriate," He thought.

The sheriff stopped when he saw the Indian sitting on the lawn. His curious look did not phase the munching Indian. The young girl hushed when she saw his dark silhouette and Morrison reflexively drew his pistol. Bailey chuckled, "What are you doing here?"

White Feather just grinned, "Want some pizza?"

His childlike jest triggered sniggers from the uptight party. The sheriff nudged David toward the SUV and Morrison trailed behind with his daughter. David looked back and grimaced as he pleaded, "I'm sorry, White Feather."

White Feather watched them drive off, picked up the box of pizza, and slipped inside the Ludwig house.

Part VI
Tuesday

Chapter Fifty-Six
Missing Slug in PC

JEREMY LUGGED THE BULKY PC into the evidence room. The camera case bounced against his hip. As he lifted the PC to place it on the shelf, he heard a jingling noise inside the computer, like something metal falling down through the inside. He found a vacant desk to set down the computer and laid the camera next to it. He studied the tall, rectangular box and determined he would need a screw driver to remove the cover. He pulled open a side drawer and retrieved the tool.

With the deftness of a computer tech, he popped the cover off revealing the metal frame cradling the cards and circuits of the PC.

As the clerk approached, Jeremy explained, "I heard something metal rattling around inside the thing as I was bringing it in."

The two men closed in to search for something in the base of the computer. Jeremy reached in, pinched something in his fingers and held it up to his face to analyze. "It's a slug," he declared.

The clerk's forehead furrowed, "Yeah."

Jeremy touched a bulge in the back of the metal frame, "One of the missing bullets from the Ludwig shooting. Looks like it entered through the disk reader and impacted in the back plate."

Jeremy pressed his cell phone to the side of his face, "Yeah, it was in the PC. It passed through the disk drive and lodged into the back plate. When I was hauling to the evidence room, it dropped to the base."

Buster thanked his CBI friend and headed for Bailey's office. "Jeremy found a slug in the PC."

Morrison overheard the Chief and rushed to Bailey's office, "They found one of the missing slugs?"

Buster confirmed it. Bailey smiled, "It was fired into that laundry slash office in the back of the house and hit the PC."

Morrison's eyes rolled up toward the ceiling, "So that bullet is probably from one of the shots fired at Jon Ludwig."

Buster nodded, "Yeah, missed him and lodged in the computer."

Morrison focused on the sheriff, "That proves Jon was shot first."

Buster and Bailey frowned at Morrison, he reminded them, "There were three quick shots, followed by a single shot, then by another."

Chapter Fifty-Seven
Bailey Calls the D.A.

Bailey SAT AT HIS desk and looked out over the office. Melton had his feet resting on his desk and was reading the paper. Calhoun was returning from the break room cradling steaming coffee in his over-sized cup. Morrison was doing some paperwork on a computer. Buster Crab was chatting with the Administrative Assistant. Bailey, reflecting, shook his head. Things were almost normal.

But Bennet and Wooten were wearing orange jumpsuits sitting in detention in Canon City. He would have a hard time finding replacements for them, especially in Rockcliffe. And who would want to come to Rockcliffe to do the dangerous job of drug enforcement for so little pay and with so little equipment and backup?

What they did was a terrible thing, of course. Two more lives; two more families ruined by a ruthless, manipulative, evil man.

He felt bad for their families. Bennet had a wife and three girls. They were pretty little girls, quiet, and very polite. Wooten was married and had a three-year-old boy.

Contrary to his aloof, tough-guy personality around the office, he doted over the boy more like a proud grandfather than a stern father. From all signs, Bennet and Wooten were good family men. Their families did not deserve to have their loved ones in prison.

They had been just another of Ludwig's victims and they deserved another chance. He spun his rolodex with his index and pointing fingers and found the card for the District Attorney. He glanced at his watch, picked up the phone and dialed. The D. A. was a good friend, "Martin? This is Sean ..."

"Yeah, Sean, what can I do for you."

"I'm thinking about Bennet and Wooten. Good guys, really. Nice families. Is there anything we can do?"

There was a short pause before Martin got to the point, "The Brady Code, Sean. They falsified their report. They'll never work for law enforcement again. We can't ignore the Brady Code, it speaks to the integrity of all of us. We are governed by a higher principal and that is the foundation of our trust and respect with the public."

"Oh, I understand that, Martin. I wasn't suggesting ... I was just wondering what we can do for them, you know? Lighter sentences, maybe? What are they going to do now with this hanging over their heads?"

"Truthfully, we should throw the book at 'em."

Sean sat back and took a deep breath. Martin was right. He was letting his heart get in the way. Those cute, innocent little girls; that happy, energetic little boy; their lives and their futures suddenly devastated. "Sorry, to bother you, Martin."

Martin was silent. Sean huffed, "Thanks, Martin, talk to you later."

"It's tough, Sean. It's good you have a heart, but our hands are tied. We have to think of the better good, Buddy."

"I know, Martin. Thanks for listening to me."

Chapter Fifty-Eight

White Feather Examines the Crime Scene

Wʜɪᴛᴇ ꜰᴇᴀᴛʜᴇʀ ᴡᴏᴋᴇ ᴜᴘ shivering from the cold. The blanket he had pulled from one of the bunks in the Ludwig boy's bedroom had managed to slip off. He pulled it over his body and waited for warmth. He closed his eyes and "listened" for spirits.

It had been a restless night for the creaky old elder. He tried sleeping on one of the beds in the boy's bedroom; he tried sleeping on the couch, but the spirits of the dead danced around the room; so, he resorted to sleeping on his blanket on the floor in the boy's bedroom. But, even after retiring to the floor, sleep alluded him as he struggled to decide what to do about his friend trapped in a cage at the sheriff's office.

When Grandmother Sun finally illuminated the dark Ludwig house, White Feather was grateful to have an excuse to rise and get dressed. The light from the sun now illuminated the interior of the house and everything was becoming visible. He was surprised again to find the house in complete disarray.

The old wizard followed the path of the searchers into the bedrooms, bathroom, anteroom, kitchen, dining room, and living room. He resolved again that they had not found what they were looking for, since the item was most likely in the master bedroom where they started, but they had searched the entire house. If they had found whatever they were looking for, he reasoned they would have stopped searching.

As he stepped down into the anteroom, his eyes spotted the rectangular area on a small desk in the corner. It was clean while the rest of the desk was dingy. Something had rested on the desk recently. The loose cables from the monitor and keyboard told him they had once been attached to a computer.

White Feather looked back into the living room and pointed his finger. There was a clear trail back to where the shooter could have held the gun from the floor.

He returned to the living room and remembered what he had overheard from the two deputies. *The man, David's father, was lying on the floor next to the couch. David's brother and mother were sitting on the couch.* He remembered the autopsy report. *The father was shot in the head, no powder burns, the angle suggested someone shot him from the floor.*

White Feather studied the blood stain on the hardwood floor. He could see the outline of the body, the faint outline of the gun David had dropped by the park bench, and the faint imprint of David's shoe.

White Feather knelt to the floor and touched the dry blood stain. Like a bolt of electricity, he felt a sense of shock.

This man's last feeling was one of utter shock, disbelief, and confusion. The old wizard closed his eyes and softly touched the stain again. The feeling was unmistakable.

Jon Ludwig was completely surprised by the person who shot him. He had no suspicion that the person was going to shoot him. He had no suspicion that the person was capable of shooting him. He did not believe that the person could or would shoot him.

White Feather sat back cross-legged to think about this revelation.

As he sat there, he pointed his finger at the imaginary man standing in front of the end table by the couch. His eagle-eyes spotted a square hole in the wall above the entry into the anteroom consistent with the line of fire. He got up to investigate the hole. The dry wall had been removed. This was the hole the deputy had discovered. He then remembered that they had found only two bullet holes but five shots had been fired. One bullet had lodged in the woman's stomach.

He dragged a chair over to stand on. As he stood on the chair, he glanced around the room. He remembered that the deputies had searched the walls thoroughly for the other two bullet holes to no avail. So, where else could the bullets have gone?

If the shooter was shooting from a prone position, especially if he had been knocked down, it was unlikely his shots would be accurate. The mother and the boy had been shot from close range. No other shots would have been needed to hit those targets.

He stepped down off the chair and walked over to where the shooter might have been knocked to the floor. He lay down and pointed his finger like a pistol. Again, he noted that there was a clear path into the anteroom where the computer sat. He aimed into the room.

He sat up and then rocked back, "Pow." He muttered as he examined where a bullet might have gone if fired while falling back. His finger was pointing to the window behind the end table. "The lamp." The lamp was lying in pieces behind the end table.

"Shot one," he muttered.

Then he turned onto his back, "Pow." His finger was approximately in the direction of the anteroom and where the computer had been. "Shot two."

He lay back on his back and grasped his hands together as if pointing a gun, "Pow." He was aiming at the imaginary chin of Jon Ludwig. It aligned with the bullet hole near the ceiling above the entry way into the anteroom.

He remembered that the deputy had said there were three quick shots first, a pause then another, a pause then another. *Jon Ludwig was shot first by someone lying on the floor.*

He got up to examine the broken lamp. A strange material had been in the glass container of the lamp. He touched the goop. It was a "lava lamp." He examined the shards of glass and then picked up the metal base. Something was rattling around in it—a slug. The bullet had hit the lamp and the thick liquid had stopped it.

He walked around to the front of the couch. The woman had been shot in the stomach. He walked over to the couch to touch the blood where Matilda Ludwig had passed her last breath.

As a Cherokee wizard, he knew what the white man did not know about a person's souls. That a man has four souls and the soul of consciousness leaves the body first in death. The soul of consciousness resides in the saliva and brain and, therefore, is released from the body when the person exhales his last breath.

The Cherokee know that this soul must blindly search for the ancestors in the Nightland. That is why the Cherokee do not speak the name of the deceased, for that might call them back from their search. He could feel that the souls of this family were lingering.

Some white men could sense these lingering souls and called them "ghosts." The white investigators had carelessly spoken their names many times at the crime scene calling them back from their journey. He felt their confusion and despair. Until their names ceased to be spoken, they were doomed to linger.

The third soul, the soul of circulation, resides in the blood and the heart. It is the soul of feelings and it lingers for the length of a moon cycle. He placed his hand on the dried blood of Matilda and felt the sting of her last feelings. She had felt remorse; she had felt guilt. Not only for herself but for someone else.

On the floor were the remnants of blood splattered in front of the couch. At the point of the first drops, he reached down and touched the remnants of her third soul and felt her desperate struggle to protect someone and the shock of a bullet penetrating her stomach.

He concluded that she was standing in front of the couch looking toward her husband. He pretended to be the father and aimed at the imaginary mother. He shook his head. It did not work; the father was too tall to shoot her with that line of flight; a shorter man, holding the gun waist high maybe, or rising from the floor. Maybe she struggled with the shooter getting up from the floor and the gun went off.

The son, David's brother, was shot from close range in the side of the head, with the bullet exiting at an upward angle. White Feather aimed his finger at an imaginary boy standing in front of the couch. "Pow." He looked around, but the blood spatters were wrong. All of the boy's blood was splattered on the top of the couch. The boy had to be sitting when the shot was fired.

The old wizard climbed onto the couch on his knees and imagined being the shooter. He extended his arm and aimed at the boy's head. He was pointing into the dining area of the house. He followed the line of flight and found the square hole next to the picture of the Last Supper hanging on the wall.

He nodded to himself, it all made sense to him now— except for the pistol on the floor. How did the gun wind up beside the body of Jon Ludwig?

Chapter Fifty-Nine

White Feather Visits Jail

WHITE FEATHER DECIDED TO walk the few blocks to downtown Rockcliffe and indulge himself in a white man's breakfast. As he stepped into "Sunny Side Up," all of the old farmers and ranchers were clustered at their usual tables and stopped to look at the strange Indian, their morning's curiosity. He was accustomed to being an object of fascination for strangers.

White Feather found an empty table in the corner. He glanced at the newspaper still unfolded on the table. The headlines read, "HIGH SCHOOL ADMINISTRATOR ARRESTED IN CONNECTION WITH LUDWIG TRIPLE HOMICIDE."

He read the article reporting that Mrs. Pentington was being held at the county jail on suspicion that she might be connected to the Ludwig triple homicide. "Sources report that she is suspected of having been at the Ludwig house just before and possibly during the murders."

White Feather jumped up from his chair. A plump waitress lifted the newspaper and wiped off his table, "What can I get you to drink, Doll?"

She placed a menu on the table and pulled out her order book and pen. White Feather bowed humbly, "So sorry, must go!"

White Feather rushed over to the sheriff's office. It was difficult for the old man, but he ignored the pain in his legs and feet. His mind was on his mission.

Inside the small, narrow, rectangular reception area, he pushed the buzzer on the wall next to the glass window. A young girl approached the window and smiled, "Good morning, how can I help you?"

"I want to see the prisoner."

The girl studied him for a moment, "Which one?"

White Feather was perplexed. He actually wanted to see Mrs. Pentington, but decided he should say, "David Ludwig."

"Are you his attorney or somethin'?"

"Counselor."

She looked up at the plain round clock on the wall, "Well, let me see if Terry is back there."

She looked him over again before disappearing behind the partition.

After a long few minutes, the door at the end of the room opened and a uniformed lady stepped through and stared at him, "I am Detention Officer Terry Kruger."

White feather walked over and shook her hand and replied, "White Feather."

The detention officer nodded, looked him over again and then led him down a long hallway to the back of the building where they turned left. Officer Kruger escorted him into a tiny room with two chairs facing right and left in front of windows. "I'll have Ludwig come over," she pointed to a phone hanging beside a counter, "You'll need to use the phone to communicate."

White Feather sat down, scooted the chair up to the counter, picked up the phone and held it to his ear. He stared through the thick glass at the small room on the other side and waited.

Finally, the door on the opposite side of the other room opened and David Ludwig entered wearing an orange jump suit. He smiled and waved at his old friend, sat down and grabbed the phone on his side.

"You are well?" White Feather inquired of his young friend.

David peered at him sadly and answered with a shrug. White Feather nodded, "Who was that girl?"

David frowned and shrugged again. "I don't know, probably Officer Kruger."

White Feather chuckled, "The girl last night."

David smirked, "Oh, that was Tammy. My girlfriend. I called her after you went after the pizza and she drove over."

White Feather remembered, "She called the deputy 'Daddy'."

"Yeah, her father just moved here from Denver. Deputy Morrison. He's investigating the murders."

White Feather pointed to the boy's head, "Did they ask you about ..."

David ran his fingers through his short hair, "Yeah. They asked all kinds of questions. I don't think they're buying my amnesia."

White Feather nodded. Someone passed by in the hallway jangling keys. White Feather turned to see Officer Kruger stroll past the windowed door to the hallway. After a few moments, Kruger passed back by escorting the lady from the school, Mrs. Pentington.

The stoic woman glanced through the window in the door and stopped when she saw David. She spoke to Officer Kruger and then opened the door to the visiting room and stepped in behind White Feather. She waved at David and snatched the phone from White Feather, "How are you, David?"

David shrugged, "Fine. Thank you, Mrs. Pentington."

She forced a smile, "I'm sorry about your family."

David nodded, "Thank you."

White Feather looked up at her, "You are ...?"

Mrs. Pentington gave him a cold look, handed him the phone, turned, and contemptuously returned to the hallway.

White Feather turned back to David, "She was in the paper; suspected of being involved in the murder."

David looked concerned, "She is?"

White Feather nodded, "But, they let her go?"

David looked in the direction of the hallway. White Feather continued, "Says she was at the house just before and possibly during the murders."

Ludwig shrugged. Memories of the murders were lost in his fugue. She could have even been there when he was, but he could not remember that part of his life.

Chapter Sixty

White Feather Interrogated

Morrison was in the break room when the sheriff walked in. Bailey updated him, "We've released Pentington on bail. Kruger tells me Ludwig has a visitor this morning."

Morrison paused before filling his coffee cup, "We know who?"

"Says he looks like an Indian. Gabby told her he claimed to be Ludwig's counsel."

Morrison filled his cup, "Same one from the morgue?"

Bailey shrugged, "Let's go see."

White Feather was coming down the hall from detention when Bailey and Morrison intercepted him, "Sir! Could we have a talk with you?"

White Feather paused and nodded passively. Bailey waved his hand toward the interrogation room, "Please. In here."

They escorted the old Indian into the interrogation room and sat across the bare, metal table from him. Bailey turned on his body cam and started, "Could you state for the record, your name, occupation and address."

White Feather was mildly perturbed, "Ugidahli Unega, Ani Gilohi clan. I am a medicine man and I have no residence."

Bailey tried to repeat, "Oo-gee ..."

White Feather rewarded the sheriff for trying, "Just call me White Feather."

Morrison tried to pin him down, "You've been living at the train depot?"

White Feather closed his eyes and his mouth and gave an almost imperceptible nod.

Bailey decided to move on, "So, how do you know David Ludwig?"

White Feather studied the two men. He could sense the intentions of men and sensed good vibes from these two. "I found him in the park."

Bailey cocked his head to one side, "Which park?"

"Coke Park." White Feather pointed northeast.

"When was that?"

White Feather folded his arms and maintained eye-contact, "Thursday."

Bailey frowned, "What was he doing in the park?"

"Sleeping on my bench."

"Your bench?"

White Feather closed his eyes, "I like that bench. Looks out over the pond. Secluded, quiet."

The old Indian opened his eyes and focused on the sheriff, "Grandmother Sun had just started her journey across the sky vault. I woke him up. He seemed confused."

"Confused?"

White Feather clarified, "Disoriented."

Bailey glanced at Morrison. Morrison took over, "What did you do?"

White Feather looked at Morrison, "Showed him a newspaper article with his picture, but he didn't recognize himself. Had him look at his reflection in the pond."

Bailey was curious, "If you knew who he was, why did you risk approaching him? A possible murderer."

White Feather focused on the sheriff, "I knew he was not the murderer."

Morrison jumped in, suddenly focused; "How did you know that?"

White Feather smiled pertly at the deputy, "The blood on his shirt was not splattered on, it was wiped on. Blood was not splattered on the back of his hand but was on his palm where he had picked up the bloody gun. Blood on the bottom of his shoe, not on top. David arrived after the murders."

The sheriff and the deputy looked at each other. They were impressed. They looked back at the Indian for a moment. The deputy picked up the questioning, "How did he react?"

White Feather looked at the young man. Would he understand? "His reflection shocked him."

White Feather closed his eyes again as he related the story, "I sensed he knew nothing about the murders. I sensed that he was helpless. Took him home with me."

Morrison probed, "What did he tell you about the murders?"

White Feather opened his eyes and studied Morrison, "At first, he couldn't remember anything for more than a few minutes."

Morrison followed up, "At first?"

White Feather nodded, "Then, Saturday, he woke up and remembered everything up to football practice."

Morrison was skeptical, "But, nothing afterwards?"

White Feather explained, "Now, he remembers everything since Saturday, but not that gap between."

Bailey turned to Morrison, "Convenient."

White Feather ignored their skepticism. The sheriff asked him, "Then what did you do?"

"Searched for the truth."

Bailey nodded, "You visited the autopsy in Springs."

White Feather frowned, Morrison clarified, "The building where the bodies were taken in Colorado Springs. You listened in on the examination?"

White Feather nodded. "And at the crime scene. And at the school."

Morrison's eyes lit up as the image flashed into his head, "You were the janitor?"

White Feather closed his eyes and nodded. Morrison sat back and studied this curious man who suddenly has become a significant part of the case investigation, possibly knowing or understanding as much as they did. "So, who do you think did it?"

White Feather opened his eyes and smiled. "It is obvious. Murder, suicide."

Morrison and Sheriff Bailey raised their eyebrows. The sheriff challenged him, "You think that Jon Ludwig shot his wife and boy and turned the gun on himself?"

White Feather shook his head and spoke slowly, "Son did it."

Bailey was surprised, totally. "So you now think that David shot his family?"

White Feather frowned, "Other son."

They had not seriously considered that possibility. Morrison smiled, "Why him?"

The old man explained, "Witness said three shots fired first. Bullet in the lamp, bullet in the computer, bullet hole above entry into little room. Father was shot first."

Morrison interrupted, "Bullet in the lamp?"

White Feather shrugged. The sheriff turned to Morrison with understanding in his eyes, "The lava lamp. We thought it was knocked off the table in the scuffle."

Morrison was clear now, "The thick gunk in it stopped the bullet."

Bailey smiled brightly and then frowned, "How do you know about the computer?"

White Feather shifted uneasily, "Dirt free rectangle."

The sheriff and his deputy chuckled, glanced at each other, Bailey nodded, "Ok. Why do you suspect the other son?"

"Son came home, parents were fighting. Tried to stop fight, father knocked him down. Son pulled out gun, shot three times, hit father once in head. Mother grabbed gun, went off, shot her in stomach. She fell back on couch. Son sat by her, felt remorse, shot himself."

Morrison was impressed, "Sounds plausible except for one thing. How did the pistol wind up beside Mr. Ludwig?"

White Feather nodded and held up one finger, "Mother."

Morrison responded, "Not likely."

White Feather agreed and held up two fingers, "Someone else was there."

The sheriff nodded and suggested, "David Ludwig, maybe?"

White Feather closed his eyes, "Pentington."

Morrison liked this old sleuth. He and the sheriff sat back to absorb the old man's hypothesis. Morrison asked, "Did David have a gun with him when you found him?"

White Feather opened his eyes and nodded. "Under bench in park."

The sheriff rubbed his mouth with his hand and stared at Morrison. Morrison could see that something was troubling his boss. Bailey nodded toward the door. Morrison followed Bailey into the room behind the interrogation room, "We have a problem."

Morrison waited, Bailey clarified, "He's a likable old man. Got a good heart. But he has admitted to harboring a fugitive, breaking and entering, and who knows what else."

Morrison looked down. Bailey shook his head, "We have no choice, we have to ..."

He was interrupted by Deedie's horrifying scream. The two men raced to the dispatch area to find the young girl standing, trembling, pressed against the corner behind her desk. Her arms were wrapped around herself and her paperback novel was lying on the floor spayed open.

Bailey ran to her, "What is it, Gabby?"

Gabby took a deep breath, "I heard the door open and looked up. A huge black bird flew out!"

Morrison ran to the door and tried to jerk it open but it would not budge. He remembered that it required a code even from the inside because of the trustees that worked outside detention. He keyed in the code and rushed into the reception area to look out the windows but saw nothing in the parking lot or in the air. *A big black bird!* That sounded familiar. Where had they seen a big black bird?

Then he remembered that there had been a raven at the crime scene that first day. White Feather's words flashed into his mind, "... at the crime scene."

Morrison returned to meet the sheriff. Bailey was staring at him with an odd look. "White Feather is gone!"

Chapter Sixty-One
The Missing Pistol

When Morrison and Sheriff Bailey entered the office area, they were greeted by Deputy Melton, "I just got a call from Scotty McCollough. A pistol was stolen from his collection."

Melton glanced at his notes, "A U.S. Army issue, M1911A1."

Morrison and Bailey spoke simultaneously, "Forty-five caliber."

Bailey nodded to Melton, "We've got this one."

He started for his office, stopped and turned back to Melton, "You and Calhoun go over to Coke Park. Look for a hidden bench next to the pond and search underneath for a pistol."

Melton challenged the sheriff, "Got a tip?"

The sheriff raised his shoulders and held out his hands, "Just a hunch based on some info we got this morning."

"Right," Melton answered.

Bailey and Morrison started to rush out, when Deputy Calhoun hung up his phone and hailed the sheriff, "That was Agent Blakeley. The ballistics don't match on Coach's or Ludwig's pistols. Said he'd be here in about an hour."

The Sheriff nodded, "Go with Melton to look for the murder weapon." He held up his hands to stop Calhoun from asking the obvious questions, "He'll explain. When you find it, run it over to Springs and for ballistics, prints, and DNA."

On the way to his car, Bailey confirmed what Morrison suspected, "Scotty McCullough is the father of that kid you interviewed at school, Freddie, David Ludwig's friend."

When they knocked on the door, a pretty, auburn-headed woman in her mid-thirties answered. She put her hand up to shade her eyes from the sun and squinted up at them. The sheriff explained, "I'm Sheriff Bailey and this is Deputy Morrison. We're here to investigate a stolen pistol."

"Oh," she answered as she pushed the screen door open for them. "I'm Debbie McCullough. Scotty is downstairs in his gun shrine. I'll show you."

They followed the attractive woman to the basement. Shrine was an appropriate name for the room. There were guns in cabinets, guns on the walls, guns in display cases. There were pictures of Scotty and other hunters bagging all manner of game below the busts of exotic animals. Scotty was at the far end of the room cleaning a rifle. He waved them over, Bailey reached out his hand, "Hi, Scotty, good to see you again. This is Detective Morrison, Sam this is Scotty McCullough."

Scotty reached out, "Good to meet you, Sam." He grabbed Morrison's hand and shook it vigorously, failing to let go immediately.

Morrison could smell the gun oil and feel it on his hand. He nodded and struggled to retrieve his hand. "So you're missing an M1911?"

"Oh! Yes. Government Issue M1911A1, Vietnam era. I just discovered the missing pistol today. I have a schedule for cleaning the weapons and it was time for M19."

"Schedule?"

Scotty waved his hand pointing out his huge collection. "I can't clean them all at the same time. So, I schedule a few each day."

He walked over to a display case, "I keep it in here. Today was the day to clean these in this case. That's when I discovered it was missing."

Morrison jumped in, "When was the last time you saw the pistol?"

Scotty raised his hands, "I guess the last time I cleaned it, four weeks ago."

Morrison continued, "Who has access to this case?"

Scotty shrugged, "Well, I keep the key in that closet. So, technically, anyone who knows where to look."

Morrison narrowed his question; "So, who has had access since the last time you cleaned it?"

Scotty shook his head. "Well, actually, just my family."

Morrison made notes, then flipped to another page in his notepad, "Your son is Freddie?"

Scotty looked quizzically at the deputy. Morrison realized that he should probably explain, "I questioned Freddie at the school. We learned that he was one of David Ludwig's friends."

Scotty raised his eyebrows and smiled, "Oh, yes, David. We used to live next to the Ludwigs and Freddie and David have been close friends ever since."

"Were you friends with Jon Ludwig?"

Scotty shook his head and whistled, "I don't know how anyone could be friends with that thug."

"When was the last time David visited?"

Scotty scratched his beard, then shook his head, "It's been ages."

He turned and yelled at the stairway, "Debbie!"

After a few seconds, the door opened at the top of the stairs and Debbie looked down, "Did you call me?"

Scotty walked over to the base of the stairs, "When was the last time David Ludwig visited? Do you remember?"

Debbie shook her head, "David Ludwig? Not for a long time."

Scotty turned and opened out his arms as if he had proven a point. Then Debbie dropped a bomb, "Darren was here Wednesday though."

Chapter Sixty-Two
Another Round with Freddie

Freddie sat nervously beside his mother on the couch in the living room. Debbie put her arm around him to comfort him. Morrison smiled, "Hi, Freddie, remember me?"

Freddie fidgeted, "Yes, sir."

Scotty coaxed his son, "Speak up, Freddie."

Freddie raised his voice a notch, "Yes, sir."

Morrison resumed his questioning, "Freddie, can you tell me about Darren visiting you last Wednesday?"

Freddie glanced at his dad and hesitated. Scotty encouraged him, "Answer the deputy, Freddie."

Freddie looked down, "Well, I saw him at school and asked him about his shiner."

Morrison sought clarification, "He had a black eye?"

Freddie looked up and nodded. Then he looked back down, "He said his old man was beating up his mother and he got hit when he tried to defend her."

Freddie paused again, Morrison prompted him, "How did you feel about that?"

Freddie shook his head, "It made me angry." He looked up and then back down at the floor, "Darren was angry, too. He said he was afraid that his father was going to beat him again and he was worried that his dad might kill his mother next time."

Morrison nodded, "Whose idea was it to take the pistol from your dad's case?"

Freddie glanced at his dad and squirmed. His mother patted his shoulder, "It's ok, Freddie."

Freddie shrugged, "Well, I guess it was my idea." He looked at his dad, "I was afraid that Ludwig would kill him, you know? I've seen how mad he gets. Usually, it's David that steps up and he's big enough to hold his own. But Darren ..."

Scotty seemed to be agonizing over his son's dilemma, he tried to understand, "So you brought him over here and picked out a gun."

Freddie nodded sadly, "We picked it out together. He thought the military pistol looked like one he could work."

Scotty shrugged, "Probably a good choice. Simple, safe, reliable weapon."

His wife frowned at him, "Scotty, really!"

Morrison continued, "So, did you go with Darren back to his house?"

Freddie's eyes widened, "Oh, no. After I gave him the pistol, he left. Then I heard about the shooting."

"Why didn't you mention the pistol when we talked at school?"

Freddie looked up at his mother, "I was afraid." He glanced at his father.

Morrison persisted, "Where were you between 4:30 and 6:00 Wednesday?"

Debbie answered for him, "Darren left here around 4:00. Freddie was here with us the rest of the evening."

Morrison looked at the sheriff and nodded. Bailey rubbed his hands together, "Ok. Well, you've been very helpful, Freddie."

He looked at Mr. and Mrs. McCullough, "I don't suppose you want to press charges?"

Scotty and Debbie shook their heads and Debbie patted her son on his shoulder.

Bailey stood, "Thank you for your help. We'll be going now."

Everyone stood and Bailey turned to Scotty, "I think we've found your gun. We will need to hold it for a while."

Scotty nodded, "Of course."

Bailey walked over to Freddie and put his hand on his shoulder, "You know that what happened is not your fault, right?"

Freddie shrugged bashfully, "I guess so."

Bailey and Morrison stood by their car in front of the McCullough house, "Wow!" Bailey remarked.

Morrison nodded, "Kinda changes everything, doesn't it?"

Bailey took a deep breath, "Boy, I'll say. Backs up the Indian's theory."

Chapter Sixty-Three
Blakeley Questions Ludwig

Oₙ ᴛʜᴇ ᴡᴀʏ ʙᴀᴄᴋ to the office, the sheriff's cell phone rang, "Sheriff Bailey. Hi, Penny ... Oh, ok. ... Yeah, I'll drive over right away."

He hung up and raised his eyebrows, "That was my wife, Penny. Her car won't start, gotta go over and see if it needs a boost."

Static from the radio startled him as he was trying to push his cell phone into his breast pocket and he dropped it on his lap, "Crap!"

Melton reported, "Sean, we found a gun under the bench in the park. It's an M1911, over."

Morrison grabbed the mic, "Roger."

As Bailey fumbled for his phone, he commanded, "Have Calhoun run it over to Springs for prints, DNA, and ballistics."

Morrison pressed the side button on the mic; "Sheriff wants Calhoun to run it over to Colorado Springs for prints, DNA and ballistics."

Melton replied, "10-4, out."

The radio squawked again, it was Gabby, "Miles Blakeley is here."

Bailey shook his head and picked up the mic, "We're on our way back."

They found Blakeley sitting in Sheriff Bailey's office with his feet propped up on the sheriff's clean, orderly, unblemished desk. He was cleaning his fingernails with what appeared to be a hunting knife.

As they entered the room, Blakeley ignored them. Bailey rushed around behind his desk, "You remember Sam Morrison from Denver P. D.?"

Blakeley smirked, "I remember." His eyes surveyed Morrison up and down.

Morrison took a seat without offering his hand, "You haven't changed."

Blakeley huffed, "You have."

Bailey butted in, "Deputy Calhoun is headed for Springs with another pistol. We are pretty sure it is the murder weapon."

Blakeley raised an eyebrow but appeared skeptical. Bailey quickly filled him in on their meeting with White Feather and Scotty McCollough.

Blakeley dismissed out-of-hand White Feather's theory and commented, "I hope you locked him up and threw away the key for harboring a murderer."

Bailey kept his cool, "Actually, I think his theory has merit."

Blakeley sneered, "Pshaw."

Bailey shrugged, "What you got today?"

Blakeley offered, "Just came over to question Ludwig and get this case wrapped up."

Bailey stood, "Well, I've gotta go home and boost my wife's car. You can wait or go ahead without me."

Blakeley folded the blade on his huge knife and stood, "I don't need your help to do an interrogation."

Bailey turned to Morrison, "You wanna sit with Blakeley for the questioning?"

Morrison did not want to, but nodded his consent.

Bailey picked up the receiver on his desk phone and pushed a button, "Terry, could you bring Ludwig to the interrogation room? Blakeley and Morrison want to question him. ... Thanks."

Bailey pointed at Morrison's chest, "Don't forget to turn on your body cam."

Morrison nodded as he felt of the unit. At first he felt that the sheriff was being condescending until he noticed Bailey cut his eyes over to Blakeley and back.

David Ludwig looked exhausted as he was escorted into the interrogation room by Detention Officer Kruger. Blakeley had made a detour to the restroom, so Morrison stood to greet the young man, "Hi, David."

David sat down passively as Kruger attached his cuffs to the center of the table. He replied sadly, "Hello, Mr. Morrison."

"You look tired."

David shrugged, "It's noisy at night."

"The other prisoners?"

David tried to smile, "Yeah. One of 'em likes to sing himself to sleep and it makes another one angry so they yell back and forth at each other."

Morrison felt sorry for the boy. Wet Mountain Valley contracted with the state to detain some state prisoners. The program compensated the Sheriff's Office and helped with the budget, but, it meant that David was exposed to the real criminal element.

Blakeley walked in arrogantly and took his seat. He turned to Morrison and sniped, "Body cam on?"

Morrison nodded. Blakeley got down to business, after stating the location, date, and time he added, "I'm agent Miles Blakeley with Deputy Sam Morrison. State your name for the record."

He glared across the table. David leaned forward, "David Ludwig."

"Tell us about Wednesday."

David shifted in his chair as he tried to remember the day. Well, Dad woke up in one of his bad moods and he picked a fight with Mom."

Blakeley interrupted, "What was the fight about?"

David shrugged, "Nothing, really. Something about his bacon, I think. Darren commented that his bacon was fine and Dad back-handed him."

David looked at Morrison, "That was unusual. Darren doesn't usually speak up like that."

Blakeley pressed him, "What did you do?"

"Well, I wasn't in the room, I just heard it."

"What did Darren do?"

"Nothing. When I walked in, he was sitting quietly at the table rubbing an eye. Everyone was quiet at that point. I could see that Mom was trembling; the muscles in her back were twitching, you know?"

Blakeley commented, "So, you just sat down and had a quiet breakfast with your dysfunctional family?"

David shrugged again, "Yeah, basically. When Dad's like that, it is best to just keep quiet."

"Anything else happen?"

"No. Darren and I went to school after breakfast."

"How did you feel about your dad hitting your brother?"

"Well, it made me angry, but I knew it was bound to happen. Usually, Darren is too afraid to say anything. I don't know why that day was different."

Blakeley pushed harder, "So, why didn't you stick up for your brother?"

David shook his head, "Would've just made matters worse."

"So, you went to school and got to thinking about it and decided to settle it once and for all."

David's brow furrowed, "What do you mean?"

"You left football practice early, went home and shot your old man."

David looked down and got quiet. Blakeley glared at the boy impatiently waiting for a reaction. Morrison decided to step in, "What happened at football practice, David."

David looked at Morrison sadly, "I don't remember. They say I suffered a head injury and it has affected my memory."

Blakeley slammed his fist down on the metal table, "They say? They say? You know darn well what happened."

Blakeley swiveled around facing to the side, "Now cut the crap and tell us what happened. Nobody's buyin' the amnesia crap."

David looked at Morrison with pleading eyes, "It's the truth. I don't remember anything after getting dressed for football practice until a couple of days later."

Morrison smiled and nodded and then asked, "So, when did you learn about your family?"

Blakeley glared at Morrison, "When did he learn? He was there, Morrison, we got witnesses that saw him running out right afterwards."

Morrison's neck got hot, he felt fiery heat radiating out of his collar, "What if he doesn't remember? What if his head injury on the football field affected his memory?"

Blakeley rared back, "That is a lot of hooey and you know it," he turned to David, "Now fess up, kid. I'm tired of your malarkey."

David looked down, "I'm sorry, but I'm telling you the truth."

Blakeley took a deep breath and leaned forward, "Look, kid, you aren't doing yourself any favors with this cockamamie story about amnesia. It just don't fly. Maybe you shot your old man in self-defense. Maybe your old man knocked you down and you shot him before he could come after you. That the way it happened?"

David looked up at the agent, "Maybe. I just don't remember."

Blakeley let out a breath and sat back rubbing his face with his palms. Morrison smiled at David and sat back, "Why don't we wait for the report on the pistol we found?"

Blakeley stood, "You know what we're going to find, Morrison." He looked at David, "Might as well confess. It'll go better for you."

David took a deep breath and looked down.

Blakeley shook his head and looked at Morrison, "Ludwig's the shooter. You know it and I know it. And when we get the proof back, this kid's going to prison for the rest of his life!"

The single-minded agent stormed out. Morrison stood, "Thanks, David."

David was curious, "You found a pistol?"

Morrison nodded, "Yeah, White Feather told us about the pistol you had when he found you on the bench in the park. He thinks we will find other prints on the pistol that will prove you're not the shooter; that you came along later."

David frowned, "Who's prints?"

Morrison hesitated before answering in a low voice, "He thinks they'll find Darren's prints on it."

David sensed the skepticism in Morrison's answer, "You don't think so?"

"Look fingerprints are fine for television, but in real life, they are very difficult to find. There's not likely to be any prints on that pistol at this point. Besides, courts want DNA these days."

Morrison could see that David did not fully understand the implications. He tried to explain, "That pistol could have your DNA, your brother's, your father's, your mother's, the investigating officers, the gun's owners."

Morrison pushed his hand through his hair, "Don't get your hopes up that the gun will prove anything."

David looked at Morrison like a puppy looks at his owner eating a snack, "You think I did it?"

It was like a knife in Morrison's heart. He put his hand on the boy's shoulder, "I don't know, David, I honestly don't know. But, your friend, White Feather, has proposed a very valid hypothesis. Whether or not we can prove it is another thing."

Morrison turned and exited the room before David could react. He stepped down the hall and motioned to Officer Kruger and then found Blakeley pulling on his coat in the sheriff's office. He challenged him, "You leaving already?"

"Nothing more to do here. I'll see if I can expedite the tests on that pistol you found, But this is an open and shut case and we need to get it wrapped up."

Morrison raised an eyebrow, "We'll see."

Part VII
Wednesday

Chapter Sixty-Four
CBI Directive

Bailey asked Chief Crab to call a meeting for all of the deputies involved in the Ludwig case. Morrison, Calhoun, Melton and Crab were seated at the small conference table in the open area when Bailey came out of his office to join them.

"I just got off the phone with Agent Blakeley. He is convinced that David is the shooter and wants us to put pressure on him for a confession."

Crab shrugged, "It don't make sense, does it?"

Morrison shook his head. Bailey took a deep breath and leaned forward to address Morrison, "Can you take care of sending copies of our files to CBI?"

"I'm on it."

Calhoun innocently stated what was on everyone's mind, "I thought we'd decided his brother did it."

Everyone chuckled at his naivete. Chief Crab explained to him, "We did."

Calhoun screwed up his face, "Oh."

The group chuckled again.

Bailey added, "That's not all," he had everyone's attention, "He wants us to throw the book at White Feather for harboring a fugitive, obstructing an investigation, etc., etc."

Melton's face turned bright red.

Bailey sat back. He had done his duty and delivered the message from CBI. Now he was ready to get down to business. He looked at Morrison, "What do you think of White Feather?"

Morrison was surprised, "The Indian? Well, I don't know. He's likable. Smart. I like the way he thinks."

Melton had an opinion, "Without the train depot, he's back on the streets now."

Morrison looked at the older deputy. There was something about Melton that Morrison just could not figure out. "You thinking about taking him in?"

Melton snickered. Buster turned to Morrison and added, "Bill helped get my uncle into St. Jude. He's a big wig in the Methodist Church."

Morrison studied Melton. This information did not clear things up for him. Melton was an enigma. Bailey commented, "So, you were thinking we might try to get White Feather in at St. Jude?"

Morrison was speechless. He did not understand the interest in the old Indian. Was he the only one that heard Bailey say that CBI wanted him arrested?

Bailey chuckled, "I get the feeling, Sam, you think we're bonkers."

Morrison laughed and shifted in his chair, "Well, Sean, no offense, but I'm just trying to understand what the sudden interest in this old man is. You're the one that pointed out he harbored a fugitive after we questioned him. So we've gone from thinking about arresting him, to refusing to arrest him, to trying to find a home for him?"

Bailey nodded and smiled at Melton, "He's got a point, Bill."

Melton smiled kindly, but ignored the razzing. He calmly responded, "I'm looking into it."

The Methodist big wig stood and walked away. Morrison showed concern, "Did I offend him?"

Bailey shook his head, "Nah. Bill has a big heart. He never ceases to surprise me. Want to bet where White Feather's next residence will be?"

All but Morrison laughed. But, Morrison was totally flabbergasted, "What about Blakeley? He's not going to go for that."

As if he did not hear Morrison, Buster mused, "I will say one thing. I really think White Feather's theory has merit."

Bailey nodded, "I do, too. But something is missing."

Then it hit him! Morrison almost fell out of his chair, "Wait a minute, guys. I can't believe I missed it!"

The sheriff sat up, Morrison pulled out his cell phone and dialed his wife. "Samantha, this is Sam. Just a quick question. What time did Tammy take David home that day?"

Morrison switched his phone to speaker. "Oh, goodness, Sam, let me think."

The room hushed as they waited for the answer. Melton returned to stand by the table.

"It must have been a quarter 'til six. I know that Penny left right afterwards and commented she only had ten minutes to get to an appointment at six."

Everyone smiled at each other with bright smiles. If that was accurate, David Ludwig could not have been home in time shoot his family. The 9-1-1 call came in at 5:45 p.m. "Thanks, Sam," Morrison proudly set his phone down on the table.

The sheriff slapped the table, "If Penny can confirm that ..."

He pulled out his cell phone and dialed his wife. "Hi, Hon. Got a question for you concerning the Ludwig case ... yeah," he chuckled, "What time did Ludwig leave Samantha's that Wednesday? ... Yeah, the day of the murder."

He waited while his wife strained to remember, he prompted her, "Samantha remembered you had an appointment and had to leave?"

Bailey smiled broadly and nodded his head, "Yeah, ... ok! Yeah, it proves Ludwig was with Tammy when the shots were fired. ... Ok, thanks, Hon."

Bailey put up his cell phone, and looked around the table, "Bingo! Good work, Sam."

Morrison put it together and suggested, "I think we need to put some pressure on Pentington. If White Feather's right, Dottie's hiding something."

Bailey nodded, "Shall we pay Pentington another visit?"

Chapter Sixty-Five

The Confession

Bailey was thinking out loud as they drove to the school. "Maybe there wasn't a fourth person. Maybe Darren walked in and his father and mother were fighting; he tried to separate them; Jon knocked him down and started yelling at him; Darren pulled the gun and fired three times. When Jon fell to the floor, the boy jumped up and Matilda surprised him when she tried to take the gun away from him; it went off and shot her in the stomach. She staggered over to the couch; Darren got hysterical and sat next to her, scared, panicky, remorseful and turned the gun on himself. Matilda took the gun and tossed it over by Jon to make it look like he did it."

Morrison shook his head, *What a tragic episode.* "I suppose it is possible, Sean, but not likely it would have landed in that spot. Maybe she was able to get up and place it and then return to the couch."

"Maybe David Ludwig came in, saw his brother holding the gun and planted it beside his father."

Morrison pondered the theory, "But why did he pick it back up and run?"

Bailey shook his head, "I don't know. You think the amnesia got him?"

Morrison looked at Bailey, "The amnesia? How?"

"White Feather said that he couldn't remember anything for more than a minute. Maybe he planted the gun and then when he saw Calhoun and Buster, he rediscovered the scene, panicked, picked the gun up and ran."

Morrison shook his head, "Wow, Sean, you have a very creative mind."

Sean blew out his frustration in a huff, "Yeah. Pretty far-fetched. Think we'll get any more out of Pentington?"

Morrison thought about it for a moment, "I have an idea."

Pentington was coming out of Wheeler's office as the sheriff and his deputy entered her office. Morrison shut the door. Pentington stared at them with a stiff upper lip. Bailey smiled reassuringly, "I'm sorry to bother you, Dottie, but we just need a little help wrapping things up."

Pentington frowned curiously, "Wrapping things up?"

Morrison waved his hand toward her desk, "Please, have a seat. This shouldn't take too long."

He and the sheriff sat across from her. "We were wondering if you could make a copy of David Ludwig's attendance records for us?"

Pentington was suspicious, "Sure. What for?"

Morrison crossed his legs, "Oh, it's just a formality. Details for the grand jury."

She shifted in her chair, "Grand jury?"

Bailey clarified, "The prosecutor always wants our t's crossed and i's dotted."

Pentington did not budge, "So you think David had something to do with the murders?"

Morrison sat back, "Oh, yes, ma'am. It had to be him. Scotty McCollough is missing a pistol from his collection. It turns out to be the murder weapon. We think Ludwig stole it and used it to kill his family. David's prints were the only prints on the murder weapon. We figure he walked in on a fight between Jon and Matilda and tried to break it up."

Pentington showed disgust, "Ridiculous. Why would he shoot his brother and mother?"

Morrison continued, "Oh, we think they got in the way and were accidentally shot in the scuffle."

Morrison dropped his head as if remorseful, "Of course, shooting Jon was clearly premeditated. The prosecutor will go for the death penalty on that one."

Pentington gasped and covered her mouth with her fingers, "Death penalty?"

Bailey jumped in, "Sure, Dottie. Acquiring the gun the way he did. Well, shows he was thinkin' about it before hand."

Tears welled up in her eyes as she dropped her head into her hands. Morrison glanced at the sheriff and winked. Bailey winked back. Bailey stood, "If this is a bad time, maybe you could mail it to us. We don't want to cause you any more grief, Dottie. We've already bothered you enough."

Morrison stood and turned to open the office door. "No!" Pentington protested. "You won't need David's records."

Bailey turned, "I'm sorry, Dottie, I don't understand."

Pentington jerked a tissue out of the box and sniffled, "David had nothing to do with it."

Morrison raised his eyebrows as if confused, "Ma'am? What are you saying? His prints were on the pistol; the only prints."

She blew her nose and straightened in her chair, "I wasn't completely honest with you, Deputy."

Bailey and Morrison returned to their seats. Bailey prompted her, "Why don't you tell us what really happened, Dottie?"

Dottie straightened in her chair and pulled herself back together, "So, just as I said, I was helping Matilda pack when Jon came in and was enraged. He started to beat Matilda and when I tried to intervene, he socked me and I fell to the floor. The world was spinning and I must have passed out for a second. When I woke up on the floor, Darren burst in. When he saw Jon and Matilda fighting, he tried to stop them. Jon clobbered him and he fell to the floor. Darren pulled out a gun and started firing."

Pentington blotted her eyes and blew her nose again, "He fired three shots and Jon's head exploded."

She stopped to regain control of her emotions, "Darren started screaming 'Dad! Dad!' Matilda tried to wrench the gun away from him and it went off. Matilda grabbed her stomach and staggered back. I grabbed her and helped her to the couch. Darren got hysterical and started yelling and pacing around. I tried to talk him down and get him to calm down. Finally, I persuaded him to sit with his mother while I went to look for bandages. While

I'm in the bathroom, I hear a gunshot. I raced back into the living room and saw that Darren had shot himself."

Tears rolled down her cheeks as she popped out two more tissues and covered her face. "I ran over to Matilda to try to comfort her. She stops me and hands me the gun. Her eyes ... her eyes were pleading with me. 'Put the gun by Jon' she begged, 'Promise me no one will ever know that Darren ...'"

Pentington looked at the sheriff and added sadly, "And then she ... slumped."

Dottie shook her head, "It was her dying wish. What could I do?"

Morrison and Bailey exchanged glances, Dottie finished her confession, "At that point, I heard a car pull up. I went to the window and saw David get out of Tammy's car. I looked down at the gun and made a split second decision. I decided to grant Matilda's last wish. I wiped off the gun and dropped it beside Jon's body and ran out the back door to my car. I called 9-1-1 and reported the shots. I never thought about what David might do."

Part VIII
Aftermath

Chapter Sixty-Six
Wrapping It Up

WHITE FEATHER WAS WAITING for David Ludwig's release. The two hugged and patted each other on the back. Deputy Melton stepped up to congratulate the boy and then shook hands with the homeless Indian, "White Feather."

White Feather smiled, "Bill. Wado."

Bill frowned, White Feather explained, "Wado is Cherokee for thanks."

Melton smiled, "I think you'll like St. Jude. There's a lot of good people out there."

Buster Crab stuck out his hand to Ludwig, "Congratulations, son."

He turned to White Feather, "Bill's right. St. Jude is a great place. Any place that can put up with my Uncle Benny has a lot of heart."

White Feather nodded modestly.

As Morrison shook David's hand, he noticed the connection between the old Indian and the Methodist big wig. He was glad he had not taken the sheriff's bet.

And he was glad they had finally gotten to the truth. David Ludwig seemed like a really nice kid; which was good, since he might be a future son-in-law. As if on cue, his daughter burst in, raced over and leaped into Ludwig's arms.

Quietly, Samantha slipped through the door and strolled past the dispatch area into the office forced to deal with the county's worst. But in Morrison's eyes, her presence brought the grace of royalty to the room. She regally shook David's hand, hugged him and sincerely congratulated him.

David blushed demonstrating his humility and dignity. Sheriff Bailey barged in and blustered, "David Ludwig! Never been so happy to see someone cleared. Hope all goes well for you in the future."

David nodded and shook his hand, "Thank you, Sheriff."

Samantha slipped over to stand by Morrison and whispered, "Want to join us for lunch?"

She had no idea how much, "Yes. I would love to. My treat."

Buster's cell phone rang, "Buster Crab ... Oh, hi Naomi ... Crap!"

The big man shook his head, "Sorry, my uncle is acting up again. Gotta get out to St. Jude before we have another murder on our hands."

Sneak Peek:
It's About Time

Book 2
A White Feather Mystery

by Courtney Miller

Chapter Five
Murder Most Foul

Fʀᴀɴᴋ ʜᴀᴅ ᴛᴏᴜʀᴇᴅ ᴛʜᴇ third floor of St. Jude Methodist Retirement Home again and paced the corridor to the point his eighty-seven-year-old legs were getting tired before TJ finally arrived. The effervescent teenager flew out of the elevator and crashed into him, "Oh! I'm sorry."

Frank held her arms, "It's ok, I was just pacing."

"Mr. Roberts? You shaved! You look so different. You're ready?" she gushed as she spun out of his grasp and offered him her crooked arm, "Well, let's go."

The Dining Room was a sprawling room filled with eight large oval tables hosting six per table. The tables were covered with white table cloths, the walls hosted prints of the masters in traditional wide, wood frames, and the dark, oak walls hinted of a grand, by-gone era. Floor-to-ceiling windows lined the back wall offering a stunning view of the back lawn, small lake, and magnificent mountains. The clatter of dishes and rumble of voices was disturbing for a man who had lived for years alone in a cardboard box under a bridge. Even during rush hour, the bridge was not as chaotic or noisy.

"Where would you like to sit?" TJ asked.

Frank searched the grand room, "Do you have a window seat?"

"Ooh." She said through her puckered lips. "Let's go see."

It was obvious that a window seat was in high demand, but there was one table by the windows where one rotund black man sat by himself. TJ seemed to ignore it so Frank offered, "How about over there with the big guy?"

TJ's nose crinkled as she glanced around the room. "Well, maybe you'd prefer somewhere else."

Frank was a little put off by what he assumed was her racial bias, "No, that table's fine."

She squinted, "Are you sure? Benny is ..."

"I'm sure." Frank insisted.

Reluctantly, she led him to the table. As they approached, Benny smirked, "TJ! Come 'ere little girl and give ole Benny a big hug."

TJ grimaced and tried to introduce Frank, "Mr. Cook, I'd like to introduce our newest resident, Mr. Roberts. He wants to join you?"

Benny reached out and grabbed TJ around the hips and pulled her up to him, "Of course! Nice to meet you, Roberts."

TJ struggled to free herself as the forward man handed her his big, empty tea glass, "Would you be so kind as to bring me some more tea, perty thang?"

She elbowed her way loose and wagged her finger at him, "Don't you ever do that again!"

Benny grabbed his chest and stuck out his lower lip as if she had hurt his feelings. TJ stormed off in a huff, his tea glass still in his hand. Benny motioned to the chair next to him, "Sit down, Roberts, tell me about yourself."

Frank pulled back the chair and sat down tentatively, "Not much to tell. Been homeless since the great recession. Been livin' in a box under a bridge just gettin' by."

Benny laughed grandly, "A man with no false ego. How refreshing!"

Benny raised his hand, waved and shouted, "Woody! Over here!"

Frank turned to see a short, skinny man with a large hook nose and wild, curly hair surrounding his kippah carrying a tray of food. Despite his comical appearance, he seemed quite reserved and distinguished. He took a deep breath, nodded to acknowledge Benny and dragged himself over to the table. "This is the new guy, Roberts. Roberts meet Woody."

Woody set down his tray across the table from Benny, sat down, clasped his hands and placed them on the edge of the table, "Contrary to my jovial friend's belief, I am not Woody Allen. My name is Albert Stein."

Frank smiled and reached across the oval-shaped table to shake his hand, "I am Frank Roberts."

TJ bounded up and slammed the refilled glass of tea in front of Benny and then dashed off before he could grab her, touching Frank's shoulder as she flew by. As Benny watched her departure, he dumped about three tablespoons of sugar into the tea. He declared in a deep, melodious voice, "Now there goes a truly vivacious young girl. My, my."

He laughed uproariously at himself as he stirred his tea and turned to Frank, "Wouldn't you say, Frank?"

Frank glanced at her and nodded, "Oh, yes, she has plenty of energy."

Benny added, "She makes me tired just watchin' her," and then laughed again. He turned to Albert, "How about you, Woody, what do you think of my little TJ."

Albert took a drink of water and shrugged, "She is out of your league, Benjamin."

Benny laughed, "Woody don't talk much, but when he does ..."

Albert glanced up at Frank and winked, then picked up his fork to begin eating. Noticing that Frank did not have a tray, he stopped and glanced around, motioned to a lady wearing a white apron over a blue dress, held his hand over Frank's head and pointed. The lady nodded and headed for the cart full of trays parked by the kitchen doors in the back of the room.

Albert explained the procedure, "When you come in, you can grab a tray off the cart. There is another cart with glasses of tea and water over there." He pointed.

Frank took a deep breath. He thanked Albert and tried to make conversation, "How long you two been here?"

Benny scooped up a fork full of noodles, "I've served ninety-six days of my sentence so far." He stuffed the fork into his mouth and looked at Albert.

Albert shrugged, "Almost a year."

Benny chuckled as he took a bite of bread and gulped down half of the sweet tea.

The lady with the apron placed a tray in front of Frank and asked, "What would you like to drink, Sir?"

Frank thought a moment and then ventured, "Do you have milk?"

The kind lady smiled, "Of course."

Benny declared, "A milk man!" then laughed heartily.

Frank shrugged, "Just craved milk for some reason. Haven't had any in so long."

Frank soon learned that Benjamin liked to keep the conversation rolling even if it meant doing all the talking himself. Frank took a lesson from Albert and tended to the business of eating and tried to ignore the obnoxious, boisterous man.

Benny spotted someone, "There's Twiddle Dee and Twiddle Dumb-Dumb."

Frank glanced at the entry to see a large, distinguished looking man dressed formally in a brown suit and tie with a tall, stout, smartly dressed woman clinging to his arm. As they shuffled along, the woman appeared to be prompting him surreptitiously.

Benny turned to Albert, "What's their names, Woody?"

Albert lowered his fork and turned to look, "That is Mr. and Mrs. Benaford Wilson, Benjamin."

Benny shook his head, "Mr. and Mrs. Looney Ben." He laughed loudly and downed the last of his tea.

Albert whispered to Frank, "Mr. Wilson has dementia. Mrs. Wilson is the keeper of his memories."

Benny leaned back, "Is that what she does?" The rotund man closed his eyes and wheezed. Frank watched the couple and could not help but admire the way Mrs. Wilson helped her husband maintain his dignity. He could tell that she was a remarkable woman.

Benny scoffed loudly, "He looks so dignified. It's comical."

The couple glanced toward Benny prompting him to laugh at them. Albert kept his head down and continued eating. Frank felt very ashamed of his boisterous colleague, but Benny just mocked the proud man, "Hey, Wilson!"

The reserved man stared at Benny as his wife whispered something in his ear. Benny commanded, "Come over here, Wilson!"

Albert muttered through his teeth, "Benjamin!"

The confused man glanced at his wife. She whispered to him again. He glared at Benny. Benny persisted, "Don't be rude, Wilson, Come over here!"

The man appeared embarrassed and intimidated. He glanced at his wife, then looked around the room before shuffling over to Benny's table despite his wife's contempt. Benny motioned to two empty chairs, "Sit down, Wilson. You too, Mrs. Wilson. We have a nice view here, don't you think?"

Wilson obediently sat down. Mrs. Wilson politely whispered to her husband, "Stay here Darling, I'll go get our trays."

Benny lifted his empty tea glass, "Since you're going that way, Mrs. Wilson, would you be so kind as to fetch me some more tea?"

Mrs. Wilson glared at the arrogant man, exhaled in a huff, grabbed the glass and marched off. Benny grinned slyly at Mr. Wilson, "She's right handy, ain't she?"

Wilson turned to search for her, "Oh, yes. She is a wonderful woman."

Benny's attention turned to the next person entering the dining room, "There he is! Our token Injun."

Frank and Albert turned to see an old man with wild, straight white hair pulled back into a pony tail except for a small tuft threaded through a round deer bone at the top of his head. A white feather dangled to one side.

Benny found the stooped and weathered old Native American comical, "Good 'ole White Feather." Benny patted his mouth with his hand and shouted his imitation of a war whoop.

The Native American sporting a long, colorful shawl draped over his shoulders stopped and glared at Benny before proceeding toward the cart full of trays in the back of the room. Albert commented, "Maybe he will scalp you."

Mr. Wilson giggled giddily. Benny laughed loudly and then raised his hand to wave grandly at a hefty black woman entering the room from the kitchen. "Hi, Birdie!" he yelled.

Birdie stopped and glared at Benny with a condescending look. She shook her head in disgust as she wiped her hands on a towel. Benny was delighted, "Now that's a fine woman. A FINE woman. Lordy!"

Albert muttered, "Maybe she poisoned your noodles."

Benny feigned surprise, "Whoa, Woody. That woman loves me."

Albert shook his head. Frank watched the friendly chef stop at each table and visit. He could see that she had the ability to light up the faces of the people sitting at the table. She made them smile and laugh and they clearly loved her.

Mrs. Wilson returned with two trays and set them down on the table. Benny raised his eyebrows, "Forget my tea?"

The tall, sturdy woman glared at him and walked off. In between bites, Albert commented, "You couldn't see that her hands were full, Benjamin?"

Benny scowled at his friend, "Well, excuuuuse me. But, I'm thirsty."

Frank glanced back at the tea tray and saw Mrs. Wilson dumping a spoonful of white powder into one of the tea glasses. The old Native American stepped up beside her and set down a tea glass as he adjusted his grip on the food tray in his other hand. Frank noticed that Mrs. Wilson slid the Indian's glass over beside her glasses inadvertently. White Feather picked up another glass nonchalantly and Frank watched him find a table far from them near the back wall. Frank was privately thankful that Benny did not see the "token Injun" dodging him. Benny was too busy complaining about the bland food while at the same time shoveling it in as if he found it delicious.

Someone caught his attention across the room and with a twinkle in his eye he fluttered his fingers at her. Frank looked across the room and spotted a sixty-ish, attractive black woman fluttering her eyelashes at Benny. Frank caught Benny fluttering his eyelashes back at her grinning stupidly.

"Girlfriend?" Frank asked.

Without taking his eyes off the flirting woman he declared, "My sweet Katie Mae! MMM MMMM!"

Albert explained, "Benjamin imagines that he and Katherine are an item."

Benny frowned and retorted, "We ARE an item! In fact, Miss Katie Mae is coming over to my place right after lunch."

Benny grinned grandly and winked at Frank suggestively.

Mrs. Wilson returned with three large glasses of tea squeezed in her fingers forming a triangle. She set them on the edge of the table next to her tray and then with all eyes trained on her, placed one in front of Mr. Wilson's tray and one in front of her tray. Then, as if forgetting the other glass, sat down ignoring Benny.

Benny gasped and held out his hands crying, "What about me?" Frank and Albert laughed as Frank handed the glass across to the bewildered man.

Benny turned his attention to Frank and began a relentless oratory on the history of St. Jude. Frank remembered that Judy had told him that it was once the county hospital and had been purchased by the Methodist church when the hospital closed. The church had remodeled it and converted into a retirement home for the indigent.

Benny's version was much more sinister and mysterious. "Originally, this was a looney bin—a state institution for the insane."

He paused to laugh, "It was built in 1891 and don't ask me why, but it was modeled after that creepy Hudson River Institute for the Insane in New York. This place became notorious for the maltreatment of its patients. There were some stories there, Woody!"

Benny turned to Frank and whispered, "Woody was a newspaper reporter in his previous life."

Albert smirked and continued eating while Benny resumed his story, "When they finally closed the place, they found bodies hidden in the basement and patients running around naked, all drugged up and crazy as loons." Benny's eyes sparkled with delight at the thought.

He chortled as he glanced around the room, "It appears to have returned to its roots, hasn't it?"

His wandering eyes stopped on the stringy haired woman that had stopped by Frank's room earlier, Lizzie. She was glaring at Benny with wild, fiery eyes. Benny began to sing, "Lizzie Borden took an ax and gave her father forty whacks and when the job was nicely done, she gave her mother forty one!"

Lizzie jumped up and rushed up to their table wagging her finger at Benny, "Shut your mouth, you stupid man!"

Two of her friends jumped up and grabbed her arms, "Ignore him, Elizabeth, and come finish eating."

Elizabeth strained against their grasp, "Their ghosts still roam these halls, nigger. Mark my words, you don't want to mess with them."

Benny responded angrily, "I don't know if you're a ghost or alive, but your bigotry is alive and well, honky!"

Elizabeth's face turned to an eery calm, "One night they'll grab you around the neck and you won't know what's happening to you until they've strangled you to death!"

Birdie appeared, "Benny, what have you done now? Calm down, Elizabeth, pay no never-mind to this old blow hard."

Elizabeth glanced at Birdie, turned back to spit at Benny, then let her friends lead her back to their table.

Birdie reprimanded him, "Benny, why can't you keep your mouth shut?"

Benny was angry and restless. He grabbed his tea and gulped down the last quarter of it, slammed it down and shivered. "Where'd you get this awful tea? Must've been left over from the asylum."

Birdie frowned, picked up the glass and smelled of it, "What'sa matter with it?"

"It's bitter and tastes like it's a hunnerd years old."

Birdie gasped, "How would you know with all that sugar in it?"

A loud noise drew their attention to Mr. Wilson. His tray was dumped in his lap, food covered his suit and he had a scared look on his face. Mrs. Wilson jumped up, grabbed a napkin, laid the tray flat on his lap and started swiping the food off his tie, shirt and suit lapel onto the tray.

Birdie threw up her hands, "Oh, dear. I'll get a wet cloth."

Mrs. Wilson stopped her, "No, that's alright, Birdie. We've finished. I'll take Benaford up to the room to change."

Benny guffawed and announced to the room, "Benaford? Poor little Benaford spilled his tray." Benny glanced around and pointed at the flustered man.

Birdie shook her head, "Hush, Benny, you behave yourself or I won't get you any more tea."

Benny winked at her and slapped her behind as she left. She turned, wagged her finger and then cautiously backed away. Benny laughed grandly and then scooped up some noodles on his fork and resumed his story, "In the early sixties, they turned this place into the county hospital. That lasted until around 1975 when they built that modern monstrosity in Canon City."

Without catching his breath, he scooped more noodles into his mouth and continued, "That hospital cost me my job, you know. It sits right where the hotel was where I used to work as the con-see-urge. It was a good job too. It was the finest hotel in town. But the owners got too old and sold out to the county so they could tear it down and build that dang new hospital."

Birdie returned with fresh tea, "Try that."

Benny poured a heaping serving of sugar into it, stirred it ceremoniously and then took a little sip. Then a bigger sip. Then gulped down almost half of the rest of it. He sat back, smacked his lips, swirled the tea in the glass and then downed the rest of it. He looked up at Birdie, raised his eyebrows and proclaimed, "Worst batch yet!"

Birdie punched her fists into her broad hips and scowled at him. All of sudden he dropped the glass, vomited all over his chest, grabbed his neck and began coughing. His face flushed and he started gasping and convulsing violently. Frank and Albert were stunned, Birdie started slapping him on the back, "Somebody call the nurse!"

Benny flailed about in his chair as if something invisible had a hold of his throat and was throwing him around. Lizzie came running up shouting, "I told you! I told you they'd get you!"

In one final lurch, the bedeviled man slammed forward and buried his face in his tray leaving everyone stunned. Katie Mae dashed across the room yelling, "Benny! Benny!"

She elbowed past Lizzie and threw her arms around the collapsed man, wailing and shouting his name over and over. Nurse Nujent rushed in, pushed her aside and pulled his head back, "Call 9-1-1!"

She swiped his mouth with her fingers, "Help me get him on the floor."

Albert, Frank and several men from another table pulled the hefty man off his chair and laid him out on the floor. "Give me room!" the nurse shouted as everyone backed away. She began resuscitation.

Standing over her, the sixty-ish, attractive black woman screamed, "Benny! No!"

Lizzie threw back her head and gave out a horrifying, maniacal laugh, "I warned him!"

About the Author

Courtney Miller is the multi-award winning author of the seven-book series, *The Cherokee Chronicles*. He is considered an expert on ancient Native American culture and incorporates that knowledge into his writing. He has written over 200 articles on the art, archeology, astronomy, culture and history of ancient Native America for Native American Antiquity and other online ezines.

His seven-book series, *The Cherokee Chronicles,* has received multiple awards and widespread praise from the Cherokee community for its authenticity:

Courtney Miller has created an imaginative adventure tale, one which captures the ethos of Cherokee folklore and Myth.
> —Alan Kilpatrick, Professor, American Indian Studies, San Diego State University and Author of "The Night Has A Naked Soul"

His characters seem real to us because Miller took the time to do extensive research about Indigenous Native Americans, the Cherokee in particular."
  —K. T. Hutke Fields,
    Principal Chief, Natchez Nation

In his new series, *The White Feather Mysteries,* Miller once again shows his award-winning talents bringing to life fresh characters with a twisting plot and surprise ending.

This is a very interesting mystery novel. The idea is fresh and the storyline is compelling. It was truly an interesting read.
  —B. E. Baldwin, Librarian, judge for the
    2016 Extravaganza Draft to Dream
    Book Competition

Courtney lives in the Wet Mountain Valley with his wife, Lin. He enjoys playing golf and is active in his local Rotary Club.

CPSIA information can be obtained
at www.ICGtesting.com
Printed in the USA
LVOW08*0253280317

528657LV00004B/8/P